De

Ho ok.

Jerry Bentz

Nov. 19, 2022

OPERATION COBRA

A JOHN BENSON NOVEL

JERRY BENTZ

One Printers Way
Altona, MB R0G 0B0
Canada

www.friesenpress.com

First Edition — 2022

Cover Design Credit: Sarah Schulz Creative
www.sarahschulzcreative.com
Instagram: @sarahschulzcreative

ISBN
978-1-03-915378-3 (Hardcover)
978-1-03-915377-6 (Paperback)
978-1-03-915379-0 (eBook)

1. FICTION, THRILLERS, MEDICAL

Distributed to the trade by The Ingram Book Company

*****

"Africa's elephant population has crashed from 1.3 million in 1979 to approximately four hundred thousand today."

"I am not prepared to be part of a generation that lets these iconic species disappear from the wild. By the time my daughter turns twenty-five, there will no longer be wild elephants roaming the African savannah if the current rate of poaching continues."

"Members of CITES, do not be complacent, do not let materialistic greed win against our moral duty to protect threatened species and vulnerable communities. We need to unite by declaring the ivory trade a symbol of destruction, not of luxury."

"Over one thousand rangers have been killed in the last ten years. It makes you really angry. It makes you very sad. We know where the wildlife are that are being poached. We know how the product is moved and we know where it ends up. You've got every possible bit of research and evidence you could need to fix this."

An excerpt from HRH Prince William's keynote address during a live broadcast in Johannesburg on September 22, 2016, ahead of the Conference of the Parties of the Convention on International Trade in Endangered Species of Wild Fauna and Flora (CITES) organized by **Tusk**, a British conservation charity supported by Prince William, The Duke of Cambridge, and a Royal Patron of **Tusk**. Also partially included in the 2016 Netflix documentary *"The Ivory Game"*

*****

"If we don't stop this now, that's it. It's going to be the end of the elephants."

Dr. Samuel K. Wasser, a conservation biologist at the University of Washington, Seattle, who pioneered the use of DNA from elephant feces to track ivory poachers. Excerpt from the 2016 Netflix documentary *"The Last Animals"*

*****

For the Elephants and the Rhinos

PROLOGUE

9 p.m. Friday, April 6, 2012
Extension 29 District, Gaborone, Botswana

It was a warm and humid evening in the Extension 29 District of western Gaborone. Canadian forensic biologist and Royal Canadian Mounted Police (RCMP) inspector Dr. John Benson and his partner Sergeant Denny Bear, along with their two German shepherd police dogs, Syd and Nelle, were with four officers from the elite anti-poaching unit of The Botswana Defense Force (BDF).

They were outside the front door of a house along Kagamagadi Road, two blocks south of the Segoditshane River. A tip from an informant had led them to the house, and they believed the elephant ivory poaching ringleader, Ben Simasiku, was inside, plus at least one of his senior gang members. Three BDF officers were also waiting at the back door of the house. They all had on Kevlar bulletproof vests and were brandishing assault rifles.

Denny Bear tapped one of the BDF officers on the shoulder, signaling him to swing his battering ram back and break open the front door. A BDF officer did the same thing with the back door. As soon as the door flung open, Denny Bear gave the "Capture" command to the two dogs, and they both rushed into the house looking for the bad guys. They found two of them sitting at the kitchen table drinking beer. The two men were just getting up and reaching for their handguns lying on the table beside them when the dogs lunged at them and locked their powerful jaws on the right forearm of each man, dragging them down to the floor.

Denny Bear and the rest of the officers came into the house right behind the two dogs. While the other BDF officers spread out to clear the rest of the rooms in the house, Denny and John went to the kitchen where the two men were on the floor struggling against the dogs' firm grips on their arms. They were both shouting frantically for someone to get the dogs off them.

After taking their handguns off the table, removing the clips, and putting them in their pockets, Denny gave the dogs the "Release" command. The two dogs immediately released their hold on the men and backed away. John Benson pointed his Colt special forces assault rifle at the pair, shouting at them to get face down on their stomachs. The pair complied, and Denny cuffed them.

Seth Khama, a senior training officer with the army's Botswana Defense Force and the leader of the anti-poaching unit, came into the kitchen and said, "The rest of the house is clear. These are the only two men here."

He looked at the men, who were still face down on the kitchen floor and gestured at one of them. "That one is Ben Simasiku. We've been after him for a couple of years now and as you know, we finally got a tip that he was at this house in Gaborone. He is Zambian but travels between Zambia, Botswana, and Zimbabwe, so it has been hard to track him down."

As they were talking, one of the other BDF officers came into the kitchen and said, "We found eighteen elephant tusks wrapped in tarps in the small shed behind the house. They still have fresh blood on them, so they were probably just brought to the house from the bush in the last few days."

John Benson, looking more relaxed with his assault rifle now pointing at the floor, grinned and said to Seth, "Thanks for inviting Denny and me, and the dogs, to help in the takedown. We didn't really think we would be helping capture any ivory poachers when we came to the Botswana Law Enforcement Academy earlier this week. It's always great to get a chance to be a part of the actual arrest of the bad guys."

After a short pause, he continued, "Hopefully, we'll get to do a few more takedowns before we go back home to Canada in a few weeks."

CHAPTER 1

4 p.m. Monday, April 9, 2012
Kazangula Ferry Border Crossing, Zambesi River, Kasane, Botswana

The Kazungula Ferry was a ferry service across the Zambezi River, a width of about 400 meters, between Botswana and Zambia. It was one of the largest and busiest ferry services in south-central Africa. The service was provided by two motorized pontoon barges and operated between national border posts at Kazungula, Zambia and Kasane, Botswana.

It served the international road traffic of three countries directly (Zambia, Zimbabwe, and Botswana) and three more indirectly (Namibia, South Africa, and the Democratic Republic of Congo). It linked the Livingstone-Sesheke Road (Highway M10) in Zambia to the main north-south highway of Botswana through Francistown and Gaborone to South Africa (Highways A33 and A1) and the Kasane-Victoria Falls Road through Zimbabwe. The city of Livingstone in Zambia was sixty-two kilometers to the east via Highway M10, and the world-renowned Victoria Falls was a further twelve kilometers south of Livingstone.

The pontoon barges were quite small and only able to accommodate one or two semi-trailer commercial trucks or buses and up to six passenger vehicles per trip, plus up to twenty walk-on passengers who could sit on benches along the sides of the barge. It was common for commercial trucks to line up for several kilometers down the highway on both sides of the ferry crossing site, sometimes waiting for days before making their way up to the front of the line.

The two Canadians, Dr. John Benson and Dennis (Denny) Bear, plus their driver, Sammy Molefe, a regional wildlife and training officer from the Botswana Department of Wildlife and National Parks (DWNP), and Seth Khama, a senior training officer with the BDF, had arrived at the border crossing about thirty minutes previously in their DWNP Land Rover Defender four- by-four.

Government vehicles received special treatment at the border crossing and could go to the front of the line to board the ferry for the quick trip across the Zambesi River from Botswana to the Zambian border control facility. Sammy Molefe had successfully negotiated their passage with the Botswana border agent on the next ferry, and they were waiting for the ferry to arrive and dispatch its current occupants. John and Denny's two Royal Canadian Mounted Police (RCMP) trained German shepherd dogs, Sydney (Syd) and Nelle, were anxiously looking out the partially open back window of the Land Rover. They were extremely focused on all the commotion at the ferry terminal, with brief glances at Denny and John, wondering if there was something they should be doing to protect them.

To calm them down, Denny said, "It's okay, girls, nobody is going to hurt us."

The six occupants of the Land Rover had traveled from Francistown, Botswana, a long seven-hour drive with only one stop at the town of Nata to have something to eat and fill the gas tank with fuel. The previous day, they had driven for about six hours from the Botswana Police Training College and Law Enforcement Academy, about sixty kilometers south of Gaborone in the community of Otse, to Francistown. They had stayed overnight at the Diggers Inn, a three-star hotel close to the central police station in the downtown area.

They had attended a five-day training workshop at the Botswana Police Training College and Law Enforcement Academy for wildlife anti-poaching law enforcement personnel from several eastern and southern African countries. The Botswana Department of Wildlife and National Parks hosted the workshop, along with INTERPOL's Environmental Crime Programme, the International Fund for Animal Welfare (IFAW), and Environment Canada's Wildlife Enforcement Directorate.

They were on their way to Livingstone to meet with Roberta Mulenga, the head of intelligence for the Zambia Wildlife Authority (ZAWA), and a few of her wildlife enforcement officers. ZAWA was planning a major raid on an elephant ivory storage warehouse for the following day, and Dr. Benson and his Canadian team of forensic wildlife biologists and INTERPOL trainers had been invited to observe and assist in the operation. It also served as an opportunity to provide real-time forensic crime scene training for the ZAWA wildlife enforcement officers.

The five-day training workshop at the Botswana Police Training College and Law Enforcement Academy was part of INTERPOL's Project Wisdom, a world-wide initiative against elephant ivory and rhinoceros horn poaching and trafficking. One of the first major operations to be implemented under Project Wisdom was Operation Worthy, which involved fourteen countries across eastern, southern, and western Africa. It was INTERPOL's largest global operation targeting criminal organizations behind the illegal trafficking of elephant ivory and rhino horn.

Once the pontoon ferry arrived at the docking area and the vehicles on the ferry had driven off, a Botswana border security officer directed their Land Rover onto the ferry along with a few other passenger vehicles. One large semi-trailer truck was guided on, plus one mid-sized passenger bus. About twenty walk-on passengers were allowed to board and sit on benches along the sides of the ferry deck.

The ferry then departed for the twenty-minute trip across the Zambesi River to the Zambian side of the river. Sammy Molefe drove the Land Rover off the ferry and up to the Zambian Border Services building. The scene was very chaotic, with all manner of trucks, buses, and passenger vehicles parked in the large unpaved area around the border services building. Many people stood around either waiting to get on the ferry or just trying to sort out their permits or visas.

John, Denny, Sammy, and Seth all got out of the Land Rover and went to the entrance of the border services building. Sammy Molefe, having gone through this border crossing routine several times in the past, talked to one of the border guards. The group was then directed to another spot in the large processing area reserved for people with special status. Being law enforcement or military officers from their home countries qualified them as being in the "special status" category, and their passports were all stamped with only a cursory examination by the border service agent.

Once they were all processed, they returned to the Land Rover where they were greeted by the anxious-looking dogs, who were not impressed with all the people milling around the parking area. Luckily, no one had attempted to stick their arm or hand into one of the partially opened back windows, or they might have had a very unpleasant encounter with the two extremely well-trained and protective Canadian German shepherd police dogs.

As they were driving out of the final checkpoint at the border crossing, John said, "Well, that was certainly faster than the last time I was here at the ferry crossing. Kate Beckett and I went on a week-long vacation at Chobe National Park in June 2010. We flew from Johannesburg to Livingstone and rented an SUV at the airport. We then drove from Livingstone to the Chobi Safari Lodge, where we stayed for a week with a side trip to Maun and a spectacular helicopter trip over the Okavango Delta, courtesy of the Botswana Department of Wildlife and National Parks. Anyways, since we didn't have anyone with us to verify our "special status" as visiting law enforcement officers and INTERPOL Wildlife Crime Group trainers, we had to wait our turn at the Kazungula Ferry just like everyone else."

"Yes, there are some benefits to being a civil servant and employee of the DWNP," Sammy Molefe said. "Apparently, there are now plans to start building a bridge over the Zambesi River to replace the Kazungula Ferry service. They say it is supposed to be completed by 2020, but this is Africa, so we won't get too excited until the politicians stop making promises and the construction actually starts."

"Well, that was my first Zambesi River ferry crossing, so it all seemed pretty chaotic and disorganized to me," said Denny. "Even though I have been to Africa quite a few times now, I am still surprised sometimes about how things get done here. As Canadians, we are used to things being highly organized and following plenty of rules, so we have to adjust our thinking when we come here."

"Yes, we definitely have our way of doing things that sometimes seems strange to visitors from North America," Seth Khama said. "But that is just how things are in Africa, and we try to do our best with what we have. So, will we be meeting up with Dr. Beckett and Anna Dupree in Livingstone?"

John replied, "Yes, they should be at the Protea Hotel in Livingstone by now, waiting for us to arrive. They flew to Livingstone from Gaborone on the Cessna 425 Corsair plane we used to fly from Nairobi last week. It's one of the planes owned by the Kenya Wildlife Service (KWS) airwing and they let us use it to come to the training workshop since the KWS Assistant Director was also attending."

"We are scheduled to meet with Roberta Mulenga tomorrow morning at the Livingstone Police headquarters to go over the final plans to raid the suspected ivory storage warehouse," said Sammy. "ZAWA will be using the local Livingstone police as backup for their own ZAWA enforcement officers. They are hoping this raid will lead them to the ringleaders of the elephant ivory poaching syndicate operating in this area of Botswana and Zambia. We are happy they invited us to observe the raid, since we suspect that much of the ivory in the warehouse probably comes from elephants killed in Botswana."

"My team were all excited to assist in the raid by the Botswana Defense Force in Gaborone after the training workshop was over," John said. "It gave us a chance to demonstrate some of the forensic crime scene analysis techniques we taught at the workshop."

Seth Khama said, "We were impressed with how you worked with your police dogs during the raid at the house. We've been trying to get our own wildlife law enforcement canine unit in the Botswana Defense Force, but so far, we have not been able to get the funding to hire the specialized trainers and build the training facilities. Do you think Canada can help us out with that?"

"Syd and Nelle are sisters from the same litter and were former police dogs trained at the National RCMP canine training facility south of Edmonton, Alberta, where we live in Canada," said Denny. "The trainers thought they were a little small for RCMP police dogs and were not quite as aggressive as they needed to be for taking down bad guys. When they were just under one year old, the RCMP dog handlers decided to re-deploy them and offered our team the opportunity to re-train them for our wildlife enforcement work. We gratefully accepted, and I became their primary handler. I had to take specialized training on how to manage police dogs, especially for the type of work we do, but they are now key members of our team. You saw how they performed the other day in Gaborone?"

John said, “I will talk to people I know with Environment Canada and the big anti-poaching NGOs and maybe we can find some money for the BDF to start a canine training program. I know the Kenyan Wildlife Service have increased funding for their canine program through money provided by two of the big wildlife conservation foundations and are using dogs more in their wildlife enforcement work. We have even organized a few workshops using Syd and Nelle at the Kenya Wildlife Service Training Institute in Naivasha.”

As they were talking, they arrived at the outskirts of Livingstone, a town with a population of about one hundred and thirty-five thousand. It was named after David Livingstone, the Scottish explorer and missionary. He was the first European to explore the area in the 1850s and to view Victoria Falls, one of the seven wonders of the world, and one of the world’s largest waterfalls with a width of over seventeen hundred meters. David Livingstone was thought to have been the first European to view Victoria Falls in November 1855. Livingstone named the falls in honor of Queen Victoria of Britain, but the Sotho language name, *Mosi-oa-Tunya,* “The Smoke That Thunders,” continues to be used locally.

John had been to Livingstone a few times, and he preferred to stay at the Protea Hotel by Marriott, one of the nicer hotels in the central part of the city. His journey to his current position as one of the senior trainers and strategists with INTERPOL’s Environmental Crime Group was fascinating.

John Benson was fifty-four years old now and showing his age a little. He was just over six feet tall and tried to keep his weight under two hundred and twenty pounds. His nickname within INTERPOL circles was John “Indiana Jones” Benson because they thought he looked a little like the actor Harrison Ford and had a similar swagger about him and a keen sense of humor.

He grew up on a farm about one hundred kilometers northwest of Edmonton, Alberta. After high school, he moved to Edmonton in 1976 to go to the University of Alberta, where he got a B.Sc. in Wildlife Biology. After a few years working for the Alberta provincial government, John went back to the U of A and got his M.Sc. in Forest Science. He did his M.Sc. thesis research on Rocky Mountain Bighorn Sheep and the effects of wildfires on their habitat. After graduating, he worked in the environmental consulting industry for about three years.

While completing his master's degree, he met a professor at the U of A who was doing some interesting research in aspects of forensic wildlife biology. The professor was trying to develop genetic bioassay techniques to trace the geographic origin of ungulate trophy animals confiscated from poachers by the Fish and Wildlife Service. It was assumed that many of these animals came from National Parks, but it was difficult to prove using the current scientific tools. Since bighorn sheep were one of the most popular animals confiscated from poachers, it sparked John's interest and he ended up spending another two years in a Ph.D. program developing the genetic bioassay techniques specific to Bighorn Sheep.

After completing his Ph.D. in 1989, John was recruited by the RCMP to work in conjunction with the Environmental Enforcement Branch of Environment Canada. However, he had to first attend the RCMP Training Academy in Regina, Saskatchewan, just like any new RCMP recruit. The National Environmental Enforcement headquarters was in Gatineau, Quebec, but he was allowed to set up a small operations center and forensic lab as well as hire a small team of forensic biologists to work out of the regional criminal forensic lab at K Division headquarters in Edmonton.

His small team of RCMP wildlife forensic biologists in Edmonton, often working with the enforcement officers from the Enforcement Branch of Environment Canada and Alberta provincial Fish and Wildlife officers, concentrated their efforts mostly in western Canada. However, they soon developed a national reputation for solving some complex cases of international wildlife trafficking originating in Canada and involving the illegal harvesting of animal parts, mostly for the Asian market.

John's work in Canada eventually caught the interest of INTERPOL's Wildlife Crime Working Group. The wildlife experts who make up the group devise strategies and initiatives for law enforcement to combat wildlife crimes on an international scale. They initiate operations to capture wildlife criminals, seize poached items, and dismantle the organized networks responsible for wildlife crime. They also engage with key players in wildlife conservation and law enforcement around the world to maximize the global impact of their projects and operations.

INTERPOL's Wildlife Crime Working Group is also a member of the International Consortium on Combating Wildlife Crime (ICCWC). Its mission is to strengthen criminal justice systems and provide coordinated support at regional, national, and international levels to combat wildlife and forest crime to ensure perpetrators of serious wildlife and forest crime would face a formidable and coordinated response. ICCWC is the collaborative effort of five inter-governmental organizations working to bring coordinated support to the national wildlife law enforcement agencies and to the sub-regional and regional networks.

The ICCWC partners are the Convention on International Trade in Endangered Species of Wild Fauna and Flora Secretariat (CITES), the United Nations Office on Drugs and Crime, the World Bank, and the World Customs Organization.

Beginning around 2007, John and his team were requested by Environment Canada's Wildlife Enforcement Directorate (WED) and INTERPOL's Wildlife Crime Working Group to train local and state wildlife enforcement agencies in various countries around the world in the scientific principles of forensic wildlife biology and wildlife crime scene processing. This often involved both classroom instruction and taking part in field raids and takedowns of the wildlife poachers and traffickers.

John's RCMP Wildlife Crime Unit team technically worked as a liaison service with the WED, which is part of Environment and Climate Change Canada's Enforcement Branch. The WED is responsible for enforcing federal wildlife laws with a team of around one hundred field enforcement and intelligence officers. The WED's national headquarters office is in Gatineau, Québec, with five regional offices across Canada, including Edmonton. When requested, John Benson's RCMP team also worked with the Alberta provincial Fish and Wildlife Enforcement Branch and the Fish and Wildlife Forensics Lab.

John and his team's affiliation with INTERPOL's Wildlife Crime Working Group was technically administered through the RCMP's International Operations Branch (IOB) and the Liaison Officer Program. The IOB was part of the RCMP Federal and International Operations Directorate. Liaison Officers were stationed in certain other countries and were responsible for organizing Canadian investigations, facilitating the exchange of criminal intelligence, especially related to national security, and aiding in investigations that directly affected Canada. They often collaborated with agents from the Canadian Security Intelligence Service (CSIS), as John's team did as well.

The wildlife poachers and traffickers were often involved in criminal networks or gangs and were heavily armed, so fire fights were common. Wildlife trafficking was only one of the criminal enterprises the gangs participated in—they diversified into things like terrorism, drug trafficking, and human trafficking. The Chinese Triads were some of the nastier bad guys and operated in many countries to satisfy the insatiable demand for various exotic animal parts in China and other Asian countries. Over the years, John and his team's reputation grew, and his services were in great demand.

John had been divorced for the last ten years. He had met his now ex-wife June while he was an undergraduate science student at the University of Alberta, and she was a pre-med student. They got married in the summer of 1979 after they both graduated. He completed his M.Sc. degree, and she went on to complete her medical degree and internship. She then did her residency in trauma medicine and started her career as an ER doctor. In the meantime, he worked for three years in environmental consulting and then went back to the U of A to complete his Ph.D.

The first of their three daughters, Sally, was born in 1983, and then Angela in 1985 and Laura in 1988. They were now twenty-nine, twenty-seven, and twenty-five years old, respectively, and were all married to great guys. Sally was a senior graphic designer and art director for an advertising company and had one daughter. Angela was a physiotherapist with two daughters and was pregnant again and due in June, and Laura was also a senior graphic designer working for a different advertising company and had just had her first baby, a son. They had all settled in Edmonton, so the decision about where John's home base had to be was never really an option during his career.

Unfortunately, because of the demands of both his and his ex-wife June's careers, and his frequent absences traveling around the world, their marriage did not survive. They were divorced in 2001. John tried to be home for family celebrations like birthdays and holidays as much as possible but could not always be there if he were away on some INTERPOL assignment in Africa, South America, or Asia.

John lived in a historic bungalow on Ada Boulevard in north Edmonton overlooking the North Saskatchewan River valley. It was in the Highlands neighborhood of Edmonton, one of the older suburban areas of the city, with many houses dating back one hundred years. Ada Boulevard was a very trendy street running about twenty-five blocks along the top of the river valley and had a mixture of older historic houses and new large infill houses. John lived alone in the house when he was in Edmonton, but his housemates were his two German shepherds, Syd and Nelle.

Sammy Molefe was familiar with the Protea Hotel, having stayed there a few times himself when on Botswana DWNP business in Livingstone. He drove into the parking area in front of the main entrance to the hotel to unload their luggage and register at the reception desk. When they entered the reception area, John saw Dr. Kate Beckett and Anna Dupree sitting at a table in the adjacent lounge, having a drink of some kind. He waved at them and indicated he and Denny would just check in and then come over and join them.

Dr. Kate Beckett was forty-four years old, divorced with one adult daughter, Dianna, who attended Portland State University in Portland, Oregon. Kate was an attractive brunette and always smarter than everyone else in the room. John had known her for about eight years and had collaborated with her on INTERPOL assignments for about the last three years.

She and John had been a romantic couple off and on for the last two years as well. Unfortunately, since they were both obsessed with their demanding careers and lived in different countries, they had trouble maintaining anything approaching a normal romantic relationship. However, they had come to an understanding about the demands of their careers and private lives and had decided that when they had a chance to be physically together, wherever in the world that might be, they would live together as a couple if possible. When the time came to go back to their respective homes, families, and regular jobs, they would temporarily part ways until the next assignment brought them back together. So far, it seemed to be working for them.

Kate grew up in Tacoma, Washington, just south of Seattle. Her father was an aeronautical engineer and worked for Boeing at their facility in Renton, Washington, about a half an hour drive from their home. Her mother was a nurse who worked at St. Francis Hospital in Tacoma. Her father died of a heart attack in 2007, and her mother lived in a retirement home in Tacoma.

She had a normal upper middle-class upbringing and excelled at academics throughout school.

She was also a star track athlete in high school and went on to the University of Washington in Seattle on a full athletic scholarship. Kate qualified for the US Olympic team for the 1988 Summer Olympics in Seoul, South Korea, for both the four hundred- and eight-hundred-meter track races, but tragically tore her Achilles tendon during training two months before the Olympics. That was the end of her track career, so she put all her efforts into her academic studies. She got her B.Sc. degree in Animal Physiology and Zoology in 1989, and then her M.Sc. degree in Genetics studying DNA bioassay techniques for tracing the geographic origins of endangered wildlife species.

Kate was then accepted at the University of Southern California to do her Ph.D. and continued with her M.Sc. research concentrating on DNA bioassay techniques specifically for the Sierra Nevada bighorn sheep, a subspecies of bighorn sheep unique to the Sierra Nevada mountains of California and Nevada. Sierra Nevada bighorn sheep were designated as a federally endangered subspecies in 2000, and as of 2012, only six hundred Sierra bighorn remained in the wild. They were also a prized trophy animal for poachers and wildlife traffickers, and the science of forensic wildlife biology and genetics was being used to trace the geographic origins of the confiscated trophy heads from poachers. In most cases, the origins of the trophy animals were from National Parks in the United States.

Wildlife forensic genetics had become a critical investigative tool for prosecuting criminals involved in international trafficking in wild animals or animal parts because of all the recent technology that was available for species identification and source population identification. Forensic genetics could answer questions about the identity of the species, the origin and source population of the animal or animal part, as well as identify whether it was bred in captivity or caught in the wild.

After completing her Ph.D. in 1992, Kate spent two years at the University of Cambridge in England doing post-doctoral research with a research team working on developing genetic bioassay techniques for tracing confiscated African elephant ivory to the elephant's geographic origin in Africa. She also got her first exposure to the fascinating world of international illegal wildlife trafficking and law enforcement.

Upon returning to the US in 1994, Kate was offered a job at the United States Fish and Wildlife (F&W) Service Office of Law Enforcement. She also received training as a United States Fish and Wildlife Service special agent, with most of the same law enforcement powers as FBI special agents. The F&W Office of Law Enforcement investigated wildlife crimes, regulated wildlife trade, and worked in partnership with international, state, and tribal law enforcement agencies.

When in the United States, Kate worked out of the National Fish and Wildlife Forensics Laboratory in Ashland, Oregon, at the northern end of the South Oregon State College campus. Founded in 1988 and run by the United States Fish and Wildlife Service, the forensics laboratory was the only laboratory in the world devoted to wildlife law enforcement.

By treaty, since 1998, the forensics laboratory was also the official crime lab for the CITES and the Wildlife Working Group of INTERPOL. She was offered the job of the director of the laboratory but turned it down so she would have the freedom to travel around the world working with INTERPOL and the likes of Dr. John Benson.

Kate had been in a short-term relationship with a fellow graduate student at the University of Southern California (USC). The relationship did not last long, but she had gotten pregnant and had a daughter, Dianna, in 1992 while she was finishing her Ph.D. thesis. The father was not interested in sticking around, so Kate continued as a single parent. She had already been accepted to do her post-doctoral research at Cambridge University in England, so she and her new baby moved to England for two years. She would often bring Dianna with her to the lab at Cambridge and would also take her to the daycare provided at the University for the research staff.

Dianna was now twenty years old and living and going to university in Portland. She was single and was studying to be a graphic designer. Dianna had decided not to follow her mother into the family wildlife trafficking crime-busting business and seemed happy with her life in Portland. Interestingly, two of John Benson's daughters were also graphic designers. Ashland and Portland were about a four-hour drive apart, so Kate could see Dianna often when she was home in the US.

Kate had previously heard of John Benson by reputation and had even spoken to him on the phone several times in 1992 when she was working on her Ph.D. at USC because their thesis research topics had been quite similar. She had also seen him speak at a conference in 2001. However, she only met him in person in 2004 at an international conference on wildlife trafficking and law enforcement in Lyon, France, sponsored by INTERPOL.

They had both been invited to do presentations at the conference and were then on a discussion panel together. They had hit it off right away because of their common academic interests and similar jobs in forensic wildlife biology and law enforcement. They started a professional relationship via email and phone calls, often discussing cases they were working on or asking each other for advice about new forensic procedures. They also continued to see each other periodically at international conferences and meetings.

In 2010, they were jointly invited by INTERPOL's Wildlife Crime Working Group to work together as advisors and trainers on a new initiative named Project Wisdom targeting illegal trafficking in elephant ivory and rhino horn in Africa. The current operation they were working on was Operation Worthy and was part of the larger INTERPOL Project Wisdom initiative. Kate and Anna had also attended the five- day training workshop at the Botswana Police Training College and Law Enforcement Academy but had opted to fly to Livingstone instead of doing the two-day drive from Gaborone with John and Denny.

6 p.m. Monday, April 9, 2012
Protea Hotel, Livingstone, Zambia

After checking in at the reception desk, John, Denny, and the two dogs went over to where Kate and Anna were sitting and said hello. Kate said, "Nice to see you arrived safely. How was the drive?" There was much tail wagging and squirming by Syd and Nelle when they saw Kate and Anna, and after some pats and hugs, they eventually settled down after Denny told them to be good.

John and Denny told them about the highlights of the two-day drive from Gaborone and the Kazungula Ferry crossing experience.

Anna said, "We had a nice three-hour flight from Gaborone and arrived here yesterday afternoon. Today we decided to be tourists and hired a car and driver to take us to see the Victoria Falls. We walked on all the paths beside the Falls on the Zambia side of the Zambesi River and got soaking wet even though we were wearing rain ponchos. I've been to Niagara Falls a few times, but Victoria Falls was really something special to see. I can certainly see why the locals call it 'The Smoke That Thunders.' We also did a little shopping at the open market near the parking area. I even added to my collection of carved African animals."

Anna Dupree was twenty-nine years old and was originally from Montreal. She had completed her B.Sc. in Genetics and M.Sc. in Wildlife Forensic Biology at McGill University. After completing her M.Sc. degree, she was recruited by the RCMP to work in the National Forensic Laboratory Services out of the Environment Canada National Enforcement headquarters in Gatineau, Quebec. John first met her in Gatineau three years earlier while she was working on tissue samples he had submitted for DNA testing from the Edmonton forensics lab.

After discussions both in person and over the phone, he realized she would be the perfect person to take over the day-to-day management of the Edmonton lab. He wooed her for a year with stories of the chance to not only manage the wildlife forensics lab services in Edmonton, but to travel to all the exotic locations around the world working with INTERPOL She finally took him up on his offer and moved to Edmonton two years ago.

Anna was also an attractive brunette, about five foot, eight inches tall and weighed about 130 pounds, which was all muscle. She was an over-achiever in almost every facet of her life. While John was reading her RCMP background security checks, he discovered she had an IQ of over 150. She was not only fluent in both English and French, but she also spoke Spanish like a native Spaniard, and for something to do in the evenings in hotel rooms while on assignment, she taught herself Swahili because she thought it might come in handy on the job.

Denny often liked to joke that in addition to being the smartest person on their team, which is saying something when John Benson and Kate Beckett are on your team, she was also the most dangerous person he knew. She had an instructor-level RCMP rating in marksmanship and hand-to-hand combat. She also had black belts in both Krav Maga and Brazilian Jiu-jitsu. Most of the other RCMP hand-to-hand combat instructors were afraid to train with her. Underneath that highly intelligent, attractive exterior was a warrior who loved her work and was extremely good at it.

Although John would never dare mention it to Anna, she also had a mild case of obsessive-compulsive disorder, which turned out to be very opportune for him. She was a stickler for neatness and organization. She always seemed to know where everything was and what administrative or operational paperwork needed to be completed, which were not strong points for either him or Denny. John relied on her for many things, not the least of which was keeping him out of trouble with the numerous administrators and paper-pushers in the RCMP and INTERPOL.

Kate said, "Although I have been to Victoria Falls before and have flown over them by helicopter as well, the pure power and scope of the cascading water over the escarpment is overwhelming no matter how many times you've seen them. So, are the plans set for tomorrow's raid on the ivory storage warehouse?"

Since there were no other guests in the lounge area to overhear their conversation, John answered, "Sammy Molefe told us we are scheduled to meet with Roberta Mulenga, the head of intelligence for ZAWA, tomorrow morning at the Livingstone Police headquarters at ten o'clock to go over the final plans for the raid. ZAWA will be using the local Livingstone police as backup for their own enforcement officers. They are hoping this raid will lead them to the ringleaders of the elephant ivory poaching syndicate operating in this area of Botswana and Zambia. Sammy said he and Seth were invited to observe the raid since ZAWA suspects that some of the ivory in the warehouse probably comes from elephants killed in Botswana."

"ZAWA want us to use Syd and Nelle when they breach the warehouse in case there are armed guards inside," Denny said. "I guess Roberta was extremely impressed with Syd and Nelle when we raided the house in Gaborone and captured Ben Simasiku and his gang leader. She wants to put pressure on her superiors to start a canine training facility in the anti-poaching unit of ZAWA." Laughing, he said, "I think Syd and Nelle are becoming more important than us in these training workshops."

Denny and John had been through a lot over the previous six years and there was not a better person in the world you would want with you when the bad guys were shooting at you in the jungle, or anywhere else, for that matter.

Denny was thirty-eight years old now. He was a member of the Driftpile Cree First Nation located south of Lesser Slave Lake in northern Alberta. His father was a Chief of the First Nation like his father before him.

As a young teenager, Denny had loved to go hunting with his father and grandfather. He got his first hunting rifle at the age of fourteen and it was his most prized possession. He and his cousin, Mike Giroux, set up a shooting range in the forest and they would spend hours shooting at homemade targets. Denny saved up some money and bought the best rifle scope he could afford in the sporting goods store in the town of Slave Lake, east of the Reserve. Mike was a good shot, but Denny had a special skill for hitting the bullseye every time from ever increasing distances.

Both Denny and Mike also liked watching war movies on TV and talked about joining the military when they were old enough. Denny talked to the guidance counselor at the High School in Slave Lake, who gave him a few pamphlets about what was required to join the Canadian military. The one thing that was most important was to graduate from high school. So, Denny and Mike, although not the best students, worked harder than ever to get through high school and get their diplomas.

As soon as they turned eighteen and finished high school, they informed their parents they were going to enlist in the military. They were both accepted, and in September 1992, went off to basic training in Quebec. They both immediately took to the military lifestyle and excelled at all the training exercises. Their skill on the shooting range immediately got the interest of their instructors. Denny's sharpshooter scores were always the best of anyone in his training class. In fact, they were the best of anyone his instructors had seen for quite a while.

After their basic training was completed, they were asked if they would like to go into the specialized sniper training program. Once again, Denny completed the program as the best sharpshooter in his training class, with Mike not far behind. They both also trained as mountain warfare specialists and paratroopers, which included helicopter assault techniques.

They were then assigned to the special forces sniper unit and got their first overseas deployment to Bosnia and Herzegovina in January 1994 with Canada's NATO peacekeeping forces. They served in Bosnia and Croatia on rotating deployments for several years and were also deployed to missions in the Central African Republic and Sierra Leone in the later 1990s. Denny and Mike's reputations as snipers grew not only in the Canadian Armed Forces, but in other country's forces as well, particularly the US Army and Marine special forces.

In 2001, Denny and Mike were included among the few dozen Canadian special forces troops who took part in the US military invasion of Afghanistan. They were followed in February 2002 by an infantry battle group (approximately twelve hundred troops) sent to the southern Afghan province of Kandahar as part of a United States Army task force searching for insurgents in that area. The Canadians fought against al Qaeda and Taliban forces and provided protection for humanitarian operations and for Afghanistan's new interim government. From 2003 to 2005, the Canadian battle group's mission focused on providing security in the Afghan capital, Kabul, and helping to disarm Afghan militia units under the command of local warlords. Despite occasional insurgent suicide bomber attacks, the Canadians were mostly involved in patrolling, policing, and stabilizing the new Afghan government.

Denny and Mike, however, as special forces snipers, were deployed mostly with the US special forces in forward bases in the mountains of Afghanistan, searching for and killing senior Taliban and al Qaeda fighters. With Mike Giroux acting mostly as Denny's spotter, their kill success was usually the highest of all the special forces sniper teams. Their Aboriginal background and special forces training were particularly suited to operating in the mountainous terrain of Afghanistan. Their reputation grew and Denny became known as "The Ghost" in special forces circles. Although, he always deflected credit and seldom talked about his missions with his fellow soldiers.

John was busy with his RCMP wildlife trafficking law enforcement duties and managing his forensics lab but realized if he wanted to get more involved in international enforcement operations with agencies like INTERPOL, he needed additional specialized field training in military combat tactics. He persuaded his superiors to let him go to Afghanistan in 2005 for three months and spend time with the Canadian special forces there.

Most of his time in Afghanistan was spent at the Canadian base in Kabul, going out on routine patrols. However, he met Dennis Bear one day when he was back at the base in Kabul and since they were both from Alberta, they struck up a friendship. John talked with Denny about the type of wildlife trafficking enforcement work he was doing with the RCMP and the wildlife forensics lab in Edmonton. Denny was fascinated. He invited John to come with him on a few missions into the mountains to act as his spotter and give Mike Giroux a break. John was nervous about getting so close to the action, but during their time in the mountains waiting to get the shot at whatever bad guys they were after, they had a lot of time to talk about international wildlife trafficking and wildlife law enforcement.

Denny's latest enlistment term in the military was about to end in early 2006, and he and John agreed Denny could join John's team if Denny were to quit the military and go through the RCMP basic training program. So, both Denny and Mike Giroux ended their military careers in January 2006 and applied to join the RCMP. They were both accepted and completed their training at the RCMP training academy in Regina, Saskatchewan, in late 2006. Mike went on to become an RCMP special constable working close to home in the Slave Lake Detachment, and Denny joined John Benson's team at RCMP K Division headquarters in Edmonton.

Since then, John and Denny had traveled around the world together on various INTERPOL operations. They sometimes found themselves in some very tough spots, but always managed to survive, often only because of Denny's military rifle skills. Denny was also a fast learner, and despite his lack of any formal university training in forensic wildlife biology, he seemed to have a natural and practical understanding of the science involved. He and Anna frequently worked with local wildlife law enforcement personnel, instructing them on forensic evidence gathering and wildlife crime scene processing.

Syd and Nelle traveled with the team most of the time and stayed with John in Edmonton at his house whenever they were back home. John usually brought them into his RCMP office in Edmonton with him so they wouldn't have to stay home alone and could mingle with the rest of the office and lab staff. Since they were great at looking hungry, there were strict rules about feeding them snacks, but they got their share, anyway.

They were still young for working police dogs at only three years old, and the RCMP dog trainers had advised John and Denny that since Denny was the principal dog handler on assignments, that they try to separate their "work lives" from their "off duty" lives. So, they seldom stayed with Denny when they were not working so they knew that when they were with him, it meant they were "on duty" and their innate instincts and training kicked in. This was somewhat different from the typical handler/dog protocol in the RCMP, but it worked for the particular circumstances of John's team, and Syd and Nelle were able to adapt extremely well.

Because they were sisters, the two dogs looked very similar to each other. Weighing around eighty pounds each, they both had typical German shepherd coloration and markings, but Nelle had more black-colored fur on her head and the 'saddle' of her back and sides. At an early age, Syd became the dominant or alpha dog between the two. Although, as working police dogs, they were equals in every way.

The two dogs had very distinct personalities, which was evident to those who knew them well. Syd loved to fetch anything you threw for her. Nelle was not interested in fetching, but was an enthusiastic partner for Syd, running beside her and barking excitedly. For some reason, she thought Syd was the fetcher, and she was the helper.

Syd loved the water and would swim after sticks for as long as you wanted to throw them. Nelle didn't like getting wet, so would just venture into the water up to the bottom of her chest, and then wait for Syd to swim back with the stick. Nelle was also much more sensitive to any disapproval from her humans. She would act very offended if someone raised their voice in criticism of her for some reason, whereas it didn't seem to bother Syd. Denny and the team, soon learned how to handle the two dogs to maximize their individual strengths and accommodate their unique personalities.

6:30 p.m. Monday, April 9, 2012
Protea Hotel, Livingstone, Zambia

"Why don't Denny and I and the dogs go get settled into our rooms, have a shower, and then we can all go for dinner at the hotel restaurant," John said. "I invited Sammy and Seth to join us for dinner as well. The lady at the hotel reception counter said that I am apparently staying in the same suite as a woman named Kate Beckett, and Denny has his own suite with Syd and Nelle. It seems I probably got the better room assignment."

Laughing, Kate said, "Yes, I know how scared you get at night all by yourself away from home, so I thought I would let you stay in my room so I could keep an eye on you."

"That is truly kind of you," John said, smiling. "I will have to think of a way to repay your generosity later tonight."

CHAPTER 2

7:30 p.m. Monday, April 9, 2012
Protea Hotel, Livingstone, Zambia

The six of them gathered in the hotel dining room at about seven-thirty and had an enjoyable dinner while discussing the upcoming raid on the suspected ivory warehouse. They also discussed the current initiatives of INTERPOL's Operation Worthy and the larger problem of elephant ivory and rhino horn poaching and international trafficking in Africa.

Poaching or the illegal ivory trade was the biggest threat to African elephants' survival. Before the Europeans began colonizing Africa, there may have been as many as twenty-six million elephants. The arrival of Europeans kicked off the commercial ivory trade, in which tusks were used for piano keys, billiards balls, combs, and all kinds of other items. By the early twentieth century, elephant numbers had dropped to ten million. Hunting continued to increase, and by 1970, their numbers were down to 1.3 million.

Between 1970 and 1990, hunting and poaching put the African elephant at risk of extinction, reducing its population by another half. As of 2012, the International Union for Conservation of Nature listed them as vulnerable to extinction. As few as four hundred thousand remained in the wild.

Although the CITES banned the global commercial ivory trade in 1989, the illegal tusk trade remained strong, and poaching continued across the continent.

Compounding the problem is how long it takes for elephants to reproduce. With reproduction rates hovering around five to six percent, there are simply not enough calves being born to make up for the losses from poaching.

African rhinoceros' species are in even more jeopardy. The most recent thorough and comprehensive studies and census estimates suggest there are roughly 20,700 southern white rhino and 4,885 black rhinos' remaining in the wild in Africa, including their subspecies. South Africa's Kruger National Park was home to 7,000 to 8,300 rhinos as of 2012.

The northern white rhino subspecies has been reduced to just three living animals in a reserve in East Africa, and one each in zoos in San Diego and the Czech Republic. The three species of rhino in Asia are also threatened by the demand for rhino horn as a symbol of wealth or to be used for traditional oriental medicines. As of the end of 2011, there were an estimated 3,333 greater one-horned rhino (Indian rhino), only sixty-seven of the Javan species, and as few as thirty rhinos of the Sumatran species left in the wild.

Africa's white rhino species are the largest of the living rhinoceros' species, weighing up to 3,600 kilograms, and are the continent's third-largest species after the African bush elephant and African forest elephant. The black rhino, which is actually grey, can weigh up to 1,400 kilograms. The lifespan of a wild rhinoceros is thought to be thirty-five to fifty years for any of the species.

Rhinoceros horn is comprised largely of keratin, a substance that scientists describe as a "fibrous structural protein." In lay terms, it is the same material found in fingernails. It has no proven health benefits. Despite this, it has long been an ingredient in traditional Asian medicine, used to treat everything from fevers to gout. This demand for rhino horn has contributed to a trend that had seen rhino populations plummet from half a million to fewer than thirty thousand in less than a century.

International trade in rhino horn was banned in 1977 and demand for the substance seemed to be steadily declining. However, around 2009, a rumor began circulating of an unnamed "Vietnamese official" who had ingested rhino horn and been cured of liver cancer. Demand spiked and the poaching industry went into overdrive. Statistics published by South Africa's Department of Environmental Affairs show that in 2007, poachers killed just thirteen rhinos. In 2011, the figure was over one thousand.

Today, demand for rhino horn is as strong as ever. Wealthy consumers in Vietnam, China, and Taiwan buy it for medicinal purposes, as a hangover cure, and even for use recreationally. According to a report commissioned by the World Wildlife Federation, by 2012, the black-market price of rhino horn had risen to $57,000 per kilogram, more than gold, platinum, diamonds, or cocaine.

10 p.m. Monday, April 9, 2012
Protea Hotel, Livingstone, Zambia

At about ten o'clock, the group said goodnight to each other and dispersed for the night to their individual rooms. They agreed to meet for breakfast at seven-thirty before going to the Livingstone Police headquarters for the briefing with the Zambia Wildlife Authority at ten.

When John and Kate got into their suite, Kate said, "That was an interesting evening. It's always nice to get a candid perspective of the anti-poaching situation from local wildlife law enforcement people. They are always underfunded and mostly rely on money from international environmental foundations and trusts to do their work on the ground. It often seems like we're fighting a losing battle with the much better funded and organized wildlife poaching and trafficking syndicates."

"I know it seems discouraging sometimes, but we can't give up and let the wildlife poachers and traffickers win," said John. "We can only hope that the politicians and bureaucrats in Africa and in the West and Asia realize that the world would be a much less interesting and sadder place if our children and grandchildren could only see elephants and rhinos in zoos. As we both know, the African northern white rhino is now down to the last five animals alive in the world. After they die in a few years, we will have lost one of the most magnificent animal species in the world forever."

"I know, but let's not dwell on that. It's too depressing," Kate said. "This suite is much nicer that the spartan married couple dorm rooms at the Botswana Police Training Academy. And look at that big king-sized bed. Maybe we should try it out."

CHAPTER 3

10 a.m. Tuesday, April 10, 2012
Livingstone Central Police Headquarters, Livingstone, Zambia

John, Kate, Anna, and Denny met Sammy Molefe and Seth Khama for breakfast at the hotel and then drove the short distance to the Livingstone Central Police headquarters. Roberta Mulenga, whom they met at the training workshop in Gaborone, introduced them to her team of six wildlife enforcement officers. She also introduced them to the chief of detectives, Joseph Banda, at the Livingstone Police headquarters.

After everyone had assembled in the cramped meeting room at the central police station, Roberta started with the briefing for the upcoming raid on the suspected ivory warehouse in the Mwandi District in the northern part of Livingstone, south of the Harry Mwanga Nakumbula Airport.

She said, "The raid is scheduled for one o'clock this afternoon. Surveillance of the warehouse by undercover Livingstone police officers over the past few days revealed there is usually a lookout stationed at the entrance gate into the fenced compound. The undercover officers saw at least two armed men going into and leaving the warehouse in twelve-hour shifts around seven o'clock in the mornings and evenings. We plan to surprise the lookout and take him into custody before he can warn the men inside."

Pausing to look around, she asked, "Any questions?" Everyone shook their heads, so she continued, "We will then go into the compound in force, set explosives on the outside of the main steel re-enforced access door and blow it open."

Gesturing towards Denny, she said, "Denny's dogs, Syd and Nelle, will then go into the warehouse and hopefully take down the two men inside. At which time, we will enter and apprehend them."

She then asked Denny and John, "Is this plan alright with you and are you okay with using your dogs to take down the two guards inside the warehouse?"

Denny answered, "Yes, it sounds okay as long as you can take out the lookout at the gate before he warns the guards inside. If they are alerted, and are ready for the raid, then it will be too dangerous to send the dogs in first. You will just have to use your officers to breach the warehouse and be prepared for resistance from the guards. Otherwise, they will not be too alert if they do not suspect anything is going to happen, as is usually the case, I'm sure."

Roberta continued, "All right, if no one has questions or anything else to add, we will head out at noon in four unmarked vehicles. Three plainclothes officers in a small panel van and a driver will pull up to the gate of the compound and grab the lookout at one o'clock and put him in the van. We will then enter the compound and our explosives expert will set the charges on the door and blow it open. After that, we will proceed as we have discussed."

Outside in the parking area, Denny and John put on their Kevlar vests and then placed canine vests on Syd and Nelle. The two dogs were getting excited, sensing they would be going into action soon. John and Kate had decided that Kate, Anna, Sammy, and Seth would hang back a few blocks in the DWNP Land Rover until the raid was over and the guards were in custody before coming into the warehouse compound.

Shortly after noon, they all started out for the fifteen-minute drive via Airport Road to Njiba Street, where the warehouse was located. John, Denny, Syd, and Nelle were in an SUV with Roberta and Joseph. They parked a few blocks away to wait until the "all-clear" was transmitted on the radio by the officers who were going to apprehend the lookout. Both John and Denny had been issued police assault rifles to use if required during the raid.

A few minutes past one o'clock, the call came from one of the officers in the panel van. They surprised the lookout who didn't have a chance to use his radio to warn the guards inside the warehouse.

All four SUV's immediately drove the few blocks to the warehouse compound, went through the gate, and parked outside the access door. The explosives expert jumped out of his vehicle and set the three charges on the outside of the steel re-enforced door — two next to the hinges and the third by the deadbolt. Denny was in place a few feet from the side of the door with Syd and Nelle, crouched down behind the shield of one of the tactical officers, ready to send the dogs into the warehouse as soon as the door was blown.

As they had discussed at the police station, Denny gave the explosives expert the "thumbs-up" signal. The officer pressed the detonator switch, and with a loud explosion, the door blew off its hinges into the warehouse. Denny then released Syd and Nelle and shouted "Capture"—the signal he used to send the dogs into action.

Both dogs rushed into the warehouse. They were trained to seek out criminals and always assumed anyone they encountered were bad guys. They immediately saw two men come rushing out of an office doorway carrying rifles. They were on them in seconds. They each selected a man and went for one of their arms. They clamped down on the men's arms as hard as they could and pulled them down onto the floor before the men aimed their rifles.

Faced with a dog locked onto their arm, both men immediately dropped their guns and started frantically howling in pain. Denny and several of the Livingstone police officers rushed into the warehouse right behind the dogs. When they got to the two men writhing on the floor, Denny quickly glanced around to make sure the scene was secure and there were no other guards in the office area. The dogs continued to grip the men's arms and hold them on the floor until they heard the command from Denny to let them go. After a few frantic seconds, Denny shouted "Release," and both Syd and Nelle immediately released their grip on the two men's arms and backed away.

The tactical officers immediately surrounded the two men with their assault rifles pointed at them. One of the officers picked up the two rifles. Another officer shouted at them to roll over on their stomachs and put their hands behind their backs. Two officers then handcuffed both men and instructed them not to move.

With the situation now secure, Denny patted both dogs and told them what good dogs they were. He gave each of them some beef jerky from the bag he had in his pocket. This was their special treat after each successful takedown, and they knew they had done their job. John came into the warehouse right after the first police officers and stood beside Denny and the dogs. After patting the dogs and telling them what good dogs they were, he nudged Denny, and they both started looking around the warehouse. There were shelves filled with what looked like over one hundred raw elephant tusks of assorted sizes.

Roberta walked over to where they were standing looking extremely pleased and said, "Congratulations, your dogs performed perfectly, and it looks like we discovered one of the major ivory storage and distribution sites in this region of Zambia and Botswana. This is an extremely big day for us, and hopefully it will lead us to the ringleaders of the poaching syndicates operating in this area."

Smiling and gesturing to the elephant tusks that filled the shelves around the warehouse, she said, "We will take all the tusks back to the ZAWA headquarters in Lusaka and then try to get Dr. Saul Waters from the University of Washington in Seattle to come to Lusaka and take samples for DNA testing so we can try to figure out what regions they came from."

John called Kate and Anna on the police radio and told them it was all clear for them to come into the warehouse. A few minutes later, they walked into the warehouse with Sammy and Seth just as Roberta began talking to John and Denny.

After looking around in shock at the dozens of elephant tusks in the warehouse, Kate and Anna walked over to them and Kate said, "Congratulations everyone, your raid worked just like you laid it out."

She kneeled down beside Syd and Nelle and gave them each a few pats on the head and said, "Great job, girls. You got the bad guys again."

She then turned her attention back to Roberta and said, "I heard you mention Dr. Saul Waters. I know him well and the work he's done in developing the African elephant DNA database is extraordinary. He and his people at the University of Washington used elephant feces from all over western, eastern, and southern Africa to develop the DNA database. They can now extract DNA samples from any confiscated African elephant tusk and determine the geographic origin of the elephant that the tusk came from. Often, they can determine not only which country the ivory came from, but which specific park or game reserve it came from."

Roberta agreed, "Yes, I saw him speak last year at the University of Zambia in Lusaka where he explained how they developed the African elephant DNA database and how they've been using it to assist African law enforcement agencies. It has the potential to completely change how effective we are in tracking down and apprehending ivory poachers."

After a brief pause, she continued, "However, it costs a lot of money to collect the ivory samples and do the testing, so that's a big problem. Here in Africa, we don't have enough money to support the work, so we are dependent on the generosity of the international wildlife conservation foundations and trusts to help us save the elephants. Of course, we're also grateful for the help from INTERPOL's Wildlife Crime Unit and Canada's Wildlife Enforcement Directorate."

"We are happy to assist in any way we can," said John. "These past couple of weeks have been phenomenal, first helping to facilitate the anti-poaching training workshop at the Botswana Police Training College and Law Enforcement Academy, and then participating in the raids in Gaborone and now here in Livingstone. Unfortunately, we need to return to Nairobi tomorrow, but it's been a genuine pleasure to get to meet and collaborate with you and your team."

Roberta responded, "We have a lot of work to do now, cataloguing all the ivory here and transporting it back to Lusaka for processing. We also need to interrogate the lookout and these two guards in the warehouse. We know the identity of the other two guards who have been working here, and Joseph Banda has already sent his officers to their houses to arrest them.

"Hopefully, they will be able to tell us who they work for and what happens to the ivory that is stored here in the warehouse. They are just locals though, so we don't expect they will know too much about the overall poaching syndicate and how it all works. It's still a big win for us though, so we hope it will lead us closer to catching some ringleaders of the poaching syndicate."

John responded, "We can stay for a while and help your officers get started on documenting and cataloguing the ivory pieces. After that, I think we'll go back to our hotel, but maybe you could come by tomorrow morning for breakfast before we leave for the airport. We would be extremely interested in finding out how the interrogation of the guards went and what information you were able to get from them."

"That sounds like a good plan," Roberta said. "I'll see you tomorrow morning at about eight at your hotel. And thanks again for your help here today. Your dogs were amazing. I hope we can start using our own dogs soon if we get the funding to start an anti-poaching canine unit."

As they were talking, the Livingstone police officers got their two prisoners up from the floor and escorted them out to the police vehicles for transport back to the police station lock-up. With some initial instruction from John and the team, the ZAWA wildlife officers began the task of cataloguing the elephant tusks in the warehouse.

Sammy and Seth stayed to help document the ivory as well. After the process was well underway, John and the team went back to the hotel. However, Roberta, Seth, Sammy, and the other wildlife officers were all excited to implement the new wildlife crime scene documentation techniques taught by John's team at the workshop in Gaborone the previous week.

8 a.m. Wednesday, April 11, 2012
Protea Hotel, Livingstone, Zambia

Roberta arrived at the hotel as scheduled and she and the team all gathered at a table in the hotel restaurant. After some small talk and their breakfast orders arrived, she said, "So, it took all afternoon and into the evening, but we managed to get all the ivory pieces in the warehouse weighed and catalogued. There were 108 individual tusks and they collectively weighed 864 kilograms, almost a metric tonne of poached ivory."

Pausing, and flushed with emotion, she said, "That is over fifty dead elephants, just in this one small warehouse. They probably came from Zambia, Botswana, and Zimbabwe, and maybe even from Namibia. We won't know for sure until we get the DNA testing done."

Kate asked, "Did you get any information out of the warehouse guards or the lookout?"

Roberta answered, "As we suspected, they didn't know too much about the larger poaching operation, but we got the name of their immediate boss, who is the local manager of the warehouse. They said they usually only saw him a few times per month, either when someone was delivering new raw tusks to the warehouse, or when he brought the tusks to the warehouse himself.

"The guards said they didn't know where he lived in Livingstone and that he traveled around a lot. His name is Moses Oladele and we previously had intelligence reports that he was an associate of Ben Simasiku, the guy you helped apprehend in Gaborone a few days ago. An arrest warrant has been put out for Moses Oladele, but he may go into hiding when he hears what happened at the warehouse yesterday.

"We also asked the guards if they knew what happened to the ivory when it left the warehouse, but they didn't know too much about that part of the operation. They did tell us though that about once a month, some of the ivory pieces were taken to the airport in small shipments of ten or twenty pieces and flown by private planes to Dar es Salaam in Tanzania. The only name they ever heard from Moses Oladele when they were packing the ivory in wooden crates for shipment was someone with the last name Malengo. They said that sometimes Moses referred to him as 'Shetani,' which means 'the devil' in Swahili."

"Yes, we've heard of the guy they call 'Shetani,' said John. "His real name is Benjamin Malengo, and he's thought to be one of the up-and-coming ringleaders of the eastern and southern Africa ivory trafficking syndicates. They think he has direct links to the Chinese and Vietnamese importers and wholesalers of illegal ivory. Both the Kenya Wildlife Service and Tanzanian Wildlife Division have been trying to track him down, but he is very elusive, and they don't even have any photographs of him yet. His reputation is growing though, and we'll catch him, eventually."

After they finished breakfast, they said their goodbyes and went to their rooms to finish packing for the five-hour return flight to Nairobi. The assistant director of the Kenya Wildlife Service flew back to Nairobi from Gaborone on a commercial flight so John's team could continue to use the KWS's Cessna 425 Corsair plane.

They took the hotel shuttle bus to Livingstone's Harry Mwanga Nakumbula Airport to where the plane was parked on the tarmac close to the main terminal. They unloaded their luggage, including the travel kennels for Syd and Nelle, and went through the customs checkpoint out to the tarmac where the two KWS pilots had the plane fueled and ready to go. They took off at eleven for the five-hour flight back to the Wilson Airport in Nairobi, where the KWS airwing facilities and hangars were located.

CHAPTER 4

8 a.m. Thursday, April 12, 2012
Wildebeest Eco Camp, Nairobi, Kenya

John and the team had arrived at the Wilson Airport in Nairobi at about four-thirty the previous afternoon. They called their KWS driver, Simon Okafor, to pick them up in the Land Rover Defender vehicle assigned to them while they were in Kenya. When they were in Nairobi, they normally operated out of the KWS headquarters office complex at the north end of Nairobi National Park. The complex was just inside the park's main gate, a few kilometers southwest of the Wilson Airport on Langata Road.

Their favorite place to stay in Nairobi whenever they came on an INTERPOL assignment or operation was the Wildebeest Eco Camp located just five kilometers northwest of the KWS headquarters office via Langata Road and then north on Mokoyeti Road West. Although the Wildebeest Eco Camp was primarily an upscale tented camp/hotel, they generally booked three of the deluxe, stand-alone cottages, which were equipped for longer stays and were larger than the standard rooms. The cottages also had a small fridge, lounge area, and writing desk, and were located furthest away from the main bar and restaurant area. They had the choice of either eating meals at the open-air hotel restaurant, which overlooked the beautiful hotel grounds, gardens, and swimming pool, or making something for themselves in their rooms. However, there were no cooking appliances, so they were restricted to food items that required little preparation.

It was also an excellent location for Syd and Nelle because there were plenty of open spaces around the hotel for them to get a little exercise and have their doggie bathroom breaks. It was a small tropical oasis within the bustling city of Nairobi and always a pleasure to come back to.

They usually reserved the cottages for at least a month or more when they came to Nairobi, even though they were sometimes away on training workshops or field operations. The bill was generally covered by a combination of INTERPOL's Wildlife Crime Unit or Environment Canada's Wildlife Enforcement Directorate, depending on what assignment or operation they were there for.

In the morning, they got together for breakfast at the hotel restaurant so they could discuss what they were going to do over the upcoming few days. They were scheduled to help facilitate a three-day anti-poaching workshop from Wednesday to Friday the following week at the KWS Training Institute (KWSTI) in Naivasha, located next to Lake Naivasha and the Lake Naivasha National Park, about sixty miles north of Nairobi. John, Kate, and Anna were going to do a workshop for the senior recruits at the Institute on the latest methods in wildlife crime scene processing and evidence gathering.

They were to reinforce things the recruits had already covered, such as "chain of custody" procedures and the issuing of search warrants. So often, cases against wildlife poachers and traffickers broke down in African courts because defense lawyers were able to discredit the evidence gathering process and could have the charges dismissed on technicalities. This often negated months or sometimes even years of excellent investigative work tracking down and capturing the poaching ringleaders.

Denny, Syd, and Nelle were going to work with the Canine Training Unit at KWSTI. The KWS currently had three operational canine units based in Nairobi's Jomo Kenyatta International Airport and the Mombasa and Naivasha Stations, with well-trained Dutch shepherds, black German shepherd, and Belgian Malinois shepherd dogs.

The six dogs based at the Naivasha Station had all been acquired from Israel and had undergone a standard six-month training program. At KWSTI, they trained dogs to detect, track, and attack criminals found with illegal ivory and other prohibited wildlife products. Funding for the canine training program and acquisition of the dogs was provided by NGOs, such as the African Wildlife Foundation.

Denny was going to work with the KWS canine master, David Kimathi, to review and update the curriculum for the canine unit and demonstrate, with Syd and Nelle, the newest canine training procedures they had taught him at the RCMP National Canine Training Center in Alberta. The KWS was due to present an updated canine training curriculum to the KWS director of criminal investigation and the Kenya National Police Service for approval, so they were happy to get assistance from an expert from Canada, like Dennis Bear.

The other major training facility of the Kenya Wildlife Service was the KWS Law Enforcement Academy and Field Training School, established in the early 1990s. It was strategically located within Tsavo West National Park at Manyani, off the Nairobi-Mombasa Road. The school had permanent and semi-permanent barracks, which could accommodate up to six hundred trainees.

Although the facilities were at first quite basic, they were continually being upgraded as funding was available. The academy concentrated primarily on paramilitary field training for the KWS uniformed personnel combined with wildlife conservation concepts. John Benson and his team had also facilitated several training workshops at the Law Enforcement Academy in the past few years, concentrating on forensic evidence gathering and documentation.

They decided to check in at the KWS headquarters at the north end of Nairobi National Park where they had a temporary office to use when they were in Nairobi. Their primary contact at the KWS was Charles Jelani, the current head of the Wildlife Protection Department. Their KWS driver, Simon, had already arrived at the hotel with the Land Rover, anticipating that his services would be needed.

Simon was a very genial young man who spoke fluent English besides his native language, Swahili. He was an extremely good driver; he knew his way around Nairobi and had a knack for finding his way through the always chaotic and congested streets. Traffic laws and signs seemed to be only treated as suggestions in Nairobi, so it was best to have a driver who knew what he was doing rather than try to brave the traffic themselves. He was also familiar with most areas of Kenya and would often provide nuggets of information about the natural history or cultural significance of areas they were driving through.

After they finished breakfast and collected their things from their cottages, Simon drove them the short distance to the KWS headquarters. Their temporary office was in the part of the complex housing the Wildlife Protection Department head office staff. This was the primary centralized anti-poaching intelligence gathering unit of the KWS and they were in daily contact with KWS personnel all around the country. They also tracked INTERPOL, Kenya National Police Service, and Kenya Customs Service alerts involving activities related to wildlife crime.

Their temporary office was quite large and had four desks with a computer on each connected to the central KWS computer network, plus telephones on each desk. There were also two dog beds for Syd and Nelle, so they had their own space. When Joseph Mwangi, the operations manager of the Wildlife Intelligence Unit, realized John's team was in the office, he came in and said hello and asked them how their trip to Botswana and Zambia had gone.

John and Kate filled him in on the details of the operations in Gaborone and Livingstone. Impressed with their success helping to shut down a major ivory poaching operation, he said, "Those two dogs of yours are getting quite the reputation. I've heard that the KWS Canine Training Unit head at the KWS Training Institute, David Kimathi, is really looking forward to having Denny, Syd, and Nelle there next week."

He then told them about an INTERPOL alert they had just received about two Irish gangsters who had flown into Nairobi from Dublin the previous evening. He said, "The Irishmen are two brothers named Sean and Ryan Sheehan, who are members of an Irish gang named the 'Rathkeale Rovers.' Several other members of their gang were recently arrested for breaking into British museums and stealing whole rhino horns from museum exhibits, as well as carved rhino horn artifacts and Chinese jade. INTERPOL thinks the Sheehan brothers are in Nairobi to meet with local rhino horn traffickers, and intend to smuggle rhino horns back home to Ireland for eventual sale to China."

"Do they know where they went after they landed?" asked John.

Continuing with his story, Joseph answered, "The National Police Unit at the airport reviewed surveillance footage of their flight arrival from Dublin and based on photographs sent by INTERPOL, identified them as they were waiting for their luggage. They then observed them getting in a taxi and leaving the airport. They got the registration number and license plate of the taxi and then contacted the taxi company to find out where the driver had taken them. The taxi company said they were dropped off at the Hilton Hotel downtown at about nine o'clock.

"So, the KWS and National Police have a team of undercover officers watching the hotel as of seven o'clock this morning. They will follow them if they leave to see where they go in case they have a meeting arranged with local rhino horn traffickers. If so, we intend to apprehend them when they are in possession of the rhino horns and then take down the local rhino poachers at wherever the exchange takes place. Anyway, we were wondering if we could use Denny, Syd, and Nelle to take down the rhino poachers at the meeting place, assuming it will be at a house or some sort of business enterprise?"

Denny responded, "Well, it just so happens that we have a few days to kill here in Nairobi before we go to the KWSTI next week, so I think we could help you out. What do you think, John?"

"I don't see why not," said John. "It would be great to take down the rhino poachers, and to also put these Irish thugs behind bars as well. As despicable as the African rhino horn poachers are, there still needs to be buyers for the product to create a market and perpetuate the cycle. So, what's the story with this Irish gang, the Rathkeale Rovers?"

Joseph answered, "As far as my investigators have been able to find out, the gang originated from a small town in rural Ireland named Rathkeale, about twenty-two miles from Limerick, the closest city, hence the name 'Rathkeale Rovers.' A sizable percentage of the population of Rathkeale is from the 'Traveling Community,' Ireland's indigenous ethnic minority, who have similarities to the gypsies in Europe. Some of them have become quite wealthy, and the source of their money is the subject of a lot of speculation.

"Although most Rathkeale residents are law-abiding citizens, one group of Traveler families, headed by the O'Brien clan, are notorious in Ireland for the scope of their illegal activities and for running some very shady businesses. Over the years, they have come to be known as the Rathkeale Rovers and they now operate all over the United Kingdom, Europe, and even in the United States, with suspected ties to the Chinese Triads. In the last few years,

Irish law enforcement thinks the gang has made millions of pounds just from stolen rhino horns and jade artifacts from British museums."

"It doesn't sound like these two Sheehan brothers are here to go on safari," quipped Anna.

"INTERPOL has quite the file on these guys," continued Joseph. "The two brothers own a popular pub in Rathkeale named Sheehan's Tavern and Social Club. Although it's a popular and successful tavern, the Irish police think it's also a meeting place for the Rathkeale Rovers' gang members.

"The Sheehan's are cousins of the O'Brien's, the head family of the gang. Sean Sheehan is thirty-four years old, and his younger brother, Ryan, is thirty-two. A few of their Sheehan relatives have spent time in Irish and English jails for a variety of offences, from home burglaries to bank heists. The brothers took over the operation of the tavern from their father and uncle when they were sent to jail for ten years for holding up an armored truck outside a bank in Dublin.

"INTERPOL thinks the brothers are a little more sophisticated than most members of the Rathkeale Rovers, both having attended University College Cork studying business administration. Sean was one year ahead of Ryan at the university. They also played for the University College Cork Rugby Football Club. However, neither one finished their degrees because they were caught operating various illegal gambling enterprises out of their campus dormitory rooms. INTERPOL believes they are now in charge of the distribution and fencing of stolen goods for the Rathkeale Rovers gang, besides running a sports and horse racing betting operation from the upstairs rooms in the tavern."

"So, what's the plan?" asked Denny.

"We are just waiting for updates from our undercover surveillance team," answered Joseph. "The last report at nine-thirty from the team inside the Hilton Hotel lobby was that the two brothers were having breakfast at the hotel restaurant. If they leave the hotel by car or taxi, we have three unmarked surveillance vehicles ready to follow them. If they leave on foot, which seems unlikely, we have agents ready to follow them as well.

"As soon as they are on the move, I will let you know, and we can have Denny and the dogs go with Esther Balo to the meeting location. Denny, I assume you have the dogs' Kevlar vests with you? We can also issue you an assault rifle for the raid if it happens. One of your team is welcome to come along with Denny and the dogs as well. Otherwise, you can have Simon take you close by if the raid goes down so you can monitor the action."

Smiling, John said, "We thought we were going to have a few quiet days before we left for the training institute next week and were wondering what to do with ourselves, but this sounds like a lot more fun. I guess we'll just hang out here until we hear that something is happening then."

Joseph responded, "Alright, I'll get back to work, but as soon as we hear something from the undercover team, Esther will come and let you know, and she'll take you to the meeting location. The exchange of the rhino horns might not happen today, so we'll just have to see what happens. The Sheehan brothers' return flight to Dublin is booked for tomorrow morning at eleven o'clock so we think that if the exchange of the rhino horns is going to happen, it will either be today or tomorrow morning before their flight so they can go directly to the airport."

Denny said, laughing, "Well, the day just suddenly got a lot more interesting. This could be a breakthrough in dismantling the rhino horn trafficking syndicate operating here in Nairobi. We know the KWS has been trying to catch a break locating the ringleaders of the syndicate for a couple of years now, so this may be your chance to finally shut them down."

With their ears cocked, and their attention moving simultaneously from person to person, Syd and Nelle were extremely interested observers of the conversations taking place in the room. Their humans also appeared quite excited, so that usually meant something was about to happen that required their services.

At about ten-thirty, Esther Balo, who they knew from previous cases, came into the room, and said, "The surveillance team just called and said the Sheehan brothers got in a taxi at the Hilton Hotel and the surveillance vehicles are following them. The taxi is currently traveling south on Langata Road, coming towards Nairobi National Park and the KWS headquarters. I will update you as soon as they get to their destination."

In about twenty minutes, she came back into the office and said, "The taxi dropped the brothers off at the Carnivore Restaurant, just a few minutes away from the KWS office. Two of the undercover agents are going into the restaurant and will try to get seated close to them."

John's team had been to the Carnivore Restaurant numerous times. It was a popular tourist destination in Nairobi. The Carnivore was an open-air restaurant in the Langata suburb of Nairobi, and, as the name inferred, its specialty was meat, featuring an all-you-can-eat meat buffet. They served a wide variety of meat and were famous for their wild meat until Kenya imposed a ban on the sale of game meat in 2004. The game meat served, up until the restrictions, included giraffe, wildebeest, several antelope species, ostrich, and crocodile. The animals were raised on the Hopcraft Ranch, located forty kilometers outside Nairobi.

Since the sale of wild game meat was banned in Kenya, the restaurant now only served meat of domestic animals such as beef, pork, lamb, and chicken, as well as farmed animals like ostrich and crocodile. The meat was skewered on Maasai swords, cooked on coals, and served on cast-iron plates. It was ranked as one of the 'World's Best 50 Restaurants' at various times in the past.

At about one o'clock Esther came back into their office and said, "We just got an update from the undercover agents who went into the Carnivore Restaurant. They were posing as a married couple and were seated at a table near the Sheehan brothers. They were close enough to overhear some of their conversation.

"After they were there for about twenty minutes, another man joined them. Our agents were able to take his picture with their miniature surveillance camera. The man only stayed for about fifteen minutes and didn't eat lunch. However, he did have a quiet but serious looking conversation with the two Sheehan brothers.

"Our agents were not close enough to hear much of what they were saying, but after about fifteen minutes of discussion, he got up smiling and shook hands with the two brothers and left. The brothers finished their lunch and got back in their taxi, which was still waiting for them, and drove to the main gate entrance here at the park. They then checked in for one of the private, half-day guided game drives through the park.

"So, whatever is planned will not happen until this evening or tomorrow morning on their way to the airport to catch their flight back home to Ireland. We are thinking that tomorrow morning is the more likely scenario since that would minimize the time they would be in possession of the rhino horns. Our agents will continue their surveillance throughout the evening, after the brothers are finished their game drive, to see what they are up to."

"Well, at least they are getting to see some of the tourist sights here in Nairobi while they are in the city," Kate said, sarcastically. "Hopefully, it will be the last tourist activities they will be doing for a while after today."

Esther continued, "We ran the picture of the man who joined them at the Carnivore through our facial recognition software and it came back with an ID. The guy is thirty-seven years old and is a resident of Tanzania. He has a warrant out for his arrest there for suspected ivory poaching. His name is Samson Kanumba, and he has a long record of 'person of interest' detainments and arrests in Dar es Salaam and Arusha, but no convictions, and no time served. We had two of our surveillance teams follow him after he left the Carnivore Restaurant. Hopefully, we'll find out where he's staying here in Nairobi."

"I think we might as well go back to the Wildebeest Eco Camp for the afternoon since it looks like nothing will happen until at least this evening," said John. "But I agree with your assessment that the exchange of the rhino horns is much more likely to happen tomorrow morning on their way to the airport. Just give me a call on my KWS cell phone if you have any updates this afternoon or evening. If nothing happens today, we'll be ready to go first thing tomorrow morning."

"Alright, that sounds like a good plan," Esther said. "There is no sense in you all spending the rest of the day here when you could be relaxing back at the Wildebeest. It's such a lovely place to stay. I always direct people there if they ask about a good place to stay in Nairobi."

7 a.m. Friday, April 13, 2012
Kenya Wildlife Services Headquarters, Nairobi

John and the team had returned to the Wildebeest Eco Camp the previous afternoon and enjoyed a tasty lunch on the patio of the hotel restaurant, which overlooked the swimming pool area and the lush surrounding gardens. They spent the afternoon on the small front verandas of their cottages catching up on reading and responding to emails from their offices and families back home.

Denny and Anna went for a swim in the pool and took Syd and Nelle for a walk. When they heard that the Sheehan brothers had returned to the Hilton Hotel after their safari game drive and had settled in the sports bar at the hotel to watch football matches for the evening, they had a nice dinner at the hotel restaurant and then spent the rest of the evening in their cottages reading and relaxing.

Esther Balo had called John on his KWS issued cell phone at about three o'clock to let him know the agents had followed Samson Kanumba to a townhouse in the Imara Daima Estate District. The townhouse development was called Villa Franca Estate and was located north of Mombasa Road, the main road to the Airport, and off Tegla Lorupe Road going into the estate area. Jomo Kenyatta International Airport was about an eight- to ten-minute drive from the townhouse, so they assumed the townhouse would be the site of the actual rhino horn purchase and exchange.

John and the team got up early and had cold cereal and coffee for breakfast in their cottages. Simon drove them to the KWS headquarters to meet with Esther and several other KWS agents at seven o'clock. They waited in their office for the undercover agents at the Hilton Hotel to let them know when the Sheehan brothers were on the move.

A couple of unmarked SUVs with eight members of the Kenya National Police Tactical Unit were already waiting a few blocks from Samson's townhouse. The undercover KWS agents had watched the townhouse for a few hours the previous afternoon and evening and discovered that only Samson and one unidentified woman seemed to be inside.

The plan was that after the Sheehan brothers left the townhouse and were in possession of the rhino horns, KWS agents and police would apprehend them before they had a chance to get back on Mombasa Road. The tactical unit would then breach the townhouse with Denny, Syd, and Nelle leading the way.

The call from the undercover agents at the Hilton Hotel came at eight o'clock informing them that the Sheehan brothers had just left the hotel in a taxi. Denny, Syd, and Nelle got into an unmarked KWS SUV with Esther and one other KWS agent and started their short eighteen-minute drive to where the Police tactical unit was waiting. Kate, John, and Anna followed them in their KWS Land Rover with Simon driving.

The police had an unmarked car with two undercover officers parked down the street from the townhouse so they could observe when the Sheehan brothers arrived and when they left, taking pictures of them entering and leaving the townhouse. As suspected, the taxi with the Sheehan brothers arrived at the townhouse at about eight-thirty. They got out of the taxi with two medium-sized, black suitcases and went into the townhouse. Twenty minutes later, they came out with the same two suitcases and got back into the taxi.

The taxi only got about two blocks before two police cruisers and two KWS SUVs blocked its path and a total of eight agents and police officers got out of their vehicles with their guns drawn. The taxi driver, not knowing what was going on, immediately put has hands on top of his head. The law enforcement officers instructed the Sheehan brothers to get out of the taxi. They were immediately handcuffed and forced down onto their knees on the road. The two black suitcases were in the trunk, along with two other smaller carry-on bags. The officers left them there until the crime scene forensic team arrived.

When the undercover agents radioed the tactical unit officers that the Sheehan brothers had left in the taxi, they immediately drove to the townhouse, with Denny and the dogs following in the KWS SUV. They all got out of their vehicles and four of the officers rushed to the front door. The rest went to the back of the house. An officer with a battering ram broke open the front door.

The dogs were tense with anticipation but waiting obediently for Denny to give them the command to go. They had no sense of fear or foreboding. This is what they had spent their entire lives training for. This was their job. Finally, they heard Denny shout the command they were waiting for: "Capture."

The dogs rushed into the house and immediately saw a man and a woman just getting up from the living room sofa. Trained to apprehend whoever they encountered as quickly as possible, they each picked one of them and grabbed one of their arms in their powerful jaws and pulled them down to the floor. Two handguns were lying on the coffee table, but there was no time for Samson and the woman to grab them.

Denny and the other officers were right behind them. Checking quickly that they two were alone in the house, Denny waited a few more seconds until one of the police officers secured the handguns. When he was sure it was safe, he gave the dogs the "Release" command. Even though they were flushed with adrenaline from the excitement of the capture, the two dogs immediately obeyed Denny's command, a testament to their training. Two police officers then handcuffed Samson Kanumba and the woman and made them lie face down on the floor.

John, Kate, Anna, and Simon watched the action from about a block away. When the "all-clear" call came over the police radio, they drove to the front of the house and rushed inside. They saw the two captives lying on the living room floor. Several stacks of US one-hundred-dollar bills were on the coffee table. They were careful not to touch anything in the house until the forensic crime scene officers arrived.

Syd and Nelle were sitting beside Denny, licking their lips from the remnants of the beef jerky Denny had just given them. The leader of the police tactical unit came over to Denny and the dogs and congratulated them for the takedown. While he shook Denny's hand, he said, "That was a well-executed takedown. Thanks for your help. Your dogs were great. When we can, we prefer using dogs, if possible, for these types of operations. It eliminates the need for the use of firearms, and the captives are still alive to be interrogated. Unfortunately, our canine unit is small and underfunded, so we don't have as many dogs as we need."

After a few minutes, John's team went back out to their Land Rover so they could go check out the other part of the operation where the Sheehan brothers were in custody. When they arrived at the spot where the taxi was stopped, they saw the two Sheehan brothers still on their knees on the road, heads slumped on their chests, looking very defeated. The police forensic team had arrived and were about to open the two black suitcases in the trunk of the taxi. After taking numerous pictures, they removed the suitcases from the trunk and opened them on the road behind the taxi.

In each suitcase, each carefully wrapped in several layers of tinfoil and a then a towel, were three large rhino horns. Each rhino horn weighed about two and a half to three kilograms. At the going rate, when sold to a Chinese or Vietnamese wholesaler for the illegal Asian black market, the six raw whole rhino horns were worth fifty thousand to sixty thousand US dollars per kilogram. A value ranging from seven hundred and fifty thousand to one million US dollars in total.

Samson Kanumba was a low-level rhino horn trafficker and did not have the Asian connections the Rathkeale Rovers had, so the Sheehan brothers would have paid him only a fraction of what the Irish gang would get by selling them to the right Asian buyers.

Just then, Joseph Mwangi, the operations manager of the KWS Wildlife Intelligence Unit, drove up to the site in his Land Rover. Smiling broadly, he came over and shook hands with everyone on John's team.

He said, "I am extremely proud of my whole KWS team today. This has been one of our best organized and executed operations. And I especially want to thank you, Denny, and these two dogs of yours for their help in capturing Samson Kanumba. Hopefully, he will lead us to other members of his poaching gang."

Denny replied, "Thanks Joseph. I'll give the dogs some special treats for dinner tonight." Laughing, he continued, "They don't know the rest of us get paid for doing this. As long as they get their treats after the takedown is over though, they seem to be happy."

John added, "We were glad to help, Joseph. We made some progress here today. You can put these Irish thugs behind bars now, and hopefully get some information out of Samson Kanumba about the syndicate he works for."

Kate, pointing at the rhino horns lined up on the road beside them, said, "Tragically, even though we caught these guys this time, those six rhino horns still represent six dead southern white rhinos. There's still a lot more work for us all to do."

CHAPTER 5

8 a.m. Saturday, April 14, 2012
Wildebeest Eco Camp, Nairobi, Kenya

John and the team returned to the Wildebeest Eco Camp after the Sheehan brother and Samson Kanumba takedowns for some well-deserved rest and relaxation. John received a phone call after lunch from Esther Balo informing him that they had confiscated fifty thousand US dollars from Samson Kanumba's townhouse. They also searched the rest of the house and found one more rhino horn plus eight elephant tusks in the spare bedroom.

Esther also told him the woman in the townhouse with Samson was apparently his Tanzanian fiancée, and her name was Grace Sesay. They were being interrogated at the Kenya National Police headquarters, so the KWS hoped they would be able to get more information about the workings of the rhino horn and ivory trafficking syndicate.

She said the Sheehan brothers were also in custody but were refusing to say anything until their lawyers arrived. However, since they were caught in possession of the rhino horns and the case against them was strong, they did not have a lot of negotiating power. The KWS was hopeful they might get some information about who the buyers of the rhino horns were going to be. INTERPOL was also interested in talking to them, so they were sending one of their criminal investigators from Lyon, France to Nairobi to help with the interrogation.

Since John and the team had no commitments for the upcoming weekend, they decided to pay a visit to the David Sheldrick Wildlife Trust Elephant

Orphanage in Nairobi National Park near the KWS headquarters. A few years before, they became friends with Dame Daphne Sheldrick, the founder of the Elephant Orphanage.

At twenty-eight years old in 1948, David Sheldrick became the founding warden of Tsavo National Park, Kenya's largest National Park. He established the early park infrastructure such as building hundreds of kilometers of tourist and administrative all-weather roads. He also dealt with the growing problem of armed poachers.

Fascinated with the elephants in the newly established park, he studied every facet of their lifestyle in the park. Along with his wife, Daphne, they rescued and hand-reared orphaned elephants, rhinos, and antelopes. After David's premature death from a heart attack in 1977 at age fifty-seven, his widow, Daphne, established the David Sheldrick Wildlife Trust in his memory.

John, Kate, and Anna spent the afternoon at the elephant orphanage helping feed and care for the orphan elephants. They also had the chance to visit with Dame Daphne Sheldrick. Most of the orphaned elephants came from Tsavo National Park and had lost their mothers because of poaching. They were cared for at the orphanage for two to three years and then transferred to the facility at Tsavo where they were gradually re-introduced back into the park's wild elephant population. The Trust also had their own park rangers in Tsavo who helped the KWS park rangers with anti-poaching enforcement.

They spent a very pleasant afternoon at the orphanage helping the Trust elephant handlers socialize with the orphan elephants. They were fascinating animals, with complex social structures in the wild. The Trust elephant handlers had to recreate a version of the close family structures of wild elephants for the young orphans, who sometimes arrived at the orphanage only a few weeks old and extremely traumatized. Because dogs were not allowed at the orphanage, Denny stayed back at the Wildebeest Eco Camp and took Syd and Nelle for a long walk in the Ngong Forest Sanctuary just north of the hotel.

8:00 pm Monday, April 16, 2012
KWS Training Institute (KWSTI), Naivasha, Kenya

John and the team discussed traveling to the KWSTI in Naivasha on Monday so they would have a day to relax and prepare for the three-day workshop. Because Kate and Anna had never been to Lake Nakuru National Park, about an hour and half further north from Naivasha along Hwy A104, they left early in the morning so they could visit the park before going to the KWSTI.

Lake Nakuru is world famous as the location of one of the greatest bird spectacles on earth; thousands, and sometimes over a million, fuchsia pink flamingos congregate at the lake at the same time. They feed on the abundant algae, which thrive in the warm, shallow, alkaline water of the lake. There are two types of flamingo species that inhabit the lake, the lesser flamingo, which is distinguished by its deep red bill and pink plumage, and the greater flamingo, which has a bill with a black tip. The lesser flamingos are the ones commonly pictured in African wildlife documentaries, mainly because they are generally more abundant.

Lake Nakuru National Park also has over twenty-five relocated eastern black rhinoceroses, one of the largest concentrations in Kenya, plus around seventy southern white rhinos. There are also the endangered Rothschild's giraffes, several of which were relocated for their safety from western Kenya. Waterbuck were common, and both subspecies could also be found in the park.

Among the predators were lions, cheetahs, and leopards. The park also had large pythons that inhabited the forested areas and were often seen crossing the roads or dangling from trees. As well as flamingos, there were many other bird species that inhabited the lake and the area surrounding it, such as African fish eagles, Goliath herons, hamerkops, pied kingfishers, and Verreaux's eagles.

The team arrived at Lake Nakuru at about noon, after the almost four-hour drive from Nairobi. As usual, Simon was a wealth of information. As part of his training as a KWS wildlife officer and driver, he had taken several additional courses on Kenyan natural history, geography, and wildlife conservation, and entertained them with his stories and good-natured banter on the trip.

When they got to Lake Nakuru, they were not disappointed because it just happened to be at the height of the flamingo migration, and there were perhaps over a million birds lining the entire shoreline, although it would have been impossible to count them. The surface of the lake was barely visible because of the continually shifting mass of pink. Truly a once in a lifetime sight. Even Simon, who had been to Lake Nakuru several times before, gazed in awe at the magnificent spectacle.

Kate and Anna, in particular, were amazed by the phenomena of the thousands of pink flamingos on the lake. After sitting in silence, just trying to savor what they were observing, Anna said, "Wow, this is fantastic. I've seen documentaries on TV about the flamingos in Kenya and Tanzania, but to see it in person is really something. I'm really glad we took the time to come here."

"Me too," said Kate. "I've seen some amazing things in Africa since we started coming here, but this is one thing I still hadn't seen."

After watching the flamingos for about an hour, they drove to the large, fenced sanctuary area where the eastern black rhinoceroses, southern white rhinos, and Rothschild's giraffes were enclosed. Because they were driving a KWS Land Rover, and Simon was a KWS wildlife officer escorting a group of KWS trainers, they had special permission to drive into the fenced sanctuary area and observe the rhinos and giraffes more closely than the regular safari tourists. The rhinos were magnificent animals but threatened with extinction just because of their horns and the false belief they possessed some magical healing powers.

While they were slowly driving along the little-used trails in the park and watching the assemblage of animals, John remarked, "What a shame that we are in danger of losing these animals in the wild, and future generations might only see them in zoos or fenced game preserves like this one."

"Or maybe not at all, if things keep going the way they are with the poachers," said Simon.

After a couple of hours driving on the trails in the sanctuary, observing the rhinos and other assorted species of wildlife and birds, they decided it was time to leave for the KWSTI.

Lake Naivasha is a freshwater lake in Lake Naivasha National Park outside the town of Naivasha and is part of the Great Rift Valley. The name comes from the local Maasai name "*Nai'posha,*" meaning "rough water" because of the large waves on the lake that are created by sudden storms.

The lake supports diverse types of wildlife, including over four hundred species of birds and a sizable population of hippos. Hell's Gate National Park is located just south of Lake Naivasha. Hell's Gate was named for its massive, red-tinged cliffs and is famous for its unique geothermically active steam vents, natural hot geysers, and bubbling springs. It is also home to an abundance of plains wildlife and birdlife, including eagle, buzzard, and vulture breeding grounds.

They arrived at the KWSTI at dinnertime and got checked into their spartan visitor rooms in the dormitory building reserved for institute staff and visiting trainers. John and Kate got a larger room reserved for married couples and the rest of the team got standard single rooms. Syd and Nelle bunked in with Denny as usual. Their travel kennels doubled as beds.

They found their way to the staff cafeteria and were joined by the head instructor at the institute, Robert Diallo. The KWS Canine Unit head trainer, David Kimathi, also joined them at their table. Over dinner, they discussed the plans for the upcoming three-day workshop for the thirty-member senior graduating class of wildlife enforcement officers. It was to be one of their last training workshops before graduating and going to the KWS Law Enforcement Academy and Field Training School at Tsavo West National Park. While at the Field Training School, they would take six weeks of advanced field-based paramilitary training to prepare them for the realities of their often-dangerous anti-poaching duties while on the job.

Both Robert and David were also anxious to hear more about John and the team's adventures since arriving in Africa on this trip. While they were eating, Robert said, "I was talking to Joseph Mwangi this morning and he filled me in on what you guys have been up to over the last couple of weeks. It sounds like you've had quite the trip, so far."

David added, "Yes, Robert and I love our work here at the training institute, but we miss the action in the field." Smiling, he continued, "Please indulge us with a recap of your adventures in Gaborone, Livingstone, and Nairobi. From what Joseph told us, you managed to help take down some major players in the wildlife trafficking world."

Laughing, John said, "I think Joseph may have exaggerated our importance in the takedowns a little. Actually, it was Syd and Nelle who did most of the dangerous work. The rest of us mostly just observed the local law enforcement people doing their jobs. But we'd be happy to give you a rundown of what happened."

While they finished dinner, they gave them a blow-by-blow recap of each takedown, much to the appreciation of both Robert and David. After dessert and tea, they all finally said goodnight and went to their rooms for some much-needed sleep.

In the morning, they got down to business. John and the team had done various versions of the workshop before, both at the KWSTI and in several other African countries. They concentrated mostly on teaching the latest techniques in wildlife crime scene evidence gathering. Proper documentation of evidence was critical and was often the reason wildlife poachers and traffickers were able to get off on all charges. Particularly when represented by experienced defense lawyers. If crown prosecutors were unable to verify the chain-of-custody of key evidence, then their cases against the poachers often broke down, and the poachers were acquitted.

They also covered the proper issuance and execution of search warrants and how to make sure that any illegal wildlife or wildlife parts, or other contraband seized or confiscated, was covered by the search warrant. This was another weak link exploited by experienced defense lawyers. The KWS wildlife enforcement officers also worked with the local police or military when they were apprehending criminals, so they had to be aware of the specific laws involved and the applicable criminal codes, although that had also been covered in the standard courses taught at the institute.

Denny had taken part in canine training workshops in Africa several times over the past year since Syd and Nelle became part of the team but did not have any set instructional program. He usually observed what the canine unit trainers were doing and tried to give them advice about the techniques they were using.

Often, when the canine training units received their dogs, they were young adult dogs already and had received some basic training from the canine trainers in the law enforcement agencies in the counties where they were raised. The six dogs currently in the canine training unit at the KWSTI were just over one year old and had come from Israel. Funding came from an environmental conservation NGO, the African Wildlife Foundation.

Denny also reviewed the KWSTI Canine Training Unit curriculum with the head trainer, David Kimathi, and the other training officers. Each of the six dogs at the KWSTI was assigned a KWS dog handler who would partner with the dog when they were deployed to their respective field units. Creating and reinforcing the bond between the dog and its handler was one of the most important aspects of the canine training program.

Denny showed various dog training techniques he was taught at the RCMP canine training center, using Syd and Nelle as examples. They were raised from puppies at the RCMP canine training center in Alberta, which was one of the top canine training facilities in the world.

The KWS trainees were extremely impressed with the bond that Denny had with Syd and Nelle as they demonstrated various techniques and exercises. Their obedience was unwavering, and they would do anything asked of them, even sacrificing their own lives if required to protect Denny and other members of his team.

They were working police dogs, bred, and trained from birth for this specific type of deployment, with the temperament and intelligence to not only be extremely effective at their jobs but also to be loving and playful companions when not "on duty." Dogs unable to separate these two parts of their lives rarely lasted long in the canine law enforcement units, not unlike soldiers or police officers.

CHAPTER 6

2 p.m. Saturday, April 21, 2012
Wildebeest Eco Camp, Nairobi, Kenya

John and the team returned to Nairobi from the KWSTI in Naivasha on Saturday morning after successfully completing the three-day training workshop. They had just finished a late lunch on the patio of the Wildebeest restaurant and were discussing their return to Canada, scheduled for the following day. Kate was going to take the same flight as them from Nairobi to Calgary, Alberta, via KLM Airlines, with an overnight stopover in Amsterdam, and then take a flight to Portland, Oregon so she could have a visit with her daughter Dianna, before driving home to Ashland.

Although they all enjoyed their time in Africa working on INTERPOL operations and training assignments, they still had their regular jobs back home in Edmonton and Ashland. John, Anna, and Denny were RCMP officers and responsible for the operation of the Wildlife Crime Unit at the RCMP K Division headquarters in Edmonton. They were also involved in working on active wildlife-related law enforcement activities in Alberta and the other western Canadian provinces, often in conjunction with Environment and Climate Change Canada's Wildlife Enforcement Directorate and provincial Fish and Wildlife agencies.

Kate was one of the senior forensic wildlife biologists and law enforcement agents at the National Fish and Wildlife Forensics Laboratory in Ashland, Oregon. When she was home, she supervised activities at the forensics laboratory, and worked with the United States Fish and Wildlife Service Office of Law Enforcement on wildlife law enforcement operations within the US. Domestic wildlife poaching and trafficking in the United States was also a big problem, as was the importing of illegal wildlife products such as ivory, rhino horns, and restricted live animals, birds, and reptiles.

7 p.m. Sunday, April 22, 2012
Amsterdam, Netherlands

The team's flight from Nairobi landed in Amsterdam at five o'clock Sunday afternoon. It was one of their favorite cities in Europe and the overnight stopover helped break up the long trip back home for them and Syd and Nelle.

Their hotel of choice was the Hyatt Regency Amsterdam because it was pet friendly and located in the city center near the main metro station. The concierge and front desk staff, after several stays, got to know the team and what their particular needs were, especially regarding Syd and Nelle. The staff were impressed that the dogs were working police dogs and were more than happy to accommodate them a few times a year on their stopovers to and from Africa. There was also a small park nearby with a grassy area for doggie bathroom breaks.

After checking in to their rooms, they went for a short walk to a nearby restaurant they liked where the dogs were welcome in the outdoor patio area. After dinner, they went back to the hotel for a much-needed good night's sleep.

The next morning, they took the hotel shuttle bus to the airport and boarded their KLM flight to Calgary. They parted ways with Kate in Calgary, where she caught a flight to Portland. After spending several weeks together, it was difficult for John and Kate to leave each other. Before separating to catch their flights, they found a quiet place in the Calgary terminal to talk.

Seated next to each other in a quiet lounge area, John took Kate's hand and said, "So, I guess it's back to our other lives. These separations are getting harder all the time. It could be a few months until we see each other again."

Smiling at John, Kate replied, "I know, it's getting harder for me too. We make a wonderful team, but unless one of us can change where we work and live, we'll just have to make the best of the way things are right now."

"I know, changing our careers and where we live just isn't in the cards for either one of us right now, but it's still going to be hard not seeing you every morning when I wake up," said John.

"Yes, for me too," said Kate, squeezing John's hand. "Well, I guess I have to get going. I see on the monitor that my flight is boarding. I'll call you tonight from Portland."

With that, they got up and hugged for a few minutes. After a short kiss, Kate left for her boarding gate and John returned to join Denny and Anna at their gate for the flight to Edmonton. Syd and Nelle were already secured in their travel kennels for this last leg of the journey home.

8 a.m. Wednesday, April 25, 2012
RCMP K Division Headquarters, Edmonton, Alberta

John, Anna, Denny, and the dogs arrived back in Edmonton on Monday evening. They spent Tuesday getting unpacked and settled back in their homes. Denny stayed Monday night at John's house and then drove back to his cabin at Slave Lake to spend some time with his family and his long-time lady friend, Mary Woods. Their relationship was like John and Kate's. They were together as much as possible when Denny was home in Alberta, but it was understood that he had to be away from home for extended periods of time on assignments for his job. They had managed to resolve this reality and still be a couple, although the subject of marriage was discussed as a possibility when Denny was finally ready to retire and settle down. Between his military service and his RCMP career, he had been traveling and working around the world since the age of eighteen.

Both John and Anna had piles of reports on their desks they needed to review and dozens of emails to read and respond to. They also had to prepare and file briefing and expense reports for their latest INTERPOL assignments in Botswana, Zambia, and Kenya. John also had a briefing session scheduled with Michael Alden, the current RCMP superintendent of K Division headquarters in Edmonton.

John and Michael had a long history together, having attended the RCMP Training Academy in Saskatoon, Saskatchewan, together in the same graduating class. John was a few years older and a little more "world wise," but

Michael was one of the smartest people he had ever encountered. He breezed through all the academic stuff at the academy but struggled with his firearms certification and the more physical parts of the training. Those were the parts that John had excelled at, so he had worked with Michael after hours and he eventually got through the training program.

After graduating, they went their separate ways, John to the Wildlife Crime Unit, and Michael to begin his path upwards through the RCMP ranks. He was eventually promoted to the position of superintendent of K Division in Edmonton, where he and John were able to renew their friendship. Rumors said he was next in line to be promoted to the office of RCMP commissioner in Ottawa. John and Michael always kidded each other about their days at the RCMP academy, but John knew that Michael Alden had earned every accolade and promotion in his distinguished career.

After exchanging some friendly banter about their current jobs in the RCMP, Michael told John about a recent surge in illegal black bear poaching in northwestern Alberta and northeastern British Columbia. Michael explained, "Fish and Wildlife and the enforcement officers from Environment Canada's Wildlife Enforcement Branch in both Alberta and BC have received reports of dozens of dead black bears discovered in backcountry areas by forestry and oil and gas workers, as well as F&W officers. They suspect an organized ring of poachers is operating in these areas and are killing the bears for their gall bladders, and sometimes their paws and claws. They think the gall bladders are being sold to Asian buyers in China or other Asian countries for medicinal purposes."

John said, "That's interesting, we've worked on a few bear-poaching cases over the years, but this sounds bigger and more organized."

"So, what makes the gall bladders so valuable?" asked Michael.

John responded, "The bile within the gall bladders is the most coveted medicinal part of the black bears, which, gram for gram, can exceed the cost of narcotics. Bile and gallbladders have been used for thousands of years in Asian countries for the treatment of numerous ailments including cardiac problems, eye puffiness, asthma, cancer, burns, and impotence. A poacher in Canada can get up to two to three hundred dollars for a single bear gallbladder, but the organs can fetch from five to ten thousand dollars in the Asian end-market once they are processed into a powder."

"Wow, I see the incentive for the poaching. There's lots of money to be made with the right organization," said Michael.

John said, "As you know, in Canada, it's legal to hunt black bears. A permit to hunt is inexpensive, and a licensed hunter is permitted to kill up to two black bears each year. Initially, it was also legal to trade bear parts, but only if it was done through a licensed fur trader and exported with a permit.

"However, there are many incentives to get and trade bear parts illegally. Given their small size, gall bladders and paws can easily be smuggled across borders or out of the country with little chance of detection. In addition, there is more profit to be made by avoiding taxes and export duties. Also, the large, forested areas and the low population densities in Canada reduce the risk of illegally killing the bears. Even if they get caught, poachers only face, at most, a few months in jail, or more likely, a fine, which is insignificant compared to the potential profits to be made."

"You know a lot about bear poaching, John. So, how do these syndicates usually work?" asked Michael.

"From what I know about them, the more well-organized operations exist as a network comprised of three levels: the shooters, the suppliers, and the traffickers. Shooters include both legal hunters and illegal poachers. I've read that up to forty thousand black bears are legally killed each year, and just as many or more are slaughtered illegally."

"How does the illegal bear hunting work?" asked Michael.

"The illegal killing of bears is typically done with hunting dogs or by baiting. Many hunters equip their dogs with hi-tech radio collars which allow them to follow the dogs as they search for bears by scent. Other hunters lure the bears to "bait sites" by enticing them with meat and other food.

"The suppliers are the middlemen in the business, often the guides and outfitters who arrange legal hunts and then take the gall bladders of the kills as tips or employ a group of hunters who illegally kill the bears and then harvest the gall bladders. The suppliers then sell the gall bladders to traffickers who smuggle them out of the country.

"Bear parts smuggled out of North America usually ended up in Asia, where they are sold in pharmacies and restaurants. With its native supply non-existent and more consumers willing to pay, South Korea is now considered the world's largest market for imported bear parts. Not far behind, however, are Hong Kong, China, and Japan."

Michael said, "Well, thanks for the info, John. I definitely know more about the bear poaching business now. The Alberta Fish and Wildlife Division and the federal Wildlife Enforcement Branch have requested our assistance in trying to break up the current black bear poaching operation. It's suspected the poaching ringleaders are a couple of hunting guides operating out of the Peace River area in Alberta and Fort St. John in British Columbia. Fish and Wildlife and the feds are wondering if they could use Denny Bear as an undercover agent to break up the poaching operation. They are hoping to also nail the Asian traffickers buying the gall bladders and exporting them to China or South Korea."

"That sounds like something Denny might be interested in," said John. "We are scheduled to work in Canada for a few more months before going back to Africa, so he has some time available. I'll let him know and have him come back to Edmonton next week so we can discuss the operation with the F&W enforcement people. Do you know how they plan to get Denny hooked up with these hunting guides?"

"Apparently, they already have one of the First Nation poachers working undercover for them in exchange for immunity on some outstanding charges against him. They plan to have this individual introduce Denny as one of his friends who is interested in making some extra money working for the hunting guides. They hope a guy like Denny, with all his experience in the military and as an RCMP officer, could get close to the hunting guides and find out how the whole operation works, who the Asian buyers are, and how they get the gall bladders out of the country."

"All right, I'll give Denny a call and have him come to the office next week so we can get things rolling," said John.

10 a.m. Monday, April 30, 2012
RCMP K Division Headquarters, Edmonton, Alberta

John called Denny about the proposed black bear poaching undercover operation, and Denny was excited about getting involved. He agreed to come to the office in Edmonton on Monday morning from his cabin at Slave Lake.

Arriving at ten o'clock, he was greeted with great enthusiasm by Syd and Nelle, who had not seen him for the last week. Dropping his things off in his own office first, he joined Anna in John's office just down the hall.

"Thanks for coming in, Denny," John said. "I have a meeting set up at one o'clock with Russ Paulson, the director of enforcement for Alberta F&W, and Phil Keating, the senior enforcement officer with Environment Canada in Edmonton. They will be going over the plan for the undercover operation. Russ and Phil want you to get started right away and have told the guy already working undercover to expect you to join the operation later this week. His name is George Cardinal. He is from the Woodland Cree First Nation, north of Slave Lake, although he hasn't lived on the Reserve for quite a few years."

"I've heard of the Cardinal family with the Woodland Cree, but I don't know any of them personally," Denny said. "I'm looking forward to getting involved in an undercover operation like this. It should be a pleasant change of pace, and I was afraid I might get bored waiting around until our next Africa trip. Taking down this black bear poaching ring and catching the bigger players would also be great, rather than just busting the guys shooting the bears."

Russ Paulson and Phil Keating arrived at one o'clock and they all gathered in the boardroom on the third floor, just down the hallway from the forensics lab. They had all worked together numerous times over the years so there was no need for introductions. Russ got right into laying out the plan for the undercover operation.

He said, "We've had George Cardinal operating undercover for the past six months and he has provided information about how the lower-level poaching operation works, but he hasn't been able to find out much about the larger operation. He is just one of several bear hunters in Alberta and BC working for the hunting guides who are running the poaching operation."

"So, you already know who these hunting guides are?" asked Denny.

"Yes, we know the identities of the two hunting guides. The guy operating out of the Peace River area is Tim Riley and, as far as we can tell, he operates a legitimate hunting and guiding business, primarily for US and German hunters. So, the bear gall bladder operation is a sideline thing.

"The other hunting guide works out of the Fort St. John area in British Columbia. We believe he is Tim Riley's cousin; his name is Mark Riley. He also runs a legitimate hunting and guiding business in northeastern BC, as far as we can tell. We think they are working together on the black bear poaching operation and using the same buyer of the gall bladders and bear paws. These are the guys we are after, as well as the buyer, who we assume comes from China or South Korea."

"Sounds good to me," interjected Denny. "So, what's the plan?"

"The plan is to have George introduce Denny to Tim Riley in Peace River," Russ continued. "We will supply Denny with confiscated black bear gall bladders, which he will sell to Tim at a discount as a good will gesture and then get himself on the roster of the bear hunting team. Fish and Wildlife can then continue to supply Denny with confiscated gall bladders from our evidence inventory if he needs them. Hopefully, Denny can also meet Mark Riley in Fort St. John at some point."

Phil added, "We're hoping that Denny will be able to find out how they are communicating with their Asian buyer and how they are selling the gall bladders. Ideally, once we discover who the buyer is, we can then set up a sting operation to catch them all while they are making the exchange and sale. The key will be to have Denny gain the Rileys' trust, so they divulge the inner workings of the poaching operation to him."

"It sure seems worth taking a shot at bringing these guys down. I can go undercover with an alias, so they don't trace me back to the Driftpile First Nation, because the Bear family is well known in northern Alberta. I will also have to invent a believable backstory to avoid suspicion. George Cardinal can help me out with that. I could also have Syd and Nelle with me as it is quite common for bear poachers to use dogs to locate the black bears. So, when do we get started?"

Russ answered, "I can contact George right away and you and he can get together later this week. Once you talk to him and come up with a plan, we can get the F&W gall bladders to you for your first meeting with Tim Riley."

"All right, it looks like we have a plan," John said. "Just let Denny and me know when he can meet with George Cardinal so we can get going. If you don't mind, I'd like to be there the first time Denny meets with George to ensure he realizes how serious this deal is."

"That sounds like a good idea," Russ said. "We are dealing with poachers and criminals here with a lot of guns, so it's better to be safe."

2 p.m. Thursday, May 3, 2012
Queen Elizabeth Provincial Park Day Use Area, near Grimshaw, Alberta

John, Denny, Syd, and Nelle drove from Edmonton to Denny's cabin at Lesser Slave Lake on Wednesday afternoon and stayed overnight. On Thursday morning, they continued for two hours to Peace River and had lunch at the Tim Horton's. After lunch, they drove for another half an hour further west of Peace River to the day use area at Queen Elizabeth Provincial Park at Cardinal Lake to meet with George Cardinal.

Earlier in the week, Denny, John, and Anna had discussed and developed a plan, of which John and Denny worked out more of the details on their journey to Peace River. The basic plan was for George Cardinal to introduce Denny to Tim Riley and recommend Denny work as a guide for Tim Riley's hunting and guiding business during the spring black bear hunting season, which had started in late April and would run through May into mid-June. During that time, they hoped Denny could ingratiate himself into the Rileys' businesses, both legal and illegal.

Their legitimate clients were primarily wealthy American and Germans who willingly paid the large fees to come to the wilds of Canada and hunt for black bears and various other big game animals. They were mostly after the trophies of the hunt — the heads or hides of the animals.

The Rileys were pleased to charge them a hefty overhead fee to arrange for local taxidermists to prepare the trophies and hides and ship them to wherever they came from. With black bears, there was the added benefit of being able to harvest the gall bladders, and sometimes the paws or claws, and sell them on the black market to their Asian buyers. They supplemented their income with the gall bladders harvested from illegally shot black bears.

John, Denny, and the dogs arrived at the day use area at the Queen Elizabeth Provincial Park on the eastern shore of Cardinal Lake at the scheduled time of two o'clock. George Cardinal was already there in his new-looking F150 pickup truck. After introducing themselves, they opted to have their meeting at a picnic table since it was a warm spring day.

George, who looked to be his late thirties, was wearing an expensive-looking leather jacket, cowboy boots, and an Edmonton Oilers baseball cap. It seemed working as a hunting guide was paying off for him. He explained, "I've been working as a hunting guide for Tim Riley off and on for the last two years, primarily during the spring and fall bear hunting seasons. As a reason for coming to this meeting today, I told Tim I needed to take care of some things in Peace River and meet a friend and relative of mine who wanted to work as a hunting guide. Tim needs a few more guides so he was happy to hear that he might be able to hire someone recommended by one of his current trusted employees, like me."

Denny and John went over the more detailed aspects of the plan with George after it was clear he was on board and willing to play his part. Denny said, "I will be using an alias, since my family name is well known in northern Alberta. I will be going by the name Dennis Gladue. I think it's best if we have a family connection, so maybe we can say our mothers were cousins and our grandmothers were sisters, and that we spent time together at family gatherings when we were growing up."

After George said, "Okay, that sounds good," Denny continued, "I will say that I originally came from the Whitefish Lake First Nation south of Lac La Biche but spent almost fifteen years in the Canadian military and got out in 2006, which is true so I can talk about my military career if it comes up. Since then, I worked up at Fort McMurray off and on for several years but got tired of the work camp life and wanted to do hunting and guiding work again. We can say we ran into each other again recently, and that we talked about your job working for Tim Riley. How does that sound to you?"

George replied, "That all sounds good, but I think we should be specific about some details, so we don't slip up and say different things about how we know each other. For instance, I think we should say that we used to see each other growing up as teenagers when our families visited each other but had not seen one another for a long time because you were in the military. And then we ran into each other again in Slave Lake a few times, which is when we talked about my hunting and guiding job."

"Yeah, that's a good idea," Denny said. "It's always best when using an alternate identity to keep the basics as close to the truth as possible. All right, why don't you tell Tim Riley you met with me, and I'm ready to start work right away. You can mention I can do the regular guiding work for his clients, as well as any other 'extra' bear hunting he might want me to do. Also tell him I have about half a dozen black bear gall bladders in my freezer I can sell him if he's interested in buying them at a discount as a show of good faith on my part. You can also tell him I have two German shepherd dogs I can use for bear hunting if he wants me to bring them along."

George said, "Okay, I'll talk to Tim when I get back to his hunting lodge tonight and then call you to let you know when he wants you to start, although I assume it will be right away since this is prime bear hunting season, and he has quite a few American and German clients coming in the next few weeks."

8 p.m. Saturday, May 5, 2012
Tim Riley's Hunting Lodge, 42 km north of Peace River, Alberta

Denny was at his cabin when he received a call from George, stating he had talked with Tim Riley and Tim had agreed to hire Denny. He was to come to the hunting lodge on Saturday afternoon so they could meet and talk about the guiding job. John and Denny went to the F&W office in Peace River on Friday and picked up six frozen black bear gall bladders they had stored in their evidence freezer so he could sell them to Tim Riley.

They also went out in the forest south of Slave Lake with Syd and Nelle to make sure the GPS tracking devices in their special collars that the RCMP techs in Edmonton had put together were working properly. Denny planned to use them to find, chase down, and tree black bears, so they could be shot legally by Tim Riley's clients.

Once they were all set, John returned to Edmonton on Saturday morning with their RCMP unmarked SUV. Denny decided it was best to use his own personal Ford Explorer four-by-four while he was working for Tim Riley. Denny arrived at Tim Riley's hunting lodge in the late afternoon. The lodge was about forty-five kilometers north of the city of Peace River along the banks of the Peace River. He was in time to get a tour of the camp facilities before having dinner in the lodge's dining room with Tim Riley and the other three hunting guides working there, including George Cardinal. There was also a group of four well-to-do Germans at dinner who had come from Frankfurt for a week of bear hunting in the wilds of northern Alberta.

The lodge was built of logs and was rustic but had all the conveniences of modern urban homes like indoor bathrooms, hot showers, large-screen TVs, a pool table, and a comfortable lounge area for relaxing in the evenings. There were six bedrooms upstairs with private bathrooms for the guests, plus a large master bedroom and office area for Tim Riley. There was also an adjacent guest cabin with sleeping accommodations for eight and two large, shared bathrooms for male and female guests.

The hunting guides and camp workers had their own rooms in three, four-room camp trailers located a short distance from the main lodge. Tim Riley purchased them from a local oil and gas company that went out of business and sold off their remote camp facilities. There were also several large sheds for storing equipment, ATVs of several types, three boats, and a large walk-in freezer for storing meat, hides, and trophy heads of animals shot by the guests. Overall, it seemed like a well-managed, high-end, comfortable hunting lodge operation, based on similar operations Denny had seen.

Denny had a pleasant discussion with Tim upon arrival and while he was getting a tour of the hunting lodge facilities. Denny went through the cover story he had discussed with George, and Tim seemed impressed with his background and especially his years spent in the military as a special forces' sniper.

They seemed to hit it off right away, particularly when Denny told him about his own little sideline business of killing black bears and selling gall bladders to a buyer in Edmonton, who had contacts in South Korea. Denny said, "I had a regular buyer in Edmonton, but he got paranoid about getting caught and went back to South Korea. I have been looking for a new buyer for my stuff, so this could work out really well for me too. I brought six gall bladders with me if you are interested in buying them."

Tim responded, "Sure, that sounds great. How much do you want for them?"

"How about a thousand dollars for the six gall bladders? Denny answered. "That's about half the price I could have gotten from my other buyer, but let's consider it an act of good faith to kick off our new business venture."

"Okay, it's a deal then," said Tim. "I'm impressed you have your own bear dogs. I've been thinking of getting a couple of dogs myself. A few clients have asked if they could hunt with dogs, but I haven't had any guides with their own dogs."

"No problem, that's why I brought them with me," said Denny. "So, when do you want me to start?" asked Denny.

"You might as well start right away then, if you brought all your gear with you," said Tim.

"You bet. I'm all ready to go," answered Denny.

Tim Riley's hunting and guiding business, which was named Riley Hunting and Outfitting, was a modern and sophisticated operation, designed to attract the big-money US and European clients who expected to go home with a prized trophy black bear hide, or to have a professional taxidermist prepare it for later shipment to wherever they lived. Spring bear hunting season in the Peace River area of Alberta ran from April 1st to June 15th, and the hunters could use rifles, traditional bows, or crossbows.

Tim took over the business in 2006 from his father, who first started it in the early 1990s. Since taking over, Tim had expanded it with the addition of multiple bait stations, permanent and portable blinds and tree stands, and even camera systems to record the bears visiting the bait stations.

The Riley Hunting and Outfitting designated hunting area was perfect bear habitat with a mixture of heavily forested areas, recently logged areas, farmland, and the presence of other big game animals, which provided plenty for the bears to eat so they could grow quickly and end up bigger than bears in more remote wilderness areas. The huge Peace River valley also funneled traveling male bears right to the well-positioned baiting and hunting sites.

Their bear management system within their operating area focused on attracting as many bears as possible to each baiting site, letting them grow accustomed to the sites and get comfortable with the baiting, and then selectively harvesting the biggest male bears. They used a variety of bait consisting of meat, grease and table scraps from the lodge, grains such as oats and wheat, and fish when they could buy it from the local First Nation commercial fisherman.

They set the more permanent bait sites up for either bow or rifle hunting with a fifteen- to sixty-yard shot from a two-person, bear proof, wooden box, ground blind. They had constructed the ground blinds in a position that would give bow hunters a broadside shot, lessening the chance of wounding a bear. Bow hunts were also conducted by using tree stands and ladder stands. Using portable stands instead of permanent stands allowed for more flexibility in setting up the bow or rifle hunter for the best possible shot.

Rifle and crossbow hunters used the same set ups, but with longer distance shots than bow hunters, from forty to sixty yards. Most of the bait sites were accessed by jet boat on the river and sometimes also down the larger tributary rivers flowing into Peace River. Some of the bait sites were also located off trails or abandoned logging roads, which were accessed with ATVs from the river drop-off sites.

The hunting guides often reviewed the bait station camera pictures and videos with the hunters before they left for their daily hunts so they could pick out the biggest male bears visiting the bait stations. They discouraged shooting non-breeding female bears and small young bears because it reduced the breeding bear population and scared off the smart, older male bears. It was against the law to shoot female bears with cubs.

A typical working day at the hunting lodge for the guides and hunters started with a home-cooked breakfast between eight and nine o'clock. This was often followed by skinning the bears from the previous day or evening hunts in one of the specially equipped sheds. The guests could take part if they wanted as well. If the bears were too large or shot in a more remote area, they would skin them in the bush and then bring the hides back to the lodge to finish the hide treatment and preservation.

They then had a big lunch and afterwards went to the boat dock where the hunting guests were taken by jet boat to a bait station location. They would wait in the blind for the afternoon and into the early evening, if necessary, until a suitable bear arrived. Each hunter was given a radio and once a bear was shot, the hunter would notify the guide to come pick them and their trophy up. Some hunters preferred the guides stay with them in the blinds and assist them in selecting and shooting the best bears that came to the bait station.

While skinning the bears, the hunting guides would also discretely remove the gall bladder, which was a small sac near the liver and upper section of the intestine close to the stomach.

The gall bladders were stored in a special freezer because it was illegal to sell them or export them. Although, all the hunting guides who worked at the lodge knew that Tim Riley and his cousin Mark, who operated a similar hunting lodge in northeastern BC, had a lucrative sideline business selling the gall bladders to an Asian buyer. They assumed the buyer smuggled them out of the country to South Korea or China but didn't know how that happened. Most of the hunting guides also ran their own little sideline businesses illegally poaching black bears, removing their gall bladders, and selling them to Tim Riley.

The cost of a hunting trip could be as much as one thousand dollars per day for each individual. This included pick up and drop off at the Peace River airport or hotel, the cost of all licenses and permits, all meals and non-alcoholic beverages while at the hunting lodge, and professional trophy preparation. This consisted of the complete skinning of the bear, including the protection of the lips, eyes, ears, nose, and paws of the hide, and salting, drying, and packaging of the hide so it was ready for shipping.

8 p.m. Saturday, May 19, 2012
Tim Riley's Hunting Lodge, 42 km north of Peace River, Alberta

Denny caught on quickly to the routine at the lodge and soon became one of the favorite guides with the hunting lodge guests. The guests had expanded to include two groups from the US and another foursome from Germany. Denny's stories about his years as a sniper in the Canadian military were always a big hit at mealtimes. Tim Riley seemed impressed with Denny's knowledge of big game hunting and wildlife in general. His firearm skills along with being a popular hunting guide did not go amiss either.

Denny took every opportunity to talk with Tim and felt he was gaining his trust. In fact, Tim mentioned he planned to visit his cousin at his hunting lodge west of Fort St. John in British Columbia on Sunday and then return on Monday afternoon. He asked Denny if he would like to come with him so Denny could meet his cousin Mark and check out his hunting lodge operation. Of course, Denny accepted his offer and hoped to get more information about the gall bladder poaching business, especially who their Asian buyer was and when they were going to get together with him next to sell their supply of gall bladders.

Denny and Tim left for the three-hour drive to Fort St. John at about nine o'clock on Sunday morning with Syd and Nelle in the rear cargo area of Tim's Ford Expedition. Syd and Nelle also became favorites around the lodge with both the guests and the other hunting guides and camp workers. If Denny could not take them with him during the day, he left them with the chef who spoiled them with scraps of food from his kitchen, even though Denny told him not to fall for their hungry eyes look.

Some guests wanted to try tracking the bears with the dogs and then shooting them when they were treed, rather than shooting them from the blinds or tree stands. This was something new for Syd and Nelle, but they caught on right away and enjoyed tracking the bears by smell and then confronting them so they would climb up a tree where the hunter would shoot them. Denny always stayed close with the dogs, ready to shoot the bear again if it was still alive when it fell from the tree. Wounded large male bears were extremely dangerous, so Denny did not take any chances with the dogs or the hunting guests, who were often overly excited and not aware of the danger the bear posed.

Denny really enjoyed working as a hunting guide; it was something at which he was naturally good. It was also a vastly different type of work from his service in the military and his regular job with the RCMP. He had given John a call the previous evening to let him know how things were going and tell him about his upcoming trip with Tim to visit with his cousin Mark in BC. They assumed there would be a meeting planned with their Asian buyer after the spring bear hunting season on June 15th to sell their supply of black bear gall bladders. If Denny could find out the details of the meeting and exchange, the sting operation could be set in motion. During the three-hour drive from Tim's hunting lodge to Fort St. John, Denny and Tim talked about a lot of things, mostly related to the hunting and guiding business, and Denny was careful not to seem too curious about Tim and his cousin Mark's black bear gall bladder poaching sideline business.

When they got to Mark Riley's hunting lodge, fifty kilometers west of Fort St. John at the confluence of Halfway and Peace Rivers, they were greeted by Mark, who invited them for a late lunch. The lodge was much like Tim's hunting lodge, and they told Denny that the same construction company had built both lodges. The rest of the hunting lodge operation also looked quite similar, and it was apparent that the two cousins had collaborated closely with each other over the years building up their businesses.

After lunch, Mark took them for a jet boat ride up Peace River to see some of his hunting area and to check on a few of his guests who were out in their blinds waiting for the late afternoon and early evening bear visits at the bait stations. They returned to the lodge for drinks before dinner.

After a couple of beers, Denny cautiously asked, "So, do you guys want me to keep working for you hunting bears after the official spring bear hunting season is over?"

Tim said, "We usually keep a few guides on for the summer, so if you wanted to stay, that would work for us."

"That sounds great to me," said Denny.

A little later, Denny casually asked, "So, how do you guys sell the gall bladders?"

Maybe because they now trusted Denny, and had a little too much to drink, they were more than willing to explain how that part of the business worked. They seemed quite proud of how smart they were to have devised such a sophisticated operation.

Tim started the explanation by saying, "Our buyer is a South Korean named Kwan Park. His family owns a salmon and seafood farming company in the Powell River area north of Vancouver. They export fresh salmon to South Korea for sushi, as well as fresh sea urchins and crab. They ship the seafood fresh from Vancouver every week via Korean Air cargo to Incheon International Airport in Seoul. His family also owns a seafood distribution and wholesale company in Seoul, which supplies quite a few restaurants and grocery store chains."

Mark interjected, "It's the perfect cover business for Kwan Park's family to sell the gall bladders in the Korean black-market herbal medicine industry."

Continuing, Tim said, "Kwan Park comes to Vancouver regularly for his family's business. So, about three or four times per year, he meets us, usually in Kamloops, so he can buy our supply of gall bladders. He then includes the gall bladders in the weekly shipment of seafood from Vancouver to Seoul, using the same packaging to avoid detection. Since the shipments are a regular occurrence, the air cargo customs agents at the Seoul end usually clear them with no problems. Kwan Park's family then distributes the gall bladders to their regular Korean black-market clients."

"Wow, that's a great system," responded Denny, trying to sound impressed by their business savvy.

"Everyone makes a lot of money," continued Mark. "We usually pay about three hundred dollars per gall bladder to our network of freelance black bear hunters. We also have our own supply of gall bladders from our legitimate bear hunting businesses. Kwan Park pays us one thousand dollars per gall bladder. Which adds up since we usually have at least a hundred gall bladders to sell three or four times per year."

Tim added, "On the Korean end, each whole gall bladder sold by Kwan Park's family to the Korean black-market pharmacies and traditional medicine shops is worth between three and five thousand dollars, depending on the weight. The retail businesses sell the gall bladders whole for as much as ten thousand dollars. In powdered form, it sells for as much as one hundred dollars per gram. So, everyone in the supply chain makes a lot of money, with minor risk of getting caught."

Acting like he was really impressed by the Riley's' explanation of their gall bladder business dealings, Denny asked, "So, when are you going to sell your next shipment?"

Tim answered, "We don't have the exact date confirmed yet, but probably right after the spring bear hunting season on June 15th. We always have the meetings in Kamloops because it is convenient for us and only a three-and-a-half- to four-hour drive for Kwan Park from Vancouver."

Denny congratulated them on their business acumen. Leaning forward and nodding attentively while they were talking, he gave them the impression he was genuinely interested in being involved for the long-term in their black bear gall bladder business. They both seemed impressed by Denny's commitment and genuine interest in their operation.

When Denny and Tim returned to the hunting lodge the next afternoon, Denny went to his room with Syd and Nelle to give John Benson a call and fill him in on the very productive weekend with the Riley cousins.

John said, "Great work Denny. I'll update Russ Paulson about what's going on and the meeting in Kamloops. As soon as you find out the actual date and logistics for the meeting, we'll contact the RCMP in Kamloops to finalize the plan for the takedown of the Riley cousins and their Korean buyer, Kwan Park."

8 p.m. Friday, June 15, 2012
Tim Riley's Hunting Lodge, 42 km north of Peace River, Alberta

Since the trip with Tim to Mark Riley's hunting lodge, Denny kept busy working as a hunting guide: doing his normal job duties and assisting the hunting guests in shooting their trophy black bears. Drawing closer to Tim, he was soon promoted to one of the senior guides at the hunting lodge, with additional responsibilities for supervising the less experienced guides and assigning the daily responsibilities. During an evening chat with Tim over drinks, the proposed date and location of the meeting with Kwan Park was casually mentioned by Tim. It was to be on Thursday morning, June 21st at eleven o'clock in the Costco parking lot in southwest Kamloops.

Once more alone in his room, Denny called John to let him know. They decided Denny would continue to maintain his undercover identity throughout the planned takedown in Kamloops.

The next day, Denny said to Tim, "Hey, Tim, I don't have anything planned for my days off, so I'd be happy to stay at the hunting lodge to take care of things while you and Mark are away in Kamloops."

Tim replied, "Thanks, Denny, that sounds great. I shouldn't really say anything yet, but Mark and I have decided to give you a bonus for all your hard work this spring. We really appreciate your dedication. You have proved yourself as someone we can trust in our business, which is a big deal for us."

Surprised by Tim's offer of a bonus, Denny responded, "Gee, thanks, Tim. I didn't expect any bonus, but I really appreciate that you and Mark trust me with information about your businesses."

11 a.m. Thursday, June 21, 2012
Costco Parking Lot, Kamloops, British Columbia

With the end of the spring bear hunting season, there were no hunting guests left at the lodge, and most of the other guides and camp workers left to take some time off until the fall hunting season started on September 1st.

If things went as planned with the takedown, the RCMP would issue search warrants for both Riley's' hunting lodges, and any hunting guides present at the time would be arrested and charged with a variety of *Wildlife Act* offenses. John and Denny decided the RCMP officers would arrest Denny just like everyone else, to maintain his cover identity, but then release him as soon as it was safe.

John called the RCMP staff sergeant in charge at the Peace River RCMP detachment and told him to instruct his officers to be very careful with Syd and Nelle when they took Denny into custody at the hunting lodge because the dogs would protect Denny to the death if they thought he was in danger. John notified his boss, Michael Alden, about the details of the upcoming meeting in Kamloops, and they then notified the RCMP detachment there about what was going on.

The plan was to have undercover officers begin surveillance of the Riley cousins as soon as they arrived in Kamloops the day prior to the meeting. They knew from Denny the type of vehicle they would be driving and the license plate number, and that they were planning to stay overnight at the Fairfield Inn & Suites close to Costco.

For the scheduled eleven o'clock meeting with Kwan Park in the Costco parking lot, the RCMP planned to have several unmarked vehicles with tactical unit officers ready, as well as a surveillance van. The whole exchange and takedown would be videotaped.

John, Michael, and Russ decided to fly to Kamloops on an RCMP plane so they could observe the takedown. They would also be there to discuss the plan for charging and prosecuting the cousins with their BC law enforcement counterparts. There were also issues of how to deal with Kwan Park's seafood farming business in BC and his family's businesses in South Korea. Law enforcement agencies in South Korea would need to be involved.

Tim left to pick up Mark at his hunting lodge on Tuesday afternoon. He stayed overnight at Mark's lodge and then he and Mark drove from Fort St. John to Kamloops on Wednesday. Tim packed his seventy black bear gall bladders in two coolers with several ice packs. Before leaving for Kamloops, Mark did the same with his sixty-five gall bladders.

While they drove, they talked about how well things had gone that bear hunting season. They also talked about how fortunate they were to have found a guy like Denny Bear to bring into the business. After driving for about an hour, Mark asked Tim, "Is this the ninth or tenth time we're meeting with Kwan Park?"

Tim replied, "It's the tenth time. By the way, I checked our Belize bank accounts yesterday before I left home, and the total amount in the accounts is now one point four million US dollars. With this new shipment of gall bladders, that should increase to over one and a half million."

Smiling broadly at Tim, Mark said, "Wow, that's damn good for only running the operation for four years. How much longer do you figure we should keep it going?"

"I thought we agreed to shut things down when we reached two million in the bank," Tim responded. "After that, we can sell the hunting lodges and the rights to our hunting and guiding areas and move to Belize full time. That should be enough to live comfortably for as long as we want. We can build our dream houses next to each other on the beachfront property we bought and live like kings."

Laughing, Mark said, "That sounds like a good plan to me, cousin."

They arrived in Kamloops at seven o'clock in the evening and checked into the Fairfield Inn & Suites. After eating dinner at the pub adjacent to the hotel, they watched baseball games and drank beer until closing time at midnight. In the morning, they slept until nine, checked out of the hotel, and then went for a leisurely breakfast at the nearby Cora's Restaurant.

While they were having breakfast, the RCMP tactical units and surveillance vehicles got into position in the Costco parking lot. Since they didn't know the exact location of the meeting in the parking lot, they positioned their three unmarked SUVs in different spots. John, Michael, and Russ were in their own RCMP unmarked SUV monitoring the police radio communication.

At ten forty-five, the Riley cousins left the restaurant and drove the short distance to Costco parking lot. They pulled into a spot in the furthest south section. Once they'd parked, the surveillance van drove to a spot close by with a clear view of their vehicle out of the back tinted windows. The officers inside set up their video camera and radioed the other RCMP units to let them know what was happening.

At ten fifty-five, a Nissan Pathfinder SUV drove into the parking lot and parked next to the Rileys' Ford Expedition. An Asian man, who they assumed was Kwan Park, got out of the vehicle holding a computer tablet and got into the back seat of the Rileys' vehicle. After about ten minutes, during which the RCMP officers assumed Kwan Park completed the money e-Transfer to the Rileys' bank accounts, they all got out of the vehicle and opened their respective back doors to the rear cargo areas. The Rileys then transferred four large coolers from their vehicle to the Nissan Pathfinder.

While the three men were all inside the Rileys' vehicle, the officers in the surveillance van radioed the other units to converge on the two vehicles. As soon as the Rileys and Kwan Park finished shaking hands and got back into their respective vehicles, all three of the RCMP unmarked units surrounded the two vehicles with their sirens on and lights flashing, blocking them from moving.

The nine tactical unit officers immediately got out of their vehicles with weapons drawn and ordered the Rileys and Kwan Park to get out of their vehicles and kneel on the ground with their hands on their heads. Looking shocked and bewildered about what was happening, they reluctantly complied. Once they were handcuffed, each was placed in the back seat of a different RCMP vehicle.

John, Michael, and Russ were parked a short distance away in the parking lot, listening to the RCMP radio communication. They were all tense with anticipation as the takedown unfolded. Once it was all over, they drove over to the scene and congratulated the RCMP tactical unit leader on a successful operation. They then opened the back door of the Nissan Pathfinder, and with the camera operator videoing, John opened each of the four coolers.

Inside each one, individually packaged in Ziploc plastic bags, were what looked to be about thirty to forty gall bladders. Russ and Michael, with big smiles, each shook John's hand, and Russ said, "Great work, John. This is a huge takedown for us." Making sure they were out of earshot of the three captives, Russ continued, "Denny did a fantastic job getting inside the Rileys' operation and finding out about the exchange. We could never have done this without him."

Beaming with pride for Denny's work, John said, "Thanks, Russ, I'll be sure to let Denny know."

The two vehicles, with the coolers inside, were loaded on tow truck flat decks to be transported back to the RCMP detachment for forensic examination and an inventory of the contents of the four coolers. They also took possession of Kwan Park's computer tablet and his and the Rileys' cell phones. The RCMP's IT people would attempt to trace the money transfer to the location of the Rileys' bank accounts. They would also inspect the call logs of the cell phones.

Once they were back at the Kamloops' RCMP detachment, John called Denny. After a couple of tries, Denny finally answered his cell phone. John said, "Hi, Denny, it's all over here. The Rileys and Kwan Park are all in custody. How did it go on your end?"

Denny answered, "As we expected, around twelve-thirty Alberta time, three RCMP Ford Explorers from Peace River arrived at the lodge with warrants for the arrest of any hunting guides still there, including me. Because most of the guides had already left for the summer break between hunting seasons, there were only two other guides at the lodge besides me.

"Anyway, they arrested all three of us and took us back to the Peace River RCMP detachment. The two officers who arrested me knew who I was and let me calm Syd and Nelle down and I brought them with us to Peace River. They made sure that everything looked legitimate so that the camp workers and the other two hunting guides would think I was being arrested just the same as them. Once we got in the RCMP vehicle, they took off my handcuffs and we had an enjoyable time driving to Peace River while I told them about my experience as an undercover bear hunting guide and black bear gall bladder poacher."

"You did a fantastic job, Denny. It looks like we took down one of the biggest and well-organized wildlife poaching and trafficking operations in western Canadian history. Hopefully, the Rileys will get significant jail time. Since Kwan Park is a South Korean citizen, they will need to decide where to prosecute him. Regardless, there will be significant problems for his family's businesses both here in Canada and in South Korea.

"The prosecutors also think they will be able to seize all the assets of Tim and Mark Riley related to the poaching operation, which includes their hunting lodges and all the associated equipment. They will also go after their offshore bank accounts if they can prove the funds were from the illegal poaching operations."

"That sounds great, John. It seems amazing I was able to become friends with Tim and his cousin, Mark. Tim even said he was going to give me a bonus when he got back from Kamloops. They were not your typical bad guys and were good businessmen. They could have done exceptionally well if they had just been satisfied with running their hunting lodges, but they got greedy with the easy money they could make in the illegal wildlife trafficking racket. Now they'll lose everything and end up in jail."

After a short pause, Denny continued, "I guess I'll go back to the hunting lodge tomorrow and pick up my personal stuff and my vehicle and go back home for some time off. I assume they'll let me know if I need to testify at their trials whenever that might be."

John said, "If they plead guilty and make some sort of deal, there probably won't be any need for a big trial. It's best if we try to keep you out of the public eye, in case we need to put together another undercover operation in the future. That's why we wanted it to look like they arrested and charged you, just like everyone else who was part of their poaching business. Right now, Tim and Mark Riley don't know how the RCMP, and Fish and Wildlife found out about their operation and their meeting with Kwan Park."

"I understand, John. There's no sense in blowing my cover unless we have to. So, what's next on the agenda?"

"Things are under control at the office in Edmonton right now, so you might as well take some well-earned time off. Kate and I will be heading to Geneva, Switzerland, from July 23rd to 27th as part of the Canadian and US government's delegations for the yearly Standing Committee meeting of CITES.

"We helped prepare a briefing report about the progress of INTERPOL's Operation Worthy and elephant ivory and rhino horn poaching in Africa, which is going to be presented by Donald Hogan from Environment Canada. He's now also the acting head of INTERPOL's Environmental Crime Programme for the next four years. Our next extended trip to Africa is not scheduled until early next year, so it'll just be business as usual at the office in Edmonton until then."

CHAPTER 7

11 a.m. Monday, July 9, 2012
National Fish and Wildlife Forensics Laboratory, Ashland, Oregon

Since returning from Kenya in late April, Kate Beckett had been busy with her normal job duties. While John and Denny were busy with taking down the Rileys' black bear gall bladder poaching operation, Kate was running her own sting operation trying to catch a Chinese American citizen suspected of trafficking rhino horns on the US west coast. She spoke with John regularly about the progress of his and Denny's undercover operation, so when John and Denny's operation was done, she called John to let him know that her own operation was about to wrap up soon as well.

Kate said, "Hi, John. It was great to hear that your black bear poaching operation went so well. Denny did such a fantastic job, and it sounds like you broke up one of the biggest poaching and trafficking operations in western Canada."

"Thanks, Kate, it was absolutely Denny's operation, and he did a fantastic job. We have the two hunting lodge owners in custody, as well as several of their long-term hunting guides. It looks like the Rileys will plead guilty to get a reduced sentence, three to five years in prison, and a fine equal to their gall bladder trafficking proceeds over the past four years, which could amount to over a million dollars.

"The South Korean purchaser of the gall bladders, Kwan Park, is still in custody in Vancouver. The RCMP and British Columbia provincial crown prosecutors are talking to the Korean law enforcement people about where he should stand trial. The South Korean police have closed his family's seafood distribution and wholesale businesses in Seoul and have charged some of his family members with various offenses related to smuggling and selling illegally imported black bear gall bladders."

"That sounds great, John," Kate said. "I just wanted to let you know that my own undercover operation with the Chinese American businessman, Jeong Lee, who we suspect has been importing rhino horns from Mombasa to San Francisco, is about to wrap up next week as well. Our undercover Kenyan agent at the Kilindini Harbor container terminal in Mombasa informed us about three weeks ago that a shipping container with carvings, masks, and other assorted artifacts and clothing from the Akamba Handicraft Industry Cooperative Society in Mombasa had been loaded on a cargo ship bound for Pier 80 in the Port of San Francisco. Our Kenyan agent in Mombasa confirmed that hidden in the cargo container among the various wood carvings and other stuff were approximately thirty rhino horns."

"That sounds great, Kate," said John. "This could be a huge bust for you guys."

"Thanks, John, we sure hope so. This Jeong Lee guy owns several retail gift and handicraft stores in California that specialize in merchandise from Africa, such as wood carvings and handmade clothing. He also has business interests in the black market exotic traditional Asian medicine industry in San Francisco's Chinatown district. I guess he thought he would become a major supplier of rhino horn products to the large Asian community in San Francisco and other areas on the west coast. His regular shipments of carvings and handicrafts from Mombasa made the perfect cover for getting the rhino horns into the US."

John said, "I remember we visited the huge Akamba Wood Carving Factory back in 2010 on one of our first trips to Kenya. The carving factory is the primary business operated by the Akamba Handicraft Industry Cooperative Society in Mombasa. I even bought a few wood carvings and masks from the retail store for myself and to bring back to Edmonton for Anna. There were hundreds of wood carvers in open-air, thatch-roofed kiosks producing some amazing African animal carvings, masks, and polished stone and animal bone jewelry.

"It seems like a good plan by Jeong Lee to use the container shipments of wood carvings and handicrafts as a cover for smuggling the rhino horns. We all know the Kilindini Harbor and port facility in Mombasa is one of the major East African points of exit for illegal ivory, rhino horn, and other animal products bound for China and other Asian countries. Unfortunately, it has been hard to stop when so many of the Kenyan senior harbor and customs agents are being paid off by the wildlife traffickers."

Kate said, "So anyway, the container cargo ship with the rhino horns is scheduled to arrive at Pier 80 in the Port of San Francisco on Tuesday, July 17th. We are planning to track the container once it's removed from the ship and stored in the container yard at Pier 80. We assume Jeong Lee will have a truck pick up the container as soon as it arrives and then deliver it to his distribution warehouse in San Francisco where he will unload the contents, including the rhino horns. When the rhino horns are in his possession, we intend to raid the warehouse.

"I was wondering if you would like to meet me in San Francisco the weekend before, on July 14th or 15th, so you'll be there when we raid the warehouse. Then we can spend some time together in San Francisco before we have to fly to Geneva."

"That sounds like a great idea, I would love to see you and your Fish and Wildlife special agents in action on your home turf." Laughing, John said, "Maybe I can give you some pointers about how the RCMP would execute the operation in Canada if you need some help pulling it off."

Laughing, Kate said, "You better watch yourself, John Benson. We Americans don't take kindly to pushy Canadian cops coming down here telling us how to do our jobs. You never know, maybe you can learn something from us as well."

"All right, point taken," said John. "I'll try to keep my mouth shut unless I'm asked for my input. So, that sounds like a brilliant plan. After the takedown of Jeong Lee, maybe we can spend a few days just being tourists in San Francisco. It will also give us a chance to do some final editing of the briefing report we helped prepare for Donald Hogan. He's presenting the report at the Standing Committee meeting to update them about the progress of INTERPOL's Project Wisdom."

1 p.m. Wednesday, July 18, 2012
Lindenville Light Industrial District, north of San Francisco International Airport

Kate and John were sitting in a rented Toyota Highlander SUV parked along San Mateo Avenue in the Lindenville Light Industrial District north of the San Francisco International Airport, just off Highway 101. From where they were parked, they could see the single rear loading dock bay of the one-story, ten thousand square foot distribution warehouse belonging to East Africa Imports Inc., the company owned by Mr. Jeong Lee.

The cargo ship from Mombasa carrying the shipping container with the Akamba Wood Carving Factory goods, and hopefully the rhino horns, had arrived at Pier 80 as scheduled the day before. The US Customs agents at Pier 80 were alerted about the ship's arrival and given the registration numbers of Jeong Lee's shipping container. Customs had notified Kate Beckett when the container was unloaded from the ship earlier that morning. Then, a little later, they notified her again when a truck with a flat deck trailer arrived at the Pier 80 entrance gate with the US Customs paperwork necessary to claim the container and haul it out of the storage yard.

Two unmarked F&W Office of Law Enforcement vehicles, with two special agents in each vehicle, parked on Cesar Chavez Avenue about a block east of the Pier 80 entrance gate. They were ready to follow the truck when it left the Pier 80 storage yard. At one-thirty, Kate got a call that the flat-bed truck and trailer had just left the Pier 80 storage yard and the F&W vehicles were following as planned.

With normal mid-day traffic, it would take about twenty to thirty minutes to get to the warehouse. Another F&W Office of Law Enforcement unmarked Ford Explorer SUV with three special agents inside was also parked a short distance away from the warehouse with a view of the front entrance. They reported to Kate that a BMW X5 SUV had arrived at the front door parking area. The license plate and make of the vehicle matched the vehicle registered to Jeong Lee.

Just before two o'clock, the truck hauling the mid-sized storage container passed Kate and John on the street. They watched as it slowly maneuvered into the small parking area and backed up to the warehouse loading dock. The overhead door opened and two African American men in coveralls and one Asian man in a sports jacket came out onto the elevated loading dock area.

The Asian man had a discussion with the truck driver and exchanged some paperwork. The rear doors of the container were opened and a third African American man driving a forklift came out of the warehouse and started hauling wooden boxes on pallets out of the container into the warehouse. The boxes were about four feet in each dimension. It took about forty-five minutes for the forklift to transfer them from the shipping container into the warehouse. Kate and John counted eighteen boxes. Once the boxes were all in the warehouse, the truck driver closed the rear doors of the container, pulled out of the loading dock area, and drove off.

After the truck left and the loading dock overhead bay door closed, Kate radioed her team to prepare to breach the warehouse through both the front and back doors. Kate and John drove around to the front door and met the other three agents. The two vehicles that had followed the truck from Pier 80 pulled into the rear loading dock area. The agents were all wearing Kevlar vests with 'Police - F&W Agents' written on them in large letters. They were armed with standard issue assault rifles and sidearms. Since the doors were not locked, on a signal from Kate over her radio, they all rushed into the building simultaneously, completely surprising the four men and one woman drinking coffee and relaxing in the lunchroom.

One of the men sitting at the lunchroom table was the middle-aged Asian man they had seen on the loading dock. Kate walked up to him and showed him the search warrant. She then asked, "Are you Jeong Lee?"

He said gruffly, "Yes, my name is Jeong Lee. What's this all about?"

Forcefully, Kate said, "Please stand up and put your hands behind your back."

He reluctantly complied, and while Kate was putting handcuffs on him, she said, "Jeong Lee, you are under arrest for the illegal importation of restricted wildlife products into the United States. Which of these boxes contains the rhino horns?"

After stalling for a few seconds, he finally replied, "I don't know anything about any rhino horns. There are just African carvings and handicrafts in the boxes."

Kate continued, "Look Mr. Jeong, I have a search warrant that says I can tear open every one of these boxes, and I don't care if the other stuff in the boxes gets damaged."

Jeong Lee, trying to sound defiant, but looking a little more defeated, said again, "I don't know anything about rhino horns. If you damage my merchandise, I'll sue you and whoever you work for."

"Okay, if that's how you want to play this, you can all sit here handcuffed to your chairs while my officers open up all the boxes."

While John watched them, the rest of the agents went to their vehicles and got their pry bars and hammers and proceeded to systematically open the tops and sides of the boxes, spreading out the contents on the warehouse floor. Eventually, after opening every box, they found all thirty rhino horns packaged individually in several layers of bubble wrap. They took lots of pictures as each wooden box was opened and each rhino horn was revealed.

While this was going on, Kate called her contact at the San Francisco FBI field office and told him to send a prisoner transport van to pick up Jeong Lee and his warehouse workers. She also requested a team of FBI forensic crime scene investigators.

They were hoping to find paper records or computer files that would lead them to some of the black-market customers for the rhino horns. They tended to be back-room operations of legitimate Asian traditional medicine businesses in the Chinatown districts of large cities like San Francisco. These businesses operated in a very secretive manner, with long-standing and well-known customers, difficult to penetrate by law enforcement agencies.

Kate didn't know exactly what part the other warehouse workers played in the rhino horn operation, but for now, they would all be charged and detained until the federal prosecutors figured out what to do with them. As for Mr. Jeong Lee, they had an exceptionally solid case against him. The Kenyan National Police and KWS had also arrested the African ringleaders of the rhino horn poaching syndicate in Mombasa and Nairobi. As part of their plea bargain deal, they had identified Jeong Lee as one of their principal buyers of rhino horns.

Jeong Lee had met with several of the ringleaders over the past several years in Nairobi as they were planning their business partnership. The Tanzanian poacher, Samson Kanumba, who John and the team helped take down in

Nairobi on April 13th with the Irish Sheehan brothers, was also a lower-level member of the same poaching syndicate and divulged information about the workings of the syndicate in exchange for a lesser sentence.

So, it was extremely satisfying for Kate and John to close the circle on the whole rhino horn poaching syndicate. Sadly, the reality was once again that another thirty southern white rhinos had been killed just for their horns. As long as there were people like Jeong Lee willing to buy the rhino horns, there would almost certainly be another poaching syndicate formed to take its place since the illogical demand for rhino horn had not diminished.

The FBI prisoner transport van came and took Jeong Lee and his warehouse workers away to the lockup facilities at the San Francisco FBI field office. An FBI CSI team also arrived and started systematically going through the warehouse and office area, collecting any information they thought might be useful. After congratulating them on a job well done, Kate told her team of special agents they could return to their San Francisco field office.

Although she would have to go to the FBI field office the following morning to wrap things up and talk with the federal prosecutors, she and John had the next two days off to enjoy San Francisco together before they left for Geneva, Switzerland, on Saturday afternoon.

CHAPTER 8

9 p.m. Sunday, July 22, 2012
Starling Hotel, Geneva, Switzerland

John and Kate spent the rest of Thursday, Friday, and Saturday morning exploring the sights of San Francisco, wandering through the waterfront area and riding on the cable cars. Since John arrived in San Francisco on Monday evening, they had been staying at the Hotel Zoe Fisherman's Wharf, a four-star boutique hotel in the heart of the waterfront tourist area, only a few blocks from Pier 39 and Fisherman's Wharf.

Because they had been busy planning the raid on Jeong Lee's warehouse, they had not explored the area around the hotel. So, they were grateful for the time they had to relax and just be together as a regular couple on vacation. Much of the time they spent together revolved around work assignments, often with a lot of tension and sometimes danger, planning and executing the various raids and takedowns of the bad guys. Although they both thrived on the challenges and excitement of their jobs, they also appreciated their brief periods of down time together when they could wander around like normal people just enjoying being with each other.

They started their long, eighteen-hour flight from San Francisco to Geneva, Switzerland, on Saturday afternoon at two o'clock on United Airlines, and after a six-hour stopover at London's Heathrow Airport, arrived in Geneva at five o'clock Swiss time late Sunday afternoon.

They were staying at the four-star Starling Hotel Geneva, a few minutes from the large Palexpo Geneva Exhibition and Trade Center, the site of the

62nd meeting of the Standing Committee of CITES. Being part of the official Canadian and US delegations, they usually stayed together and therefore, were assigned a comfortable, one-bedroom junior suite.

CITES is an international agreement between most of the world's governments, originally formed in 1975 after ten years of negotiations. Its aim is to ensure that international trade in specimens of wild animals and plants does not threaten their survival. Because the trade in wild animals and plants often crosses borders between countries, the effort to regulate it requires international cooperation to safeguard certain species from over-exploitation. CITES accords varying degrees of protection to over 37,000 species of animals and plants, whether they are traded as live specimens or as commercial products derived from the plants or animals.

Countries and regional economic integration organizations adhere to CITES voluntarily. A country agreed to be bound by the convention is known as a party. Although CITES is legally binding for the parties, it does not take the place of the national laws of the participating countries. However, it provides a framework to be respected by each party, which has to adopt its own domestic legislation to ensure that CITES is implemented at the national level. For many years, CITES was one of the international conservation organizations with the largest membership, with 183 parties or countries.

CITES works by subjecting international trade in specimens of selected species to certain controls. All import, export, re-export, and introduction from the thousands of species covered by the convention has to be authorized through a licensing system. Each party to the convention must designate one or more management authorities in charge of administering that licensing system and one or more scientific authorities to advise them of the effects of trade on the status of the species.

In Canada, the CITES management authority and the CITES scientific authority is the Canadian Wildlife Service, and the CITES Enforcement Focal Point resides within the office of the director general of Environment Canada's Wildlife Enforcement Directorate.

The primary administrative body of CITES is the CITES secretariat, permanently located in Geneva, Switzerland. It has a pivotal role fundamental to the convention with many functions including coordinating and administering the workings of the convention, assisting with communication, monitoring the implementation of the convention, arranging meetings for the Conference of the Parties every three years and of the permanent committees at regular intervals, and overseeing those meetings.

One of the main functional bodies of the convention is the Standing Committee, which provides policy guidance to the secretariat concerning the implementation of the convention and oversees the management of the secretariat's budget. Beyond those key roles, it also coordinates and oversees the work of other committees and working groups; conducts tasks given to it by the Conference of the Parties; and drafts resolutions for consideration by the Conference of the Parties.

The members of the Standing Committee are parties representing each of the six major geographical regions (Africa, Asia, Europe, North America, Central and South America and the Caribbean, and Oceania), with the number of representatives assigned according to the number of parties within the region. Usually, the Standing Committee meets only once a year, as well as just before and after each meeting of the Conference of the Parties, which occurs every three years at designated locations around the world. The next Conference of the Parties was scheduled for Bangkok, Thailand, in March 2013. The previous one had been in Doha, Qatar in March 2010.

The working level of CITES consists of the Animals and Plants Committees, which include scientific experts whose function is to fill gaps in biological and other specialized knowledge regarding species of animals and plants that are (or might become) subject to CITES trade controls. Their role is to provide technical support to decision-making about these species.

The Animals and Plants Committees meet twice between meetings of the Conference of the Parties. They report to the Conference of the Parties at its meetings and, if requested, provide advice to the Standing Committee between meetings. The members of the Animals and Plants Committees are also individuals from the six major geographical regions as well as one specialist on nomenclature on each of the two committees.

John and Kate, although not official members of the CITES Animal Committee, had attended several meetings of the committee as observers, in general to provide updates about current INTERPOL Wildlife Crime Group initiatives in Africa. They were presently attending the annual Standing

Committee meeting to provide support to their colleague, and John's friend and fellow Canadian, Donald Hogan, the current head of INTERPOL's Environmental Crime Programme. He was scheduled to present an update about the progress of INTERPOL's Project Wisdom and the results of Operation Worthy to date. These initiatives were currently the primary focus of INTERPOL's fight to curtail elephant ivory and rhino horn poaching in Africa.

Donald Hogan's one-hour presentation was scheduled for one o'clock in the afternoon on Thursday, so John and Kate had plenty of time to explore the many conference exhibits and information kiosks in the Palexpo Geneva Exhibition and Trade Center and to talk to representatives from other countries attending the Standing Committee meeting. They also had time to do some sightseeing in the Geneva area and to sample a few of the high-end but expensive restaurants in the city center overlooking Lake Geneva.

They even took a Lake Geneva four-hour dinner cruise on Wednesday evening, departing from the Mont-Blanc docks and touring the coastline in the Geneva area of the large seventy-two-kilometer-long lake. It was one of the more romantic things they had done over the past several years. The cruise also included an informative narrated tour and a view of the beautiful estates, mansions, and natural scenery of the shoreline in the Geneva area.

After they had finished their meal and were relaxing, enjoying the cruise and the beautiful scenery, a smiling John said, "This seems like a much more civilized place to visit than the places we usually end up spending our time together. Maybe we should try to work a little more culture into our adventures."

Laughing, Kate said, "Are you saying you would rather go on this dinner cruise than drive a Land Rover through the African savannah watching a herd of elephants or a family of giraffes? I think when it comes right down to it, that is where we would both rather be. However, it's nice to sample the finer things in life occasionally."

Smiling, John said, "You're right, we're just a couple of adrenaline junkies, obsessed with saving the world's animals from the poachers and traffickers. And you can't do that from an office in Geneva, or any other city, for that matter."

1 p.m. Thursday, July 26, 2012
Palexpo Exhibition and Trade Center, Geneva, Switzerland

Donald Hogan's presentation about INTERPOL's Project Wisdom in the main conference hall on Thursday afternoon to several hundred of the delegates attending the Standing Committee meeting was well received. The plight of elephants and rhinos in Africa and Asia was a topic of great concern to many of the delegates attending the conference. Although Donald Hogan did not dwell on it in his presentation because of political sensitivities, many people in attendance also knew that the corruption of politicians, bureaucrats, and law enforcement officials was a major problem in many of the countries with the worst wildlife poaching and trafficking histories.

Money and greed were the real culprits in most wildlife poaching and trafficking enterprises. There was lots of money to be made at all levels of the industry. From the poachers on the ground who could make as much money selling one elephant tusk as they would make in several months working at a regular job, if they had one; to the poaching middlemen who resold the ivory for several times what they paid the poachers for it; to the wholesalers and traffickers who sold the ivory to the underground carving factories in China, Hong Kong, or Vietnam; to the legal and illegal retail shop owners who sold the finished carved ivory merchandise to tourists and collectors: everyone made a lot of money.

Cumulatively, the illegal trade of wildlife and wildlife parts was worth billions of dollars every year, often more lucrative than drugs or many other types of criminal activity. The temptation of the money was often too much for the very people whose jobs were to safeguard their fellow citizens from the criminals. The result was too often the decimation of an animal species to the literal point of extinction, like the magnificent northern white rhino, which had only five living animals left on the face of the earth. Soon there would be none left.

People like John Benson and Kate Beckett, and those attending the CITES Standing Committee meeting, and thousands of others working for government and law enforcement agencies and wildlife conservation foundations and wildlife trusts devoted their professional lives to trying to stem the tide of wildlife crime. However, sometimes it seemed like they were fighting a losing battle. The lust for money was always the winner. The animals and plants became the losers. Ultimately, the losers would be the future generations who would never get to see a live northern white rhino, or a multitude of other species destined for the same fate.

CHAPTER 9

August to December 2012

John and Kate returned from Geneva, Switzerland, after the CITES Standing Committee meeting and went back to their respective homes and regular jobs. For the remainder of 2012, there were no assignments scheduled through INTERPOL, so they settled into their normal lives in Edmonton and Ashland. They talked to each other regularly on the phone, and Kate went to Edmonton for a week in October for Canadian Thanksgiving, and John went to Ashland in November for a week for American Thanksgiving.

They spent Christmas and New Years with their respective families. John's family had expanded with the birth of his youngest daughter Laura's first child, a son, in February of 2012, and the birth of his middle daughter Angela's third child, also a son, in June 2012. His oldest daughter, Sally, announced she was pregnant again, with a due date in August 2013. So, John now had five grandchildren, three girls and two boys, with another on the way in late summer. Family gatherings were noisy and chaotic, but he loved being able to spend some extended time in Edmonton for a change. He got the chance to babysit his grandkids sometimes and be there for birthdays and other family gatherings.

Kate spent the Christmas holidays with her daughter Dianna, who came home to Ashland for a couple of weeks from Portland, where she attended Portland State University. Kate took the days off between Christmas and New Year's so she could spend as much time with her daughter as possible.

Kate's mother also came for Christmas from her retirement home in Tacoma, Washington, so it was an enjoyable time spent with her closest family members. She would have liked to have spent some time with John over Christmas, but they realized their families came first, especially at times like Christmas.

Besides, they were about to return to Africa together for an extended period. Several INTERPOL sponsored training workshops were scheduled early in the new year. INTERPOL's Wildlife Crime Unit and the Tanzanian and Kenyan wildlife enforcement agencies had also initiated several critical anti-poaching operations.

6 p.m. Friday, January 18, 2013
Botswana Police Training College and Law Enforcement Academy, Otse, Botswana

John, Kate, Denny, Anna, and the dogs traveled to Nairobi on the weekend of January 12th. They then flew on the KWS airwing's Cessna 425 Corsair plane to Gaborone, Botswana, where they again assisted in a five-day training workshop at the Botswana Police Training College and Law Enforcement Academy for wildlife anti-poaching law enforcement personnel from several eastern and southern African countries.

The Botswana Department of Wildlife and National Parks again jointly hosted the training workshop, together with INTERPOL's Environmental Crime Programme, the International Fund for Animal Welfare (IFAW), and Environment Canada's Wildlife Enforcement Directorate. The training workshop was the second to be hosted in Botswana and was one of several workshops planned in 2013 for African anti-poaching law enforcement agencies in conjunction with INTERPOL's Project Wisdom and Operation Worthy.

John, Kate, and their team were also in Kenya again to collaborate on a new international initiative conceptualized in mid-2012 and code-named *Operation Cobra*, which was to be conducted in twenty-two countries in Africa, Asia, and Latin America. The idea was to organize a global and regional operation coordinated by an International Coordination Team (ICT) based in Nairobi and Bangkok, Thailand, to facilitate sharing of Information and intelligence about international wildlife crime.

Operation Cobra was initiated in 2012 during the fourth Special Investigation Group (SIG) training course held in September at the International Law Enforcement Academy (ILEA) in Bangkok, Thailand. The course participants included mid to senior level law enforcement investigation managers from wildlife crime hotspots in Cameroon, Gabon, China, the Democratic Republic of Congo, Kenya, Nepal, Thailand, Vietnam, Laos, Malaysia, Indonesia, the Republic of South Africa, and the USA, as well as members of the Lusaka Agreement Task Force (LATF).

Financial support was to be provided by the US State Department Bureau of Narcotics and International Law Enforcement Affairs (INL), the US Fish and Wildlife Service, the Canada Fund for Local Initiatives implemented through the Canadian Embassy in Kenya, the IFAW, the China Wildlife Conservation Association, and the Freeland Foundation.

Operation Cobra was to be implemented in early 2013 and was coordinated internationally from Bangkok, Thailand, by an ICT. Members of the ICT included representatives from China, the US Fish and Wildlife Service, the World Customs Organization (WCO), the South and Southeast Asia Wildlife Enforcement Networks, the LATF, and law enforcement representatives from India, Indonesia, Nepal, South Africa, Thailand, and Vietnam.

At the field and investigative level, operation participants included wildlife, customs, and police officers from twenty-two Asian, African, and North American countries, namely Botswana, Cambodia, Cameroon, China, the Republic of the Congo, the Democratic Republic of the Congo, Gabon, India, Indonesia, Kenya, Laos, Malaysia, Mozambique, Nepal, Singapore, South Africa, Tanzania, Thailand, Uganda, the USA, Vietnam, and Zambia.

John and the team were also in Nairobi to collaborate with the LATF, also headquartered in Nairobi. The LATF was an intergovernmental law enforcement agency established in 1999 and was listed as a United Nations Environmental Treaty, adopted in 1994 in Lusaka, Zambia.

The LATF was mandated to combat transnational illegal trade in wildlife and forestry resources through fostering interstate cooperation and collaboration among agencies. It had achieved significant milestones in bridging source, transit, and destination countries of wildlife contraband through executing and coordinating national, regional, and multi-regional enforcement operations.

In discharging its mandate, the LATF worked closely with and received support from national enforcement agencies and international partners of mutual interest such as INTERPOL, CITES, WCO, the United Nations, and ICCWC Secretariats and Governments.

The LATF also collaborated with research institutions such as the Faculty of Biology at Washington University and conservation NGOs such as the IFAW, TRAFFIC International, the World Wildlife Fund (WWF), the African Wildlife Foundation (AWF), and the Wildlife Conservation Society (WCS) in supporting government efforts towards combating wildlife crime.

9 a.m. Sunday, January 20, 2013
Wildebeest Eco Camp, Nairobi, Kenya

John and the team returned to Nairobi from Botswana on Saturday afternoon and were picked up at the KWS hangar facilities at the Wilson Airport by their regular KWS driver, Simon Okafor, who drove them to the Wildebeest Eco Camp. They booked their usual cottages for the next several months while on their upcoming assignments in Kenya and elsewhere in Africa.

They gathered for breakfast at a table on the deck of the Wildebeest restaurant. They were all happy to be missing the chilly winter weather back in Alberta and Ashland and were looking forward to their upcoming assignments and adventures.

Anna said, "We sure picked the right time to come back to Nairobi, I saw on my computer this morning that it was minus twenty-five and snowing back in Edmonton. The Wildebeest is as beautiful as ever and I sure am happy we won't be returning to Edmonton until March when it'll be almost spring. So, is the plan finalized to go to Tanzania for the next couple of weeks?"

Kate answered, "The LATF have asked us to help set up an initial workshop for the senior staff and a longer-term training program for the enforcement agency of the newly formed Tanzania Wildlife Authority. In the last ten years, Tanzania has been one of the worst countries in Africa for ivory poaching. Since 2006, the elephant population in the country has been reduced by two thirds.

"The Tanzanian government finally decided to transform the old Wildlife Division, which had been ineffective in stopping the wholesale slaughter of the elephant population, into a parastatal called the Tanzania Wildlife Authority, or TAWA. Parastatals are public agencies, but not directly run by the government. They are governed by boards with members appointed by the government. They have management autonomy and are much more flexible in decision making than traditional government bodies. Parastatals also keep their earnings and pay taxes.

"Last year, the Tanzanian parliament passed an act that established the TAWA. Its role will be to protect, manage, and administer wildlife on all lands in Tanzania except the national parks and Ngorongoro. Most important is that the TAWA will be solely responsible for wildlife crime law enforcement and commercial hunting. A more streamlined management structure has been implemented, and a board of directors was appointed by the government to oversee TAWA."

"Wow, they really shook things up," interjected Denny.

"Yes, they sure did," continued Kate. "The field force is to be armed and organized along paramilitary lines and will have the rights to apply force like the police or military, which is necessary to make anti-poaching more effective. It has been suggested that the Tanzania People's Defense Forces could train them to acquire the enhanced skills and techniques required to manage armed adversaries out in the field."

John then said, "We have been told that sport hunting in game reserves will still be promoted and developed since the TAWA will be self-financing, so game licenses, hunting fees, licensing, sale of trophies, and various permits and certificates for game viewing will be important sources of revenue. It is planned that the headquarters of TAWA will be relocated to Morogoro, a town about two hours west of Dar es Salaam; however, the funding has not been secured for the move yet, so the administration will remain in Dar es Salaam for the time being."

Continuing, John sad, "The TAWA has formed an elite anti-poaching unit named the National and Transnational Serious Crimes Investigation Unit, or the NTSCIU, which will be responsible for pursuing the major ivory traffickers in the country. The NTSCIU is being funded and supported by the PAMS Foundation, an NGO that provides conservation and anti-poaching support to communities and governments in Africa. The Director and co-founder of the PAMS Foundation is Will Letner, who Kate and I met at the

CITES Standing Committee meeting in Geneva last July. He invited us to come to Dar es Salaam the next time we were in Africa to meet the NTSCIU team and hopefully collaborate with them on anti-poaching cases."

Kate explained further, "The NTSCIU anti-poaching team is comprised of officials from the Tanzania Intelligence and Security Service, or TISS, police, army, immigration, judiciary, and the national wildlife service. It is headed by a TISS former senior intelligence analyst, Joseph Mitambo, who's in his late fifties, and who has been in the Tanzanian intelligence community for his whole career. The NTSCIU is also closely aligned with the Wildlife Crime Unit of Tanzania's Ministry of Natural Resources and Tourism.

"We contacted Will Letner a couple of weeks ago before we left for Africa, and he said that the NTSCIU team were close to breaking up a major ivory trafficking syndicate and would welcome our assistance in planning and executing what they hope will be the final takedowns of the ringleaders."

"Will Letner filled us in on what they knew about the poaching syndicate," continued Kate. "The syndicate operates primarily out of the Selous Reserve in southern Tanzania, one of the largest and oldest protected areas in Africa, covering a wilderness area of around fifty thousand square kilometers. Tragically, we were told that elephant numbers in the Selous Reserve area plummeted from 70,400 in 2006 to just over thirteen thousand by the end of 2012, the lowest ever recorded. The Selous has become the focal point of illegal elephant killing in Tanzania over the past decade, and based on DNA analysis of ivory seizures, it's the most significant poaching hotspot in Africa in terms of numbers killed.

"Will Letner told us that the NTSCIU sent investigators to the Selous area and, through interviews with local villagers, discovered details about the main locations for ivory trading around the reserve, the main smuggling routes to Dar es Salaam, and the involvement of local game rangers and police. DNA analysis of large seizures dating back to 2006 showed that the Selous-Niassa ecosystem was the most significant poaching hotspot in Africa. Niassa is a reserve in northern Mozambique contiguous with the Selous. The DNA results showed that Selous-Niassa has been the origin for many of the major ivory seizures in Taiwan, Hong Kong, the Philippines, Sri Lanka, and Singapore since 2006.

"TAWA suspects virtually all the ivory smuggled out of the country has been in the form of raw tusks concealed in shipping containers which exit via just three ports — Dar es Salaam, Zanzibar, and Mombasa in Kenya. Despite these known ivory smuggling exit locations, until now, more ivory poached in Tanzania has been intercepted outside the country than within it.

"It's obvious there have been major problems with chronic inefficiency and corruption in Tanzania's port controls, and within various levels of government in charge of overseeing the port operations. With these ineffective levels of enforcement and the low detection rates of ivory shipments, together with a lack of meaningful prosecutions, even if the traffickers do get caught, it's obvious why international wildlife crime syndicates have consistently targeted Tanzania. Profits from ivory trafficking are high and the risk of getting caught and successfully prosecuted are low. Over the past five years, the trafficking chain from the Selous and Niassa areas to the main markets in China have emerged as the single largest conduit for illegal ivory in the world."

John interjected, "The NTSCIU hope that with the new mandate of the Tanzania Wildlife Authority, and with additional resources, training, and support from agencies like INTERPOL and the LATF, and NGOs like the PAMS Foundation and others, the TAWA can finally start breaking up the Tanzanian ivory trafficking chain."

9 a.m. Wednesday, January 23, 2013
Tanzania Wildlife Authority Headquarters, Dar es Salaam, Tanzania

John and the team drove from Nairobi to Moshi, Tanzania, on Monday and stayed overnight at the Parkview Inn. They decided to drive rather than fly so they could bring Syd and Nelle along, and so they could see some of the Kenyan and Tanzanian countryside during the fifteen-hour drive to Dar es Salaam. They also wanted to bring their RCMP issued SIG Sauer P226 sidearms with them, and it was easier to cross the Kenya-Tanzania border with them while driving, rather than bringing them along on a commercial flight, even though they had all the required permits.

Car hijackings, although not common in the more modern parts of the large cities like Nairobi and Dar es Salaam, still happened in the poorer slum areas and backcountry roads sometimes, so the team usually liked to have their firearms with them when they were traveling. Although they would not have known it beforehand, any carjackers or thieves who might have attempted to stop and rob them would have been in for a very unfortunate surprise when confronted with a vehicle full of well trained, armed law enforcement officers, and the two extremely dangerous German shepherd police dogs.

They passed through Arusha on their way to Moshi, which had a population of around two hundred thousand and was on the lower slopes of Mount Kilimanjaro. Moshi was one of the main staging cities for people climbing Mount Kilimanjaro, and together with Arusha, was also one of the important tourist staging locations for the very lucrative safari tours of the world-renowned Serengeti National Park, the Ngorongoro Crater Conservation Area, Lake Manyara National Park, and Arusha National Park.

Although they had seen Mount Kilimanjaro quite a few times from both the ground and in the air flying close by, the top of the mountain was usually shrouded in cloud and mist. However, by chance, it was a perfectly sunny day with no clouds, and they got to see the snow-capped peak of Mount Kilimanjaro in all its splendor as they were driving from Arusha to Moshi.

The College of African Wildlife Management (CAWM) commonly known as Mweka College or just Mweka, is near the Village of Mweka on the lower slopes of Mount Kilimanjaro, about fourteen kilometers north of Moshi's city center. One of the popular descent routes on Mount Kilimanjaro is the Mweka Trail.

The College of African Wildlife Management was established in 1963 as a pioneer institution for the training of African wildlife managers. Initial funding for Mweka was provided by the African Wildlife Foundation, the US Agency for International Development, and the Frankfurt Zoological Society. Since its establishment, the college has been a leader in providing quality wildlife management training in Africa and has trained over five thousand wildlife managers from fifty-two countries worldwide. Most of the college's graduates work in protected areas throughout sub-Saharan Africa.

The college was founded with stringent academic standards, and its reputation and standing are justly renowned both within Tanzania and internationally. Excellent staff and facilities, both academic and sporting, have guaranteed a high standard of education. The two main purposes of the college are to prepare both local and international students for work within the national parks and reserves of Tanzania and the rest of Africa and to prepare students for work within the safari industries for both photographic safaris and commercial hunting.

The dean of CAWM had invited John and his team to be guest lecturers on several occasions; however, they had not been able to schedule anything so far. The current trip was no exception, but while they were in Moshi, they did go meet with the dean and got a tour of the college facilities. They promised that on their next trip to Tanzania later in the year, they would do a half-day lecture and forensic wildlife biology workshop for the senior students in the Wildlife Management and Conservation degree program.

On Tuesday, they drove the remaining nine hours to Dar es Salaam and checked into the five-star Hyatt Regency Dar es Salaam - Kilimanjaro Hotel on the waterfront, with a beautiful view of Dar es Salaam Harbor. John and Kate got a comfortable regency suite, and Denny, Anna, and Simon got standard king bed, sea view rooms. Syd and Nelle bunked in with Denny as usual. There was a park area across the street along the waterfront, which was handy for taking Syd and Nelle out for their doggie bathroom breaks.

The Hyatt Regency was in the heart of the downtown government and business center, next door to the supreme court of Tanzania and a few blocks from the High Commission of Canada building. Generally, they would not have stayed at such a high-end hotel, but since they were on official INTERPOL business through Project Wisdom and the newly launched Operation Cobra, they decided to splurge a little and stay in the safer down-town harbor front area, since INTERPOL was paying the bill.

Dar es Salaam is the largest city in and the former capital of Tanzania. It is also the largest city in East Africa and the seventh largest in Africa, with a regional population of over six million. On the Swahili coast of Africa, Dar es-Salaam is an important economic center and one of the fastest growing cities in the world. It is Tanzania's most prominent city in arts, fashion, media, music, film, and television, and is the leading financial center.

The city is the main arrival and departure point for most international tourists who visit Tanzania, including the national parks for safaris and the islands of Zanzibar, Unguja, and Pemba. The downtown area is in the Ilala District and is home to the administrative district of Dar es Salaam where almost all government offices and ministries are located, as well as the Bank of Tanzania, the Dar es Salaam Stock Exchange, the city's important Magogoni fish market, Dar es Salaam's central railway station, and the Tanzania Port Authority Tower.

The Kurasini District is close by and on the Dar es Salaam Harbor. It is the home of the Dar es Salaam Port, the Police College, Mgulani Police Barracks, and the Dar es Salaam International Trade Fair Grounds. The Dar es Salaam Port is the country's busiest port, and one of the busiest in East Africa, handling up to ninety percent of the cargo and shipping container traffic.

On Wednesday morning at nine o'clock, Simon drove the thirty minutes from the hotel to the TAWA headquarters, which was in the Ministry of Natural Resources and Tourism government building. Joseph Mitambo, who was the head of intelligence for the NTSCIU, the elite anti-poaching unit of TAWA, met them when they arrived and invited them into a comfortable boardroom so they could discuss what was going on with his unit.

To maintain its operational independence, the NTSCIU's operations center was in the Tabata-Dampo District, a twenty-minute drive to the northwest of the TAWA headquarters. It was in a converted, sprawling, one-story estate house surrounded by a solid security wall topped with razor wire in an affluent suburban neighborhood. The house's bedrooms had been converted to offices and interrogation rooms. There was a metal cage in the backyard, which served as a makeshift detention facility. The NTSCIU's operations center was referred to as the Tabata House.

After making introductions, getting everyone settled with coffee or tea, and exchanging pleasantries about their drive from Nairobi, Joseph Mitambo said, "As you know, Tanzania has a major ivory poaching problem that has been going on for a long time, unfortunately supported and enabled by various levels of corrupt politicians, government officials, and police. With the formation of TAWA, and the independently financed National and Transnational Serious Crimes Investigation Unit, we hope to start dismantling the criminal international ivory trafficking syndicates operating in Tanzania.

"We are also working with various agencies involved with INTERPOL's Project Wisdom, the newly organized Operation Cobra, and the Lusaka Agreement Task Force. The plan is to tackle ivory poaching and trafficking at all levels, from the poachers in southern Tanzania killing the elephants, to the middlemen who are buying the ivory and organizing the shipments out of the country, to the shipping companies transporting the containers with the concealed ivory, to the Asian buyers of the ivory in countries like Taiwan, Hong Kong, the Philippines, Vietnam, Singapore, and ultimately, China, the usual final market destination for the ivory."

John said, "As you probably know, we have also been working with people from those same agencies over the past several years. So far, we have been working mostly in Kenya, Botswana, and Zambia; however, we are excited to have the chance to come to Tanzania and assist you in any way we can as representatives of INTERPOL's Wildlife Crime Unit, Canada's Environmental Enforcement Directorate, and the US Fish and Wildlife Service Office of Law Enforcement."

Joseph responded, "I am also pleased to have you here to assist us in getting NTSCIU to be more effective in taking down and prosecuting the criminals in the ivory trafficking syndicates. Your reputations as INTERPOL trainers and field agents are quite impressive based on reports from people who have worked with you. As you know, my second in command, David Kiama, attended your recent workshop at the Botswana Police Training College and Law Enforcement Academy and was extremely impressed with how much current information he learned about wildlife forensic science, evidence gathering, and crime scene documentation.

"Even when we catch the upper-level ivory poachers, they often get off because of technicalities their lawyers find in the evidence documentation process. I have also talked to Will Letner, the director of the PAMS Foundation, who met you at the CITES Standing Committee meeting in Geneva last July, and he speaks highly of your team as well."

Looking down at Syd and Nelle, who were relaxing on the floor of the boardroom, Joseph continued, "I'm happy to see you brought your two dogs with you. I heard how they helped with the takedown of the poachers at the ivory storage warehouse in Livingstone and in capturing the Irish gangsters and rhino horn traffickers in Nairobi last year. We are hoping to get our own canine unit in the NTSCIU; however, we are still negotiating the funding for the dogs and training facility."

"Thanks for the kind words," Kate said. "We try to do what we can to help, but the real day-to-day anti-poaching work is still done by the local wildlife and law enforcement forces. We just try to teach and illustrate some of the new wildlife law enforcement tools to help bring the poachers to justice. We've been told that you're close to taking down some of the ringleaders of the poaching and trafficking syndicates operating out of Dar es Salaam."

"Yes, after several months of undercover investigative work, we have located two houses in the Mikocheni suburb of northern Dar es Salaam we think are being used to store the ivory before it's transported to the port facilities and loaded into shipping containers, along with whatever goods the shipping containers legally transport. We have also been able to piece together the various components of one of the main poaching and trafficking syndicates originating in the Selous and Niassa Reserves in southern Tanzania and northern Mozambique."

Joseph continued, "The process begins in several of the villages on the outskirts of the Selous Reserve in southern Tanzania. Lower-level traffickers, usually from Dar es Salaam, place orders with local poachers, even supplying weapons to them sometimes. In some cases, poachers come from outside the area like northern Mozambique and are hired by local fixers, including government officers. Poached tusks are frequently cut into sections and hidden until the buyers arrive.

"The bulk of the ivory poached from Selous is transported to Dar es Salaam, either along the main road going north, or along the coastline in traditional fishing dhows. The local poachers, often using motorbikes to travel on bush paths, bring the ivory to collection points near the main road. From there, it is transported in private trucks or SUVs, often with special compartments built in, or with vans or buses, which can make more money transporting ivory than passengers.

"The raw ivory arriving in Dar es Salaam from the south is usually kept in relatively small amounts in upscale residential homes in neighborhoods of the Dar es Salaam suburbs. Once a substantial order is confirmed from an Asian ivory wholesaler, the smaller ivory stockpiles are collected and usually taken to a warehouse in an industrial area such as Chang'ombe near the port.

"The ivory is then either loaded into shipping containers if the port of export is Dar es Salaam or Mombasa, or it's transported by boat to Zanzibar to be containerized there if that is to be the exit point. The concealment method used coincides with the usual type of freight shipped from Tanzania to Asia such as plastic waste; agricultural products such as sunflower seeds, coffee beans, garlic, or grain; or seafood products such as dried fish, seaweed, or seashells.

"In most cases, we've found the poached ivory then leaves Tanzania without any problems. Corrupt freight forwarders and shipping agents ensure all the paperwork is completed and customs officials are paid off. The containers are loaded on ships operated by one of the shipping lines regularly servicing the route from East Africa to Asia. The shipping route can sometimes involve a series of transit countries, like the United Arab Emirates or Malaysia, before reaching intermediary destinations like Haiphong in Vietnam, Manila in the Philippines, and Hong Kong. From there, the ivory is transported, either by sea or land, to the end market legal and illegal carving factories in China."

Denny said, "It sounds like you've been able to find out a lot about how the whole operation works. How close are you to taking it all down?"

"We are getting closer, but there are a lot of moving pieces in the ivory supply chain," Joseph answered. "Through the new initiatives like Operation Cobra and INTERPOL's Project Wisdom, we are tackling it on several fronts, involving the law enforcement agencies both here in Africa and in the end market countries like Vietnam, Hong Kong, and China. We're also cracking down on the domestic corruption here in Tanzania and starting to apprehend and prosecute politicians, government bureaucrats, port authority and customs agents, and police who are on the take from the wildlife traffickers."

"So, what can we do to help while we're here over the next couple of weeks?" asked John.

"We are planning to conduct simultaneous raids on both ivory storage houses we know about in the Mikocheni suburb in northern Dar es Salaam on Friday, the day after tomorrow. We would appreciate your help in working out the final logistics, and we were also hoping to use your two police dogs when we breach the larger of the two houses."

Continuing, Joseph said, "We've had the two houses under surveillance for the past week and have figured out the patterns of people entering and leaving the houses. We know there is at least one Asian man and one local Tanzanian man in each of the houses all the time. Since we started our surveillance, we've observed one van and one Land Rover SUV arriving at the bigger house and unloading several large canvas bags filled with something heavy. We're assuming it is raw elephant tusks, which were then taken into the house."

Denny said, "I would like to go over your plans for breaching the house before making a final decision, but at this point, I don't see any reason we couldn't use Syd and Nelle. It's what they are trained for, and they're extremely good at it, as I'm sure you've heard. I just need to make sure it's as safe as possible and that they won't be going into a situation that will too dangerous. If there are more than two people in the house and they're armed, it becomes too dangerous to send them in alone without any backup."

"I understand your concern," Joseph said. "We can go over the breaching plans and adjust them as necessary to make sure it's as safe as possible for your dogs and for my tactical officers. Since you will be in Dar es Salaam next week, I was wondering if you could also facilitate a training session for my team. Maybe you could go through some of the material you taught at the Botswana Police Training College and Law Enforcement Academy?"

"That shouldn't be a problem," answered Kate. "In fact, we anticipated your request that we teach the course here, so we brought along all our presentation materials. We could also help to document the ivory confiscated at the houses you will be raiding on Friday and illustrate the crime scene processing techniques we teach at our training sessions."

7 a.m. Friday, January 25, 2013
House in the Mikocheni B Neighborhood, Dar es Salaam, Tanzania

John and the team spent the rest of Wednesday and Thursday at the TAWA headquarters going over the planned raid of the two suspected ivory storage houses in the Mikocheni suburb of northern Dar es Salaam and the NTSCIU's plans for apprehending the other people involved in the ivory trafficking syndicate.

The plan was to breach the two houses simultaneously, so there was no chance for the people inside to warn each other. The Dar es Salaam Police Service Tactical Unit would be the ones to breach the houses, supported by NTSCIU enforcement officers. Denny, Syd, and Nelle would be working with the six-member tactical unit to breach the larger of the two houses. John, Kate, Anna, and Simon would observe the takedown from their Land Rover, then after the 'all-clear' call on the radio, would go into the house to help with the crime scene processing.

They got up early and had a quick breakfast at the hotel coffee shop and then drove to the TAWA headquarters building where they met Joseph Mitambo and his team of NTSCIU enforcement officers. They then drove to the affluent Mikocheni B suburb in the northern area of Dar es Salaam, close to the waterfront area of Msanami Bay, where they met up with the two tactical unit teams.

After a brief discussion with the tactical unit team leader to confirm the coordination of the breaching operation, Denny, Syd, and Nelle joined the tactical unit officers assigned to breach the larger house. As usual, Syd and Nelle were outfitted with their Kevlar bulletproof body vests, which protected most of their bodies.

Denny was given the standard-issue tactical unit protective equipment, including a vest, helmet, and Colt C8SFW (Special Forces weapon) assault rifle. The report from the undercover surveillance team who had been watching the house was that they observed only two men in the house the previous evening, so Denny decided it was all right to send Syd and Nelle into the house first to take down the two occupants before he and the rest of the tactical unit officers went into the house behind them.

At seven o'clock in the morning, the tactical unit van pulled up to the large house, which was on a corner lot on Bima Road, across the street from a primary school. They parked in front of the next house on the street and the six-member tactical unit team immediately got out of the van and separated into two teams of three officers, one team going to the front door and the other to the back door.

Denny and the dogs went with the team heading to the front door. Each team had a battering ram, and on a signal from the team leader over his radio, they each used it to break open the two doors. As soon as the front door flew open, Denny gave Syd and Nelle the "Capture" command and they rushed into the house looking for the two bad guys. One was sitting at the kitchen table drinking coffee, and the other one was standing at the kitchen counter.

The dogs each picked one of them and lunged for their arms as they were reaching for their guns, which were in holsters on their belts.

Just as each dog had clamped down onto the arms of the two men, a third man emerged from a small bathroom off the kitchen area with his gun drawn. Just before Denny got into the kitchen area, the third man shot Syd with an older model Smith and Wesson pistol. The bullet hit her just behind her front shoulder, knocking her sprawling across the kitchen floor.

Instinctively, because of his many years of service as a special forces sniper, Denny shot the third man twice in the chest, killing him instantly. He then immediately turned and shot the man who Syd had tried to subdue before he could recover and grab his gun. Meanwhile, Nelle had her man on the kitchen floor with his forearm firmly clenched in her powerful jaws. No matter what was going on, she would not release her grip until Denny gave her the command.

After shooting the second man at the kitchen table, also twice in the chest, Denny rushed over to Syd lying on the kitchen floor. She was still alive but stunned by the force of the bullet impacting her Kevlar vest at short range. He looked quickly over at Nelle and gave her the "Release" command just as the rest of the tactical unit team rushed into the kitchen, grabbed the man, and put him in handcuffs.

John, Kate, Anna, and Simon were watching the front of the house in the KWS Land Rover from a block away as the tactical team entered the house behind Denny and the dogs. They then heard the five gunshots. One right after the other. They knew immediately that something had gone terribly wrong because there was almost never any need for gunfire during one of these raids.

The last four gunshots, the first two close together with a couple of seconds in between before the next two shots, meant that Denny or one of the tactical unit officers had just killed two people. Special forces soldiers are trained to always shoot to kill, with the ominous 'double tap' to the chest being the kill shot of choice. The first gunshot was what really worried them.

They anxiously waited for the 'all-clear' call on the police radio and then drove to the front of the house and rushed through the broken front door and into the kitchen. They were horrified to see two men, obviously dead, lying on the kitchen floor with pools of blood forming underneath them.

Then they spotted Denny sitting on the floor cradling Syd in his arms, with Nelle sitting beside him whining as she looked at Syd.

As soon as Denny saw John and the others come into the kitchen, he said, "Syd's alive. She's just stunned from the force of the bullet hitting her vest. The vest did its job and stopped the bullet, but we need to take her to a veterinary hospital to make sure it didn't break any of her ribs or damage anything else."

Trembling with worry, Anna gasped, "Oh my God, we were so scared when we heard the gunshots. Are you sure Syd is okay? She doesn't look good."

Denny looked at them with tears of relief in his eyes and said, "Yes, she's alive, so that's all that matters. We all know this can happen to any of us, but she should be all right after a little recovery time."

After a few minutes, Joseph Mitambo came into the kitchen and said, "I'm extremely sorry about your dog. I hope she's going to be all right. The third man must have come to the house sometime last night and avoided detection by the surveillance team."

After looking at Syd in Denny's arms, Joseph said, "I know a good veterinarian clinic close to where you're staying at the Hyatt Regency called Vet Care Ltd. I can have one of my officers escort you there as soon as you want to go. By the way, the raid on the second house went down without problems, and we have the two occupants in custody. From my quick walk through this house, it looks like there are at least several hundred ivory tusks in the attached garage and walk-out basement area.

"My officers at the other house told me on the radio there are a few hundred ivory tusks there as well. So, despite the unfortunate events here, it looks like the raids were a success. Please take care of your dog now. We will be here for several days processing the ivory and all the other evidence. Just come back when you're ready, and you can give us a hand."

Denny carefully took off Syd's Kevlar vest and looked at the spot on her side where the bullet hit. It was red and already a little swollen, but there was no blood. Syd was awake and looking at him as he held her in his lap on the kitchen floor. Nelle was still hovering over Syd, whining a little and licking her face every few seconds. Denny said to the others gathered in a circle around him, Nelle, and Syd, "Let's get Syd to the vet clinic and get her checked over. I think she'll be okay, but I would just like to make sure."

Denny got up and, still carrying Syd, walked out of the house, and got into the back seat of the Land Rover. The rest of the team followed with Nelle and got into the vehicle as well. One of the NTSCIU enforcement officers came over to the driver's window and told Simon to follow him in his TAWA Land Rover to the vet clinic, which was about a fifteen- to twenty-minute drive south towards the city center. His Land Rover was equipped with flashing police lights and a siren, which the officer turned on so they could make good time in the early morning city traffic. Simon also had a portable red flashing light he could attach to the roof of the KWS Land Rover, which he did as well.

During the drive to the vet clinic, Syd perked up a little, got up from Denny's lap, and sat between him and Anna on the rear seat. She kept turning her head and looking into the rear cargo area to make sure that Nelle was there. Because they were sisters, they had never been apart from each other since birth.

After about twenty minutes of weaving through the morning traffic and driving through red lights when they could, they arrived at the modern-looking Vet Care Ltd. hospital. It was next to a golf course in an affluent part of the city center, so it serviced a more up-scale pet-owning clientele. Syd was able to walk, so Denny put her collar on and attached her leash, and they all walked into the reception area of the vet clinic.

Joseph had called ahead to the vet clinic while they were driving, so the senior veterinarian, Dr. Maria Juma, was waiting for them when they arrived. She said to Denny, "Please bring Syd into the examination room so we can check her over."

Anna asked, "Can I come along as well?"

Dr. Juma replied, "Sure, it's okay, but the room is quite small, so the rest of your team will have to wait in the reception area."

When they got into the examination room, Denny lifted Syd onto the examination table and Dr. Juma started looking at the area on her side where the bullet hit the vest. She carefully felt for any broken ribs and watched for Syd's reaction to judge how much pain she was in. Syd flinched and whined a little when Dr. Juma touched the spot where the bullet had hit, but otherwise, she was getting stronger and calmer.

Dr Juma said, "It doesn't feel like there are any broken ribs and she is fairly tolerant of me touching the affected area on her side; however, to be on the safe side, I would like to X-ray her ribcage area."

"That sounds like a good idea," said Denny. "Can you do it right away?"

"Yes, we have our own X-ray machine, and it shouldn't take very long," Dr. Juma answered.

She instructed Denny to take Syd into another room and position her on the six-inch high platform. After Denny stepped away from the machine, the X-ray technician took several X-rays of Syd's ribcage areas. Denny then took Syd back out to the reception area while they waited for the X-rays to be processed. Nelle was happy to see Syd again and the two dogs licked each other's faces and then sat down side by side next to Denny and Anna. John and Kate both went over to Syd and gave her a hug and told her what a brave dog she was.

After about fifteen minutes, Dr. Juma came out into the reception area and said, "The X-rays confirmed there are no broken or cracked ribs. Syd will be sore for a week or so; however, she should be fine. You should watch if she has any problems keeping food down, or if there is any blood in her stool or urine over the next few days."

As she reached down to give Syd and Nelle pats on their heads, she said, "I've seen police dogs in action on television and in movies, but I've never treated one. I would just like to say that they must be incredibly well-trained and brave to go into situations like the one that happened this morning. I'm relieved Syd's injuries are not more serious, as I'm sure you are as well. Here is my business card with my personal cell phone number. Please call me if Syd has any problems with her recovery while you are here in Dar es Salaam."

They all thanked Dr. Juma and then got back into the Land Rover. While they had been waiting in the reception area, they discussed what to do for the rest of the day. They decided to go back to the hotel for lunch and drop off Denny, Anna, Nelle, and Syd before deciding what they would do.

After getting Denny, Anna, and the dogs settled at the hotel and ordering an early lunch from room service, John, Kate, and Simon went back to the Mikocheni houses to help with the processing of the confiscated ivory and the collection and documentation of any other evidence.

After they finished lunch and John, Kate, and Simon had left to go back to the Mikocheni houses, Denny sat down on the couch and put his hands over his face. After a couple of minutes, Anna noticed Denny was quietly crying. Anna went over to him and put her arms around him and just let him cry for a few minutes until he stopped, took a few deep breaths, and wiped the tears from his eyes with a tissue.

He then said to Anna, "I'm sorry, but it just suddenly hit me that I killed two people a few hours ago and almost lost Syd because the dogs gave me their absolute loyalty and put their lives in my hands and trusted me to make the right decisions. I should have made the tactical team verify there were only two people in the house before I sent the dogs in."

Still with her arm over Denny's shoulders, Anna said, "You can't blame yourself for what happened. You made the decision based on the best information we all had. Any of us could have stopped the operation, but we all agreed with the decision to use Syd and Nelle to breach the house. Sometimes shit just happens, no matter how good your plan is. You should know that better than anyone."

Not crying anymore, but still flushed and looking upset, Denny said, "I know you're right, but it was just so scary seeing Syd get shot and not knowing if she was going to make it. I've used my guns in lots of situations since I started working with John back in 2006, but this was the first time I've killed anyone since I left the military. And there's a big difference between killing someone with a sniper rifle from a thousand yards away and killing someone who's only six feet in front of you."

Now with her hand over one of Denny's, Anna said, "Although I have been trained to do what you had to do this morning and would do it in a second if it meant saving my own life or one of you guys, so far, I haven't had to. So, I can't say that I know how you feel, but we are all here for you if you need to talk about things. I know you had a tough time with your demons after leaving the military, but you got through it then, and you'll get through this as well. Do you see those two dogs lying down and looking at us right now? They are fine, and they will be ready to do it all over again in a few days if you tell them to go into another house and take down the bad guys."

After a few minutes, she said smiling, "Let's just relax for the afternoon and enjoy the beautiful view of Dar es Salaam Harbor. If you feel like it, in a while, I can let you beat me at a game of cribbage."

Laughing, Denny said, "I don't need your 'pity win' lady, I can beat you fair and square any time."

CHAPTER 10

1:30 p.m. Friday, January 25, 2013
House in the Mikocheni B Neighborhood, Dar es Salaam, Tanzania

When John, Kate, and Simon arrived back at the Mikocheni house, the street in front of the house looked like something out of the movies. There were at least half a dozen Dar es Salaam police cruisers and TAWA SUVs with their lights flashing, two ambulances, a crime scene forensics van, and orange crime scene tape around the whole house. They assumed the scene at the other house a few blocks away was the same, minus the ambulances. They parked the KWS Land Rover down the street, put the lanyards with their INTERPOL credentials around their necks, and made their way into the house.

When Joseph saw John and Kate, he walked up to them and asked, "How is your dog doing?"

Kate replied, "Syd is doing all right. Dr. Juma at the vet clinic checked her over and took some X-rays, and she doesn't have any broken ribs or internal injuries. She will be sore for a week or so but should be fine. The dogs have been shot at twice, but this was the first time one has been hit. Luckily, Syd's canine vest did its job. Denny got shot in his vest while he was a special forces sniper in the Canadian military, so he knows how much it hurts, but his vest saved his life as well. So, how are things going here?"

"We have identified the two men Denny shot from IDs we found in the house," said Joseph. "They are both Tanzanian citizens, Emmanuel Mulla, and Julius Akyoo, and both have long criminal records for various petty crimes and assaults. They were both just hired as muscle to guard the house.

"The other guy we have in custody is a Chinese citizen, Chen Xiao, who, so far, is saying he doesn't speak English. But we suspect he is the brains behind the operation at the house. At the other house, we arrested a Tanzanian citizen, Stanley Muta, also a low-level criminal, and a Chinese citizen, Zhang Wei. He can speak English fine since he offered the police officers transporting him to the downtown police headquarters lock-up a ten-thousand-US-dollar bribe if they dropped him off on the way there. We will interrogate them all once we finish processing things at the two houses. You are welcome to observe the interrogations."

Nodding in agreement, John said, "Sure, that would be great."

Continuing, Joseph said, "We discovered a substantial stash of money, both US dollars and Tanzanian shillings, in a dresser drawer in what we assume was Chen Xiao's bedroom and office area. We also found high-end digital weigh scales at both houses and a specially modified Toyota van with a hidden compartment for concealing ivory, and three sets of license plates in the garage at the other house. It looks like both Chinese citizens were good businessmen and bookkeepers because we found ledgers with records of ivory purchases going back months and a bunch of shipping documents in files with the company name Brightline International."

"Well, that should help a lot," offered Kate.

"Yes, it's great," responded Joseph. "The CSI team leader just showed me a couple of shipping orders they found in the desk in the bedroom. They were for container shipments of dried fish, snail shells, and seashells from both Zanzibar and the Port of Dar es Salaam. The most recent shipping order or bill of lading was dated a week ago and showed a container was loaded onto a smaller barge in Dar es Salaam and transported to Zanzibar. According to the shipping order, the container is scheduled to be loaded onto a cargo ship bound for China, with a stopover in the Philippines."

"Is there time to intercept the container before it leaves on the ship?" asked John.

"We'll notify the port authority and customs agents in Zanzibar right away. They should be able to locate the container and seize it until we can get there and see what's inside," answered Joseph. "The name of the same

Zanzibar-based shipping agent, Makame Matembo, appears on most of the bills of lading. We'll also be paying Mr. Matembo a visit."

"So, why ship the container from Zanzibar rather than Dar es Salaam?" asked John.

"I'm sure you probably know, but Zanzibar is a self-governing state of Tanzania. The archipelago of islands, located off the coast of the mainland, was once the separate state of Zanzibar; however, it united with Tanganyika in 1964 to form the United Republic of Tanzania. It consists of a group of small islands and two larger ones; the main and largest island, Unguja, is the one normally referred to as Zanzibar, and the other less well-known, smaller island is Pemba Island. The major port in Zanzibar is in the Malindi District of Zanzibar City, and it handles about ninety percent of Zanzibar's shipping traffic.

"We know the Port of Malindi in Zanzibar has been specifically chosen as the preferred exit point for ivory smuggling syndicates operating in Tanzania. Unfortunately, there are several reasons for this. There is faster and easier clearance of container cargo compared with the larger Port of Dar es Salaam. There's also less effective oversight and controls, so it's easier for corrupt officials to operate in the port.

"There's also different legislation on trade in endangered species in Zanzibar compared with mainland Tanzania. Zanzibar's primary wildlife law, the Forest Resources Management and Conservation Act, protects only wildlife that naturally occurs within Zanzibar, meaning that elephants, which are not endemic, are technically excluded from protection."

"Well, that must make enforcement a lot harder for you," said Kate.

"That's not the only problem," continued Joseph. "The penalties that are now in place under the Zanzibar Conservation Act are extremely low compared to those in mainland Tanzania. The highest penalty on conviction is imprisonment for a term of no less than six months or a fine of no less than three hundred thousand Tanzanian shillings, which is only equal to about 185 US dollars. That's not a big deterrent considering the amount of money they can make trafficking the ivory. We're trying to change these laws, but it's difficult when we don't always have the support of the politicians and top government bureaucrats."

John added, "It must be really frustrating for you and your team to know what has been going on with many of these ivory trafficking syndicates and not get the support and funding from the government you need to shut them down."

"Yes, it's extremely frustrating," Joseph said emphatically. "Fortunately, the international conservation community has been very vocal the last few years about the wildlife poaching and trafficking problems in Tanzania and the inherent government corruption. The current government is basically being shamed by agencies like INTERPOL, CITES, and the LATF, and numerous high-profile wildlife conservation NGOs into clamping down on the corruption and targeting the trafficking syndicates. I assume that is partly the reason you are here in Dar es Salaam."

"Well, yes, you're right about that," John said. "As a supporter of the new initiative, Operation Cobra, INTERPOL's Wildlife Crime Group, whom we do most of our international work with, is extremely interested in trying to stop the ivory and rhino horn trafficking chain from Africa to China. Through Project Wisdom, Operation Worthy, and now Operation Cobra, INTERPOL is working with government wildlife enforcement agencies in multiple African countries, as well in the transit countries like Hong Kong, Vietnam, Malaysia, and the Philippines.

"The end market destination for much of the ivory is China, and particularly the Guangdong and Fujian provinces in southern China, which are thought to be the major ivory smuggling and processing centers. My team is just a small component of the larger international effort, but we do what we can to help."

Smiling, Joseph said, "Well, you helped us with a huge win here today. I'm just sorry your dog ended up getting hurt. Based on a quick count of the ivory pieces, it looks like there are about four hundred elephant tusks in this house and three hundred at the other house. Once we sort through the ledger books and other paperwork, we should also get information about the suppliers and poaching network in the Selous Reserve in southern Tanzania and the people involved in the ivory transport from Tanzania and Zanzibar to Asia.

"This afternoon, we are going to document and photograph each of the ivory pieces in the houses and then transport them to the TAWA headquarters where we will weigh and measure each piece, so we have a complete inventory for the prosecutors when the case goes to court. If you don't mind, my forensics people would really appreciate your opinion and advice about our crime scene documentation techniques, since I know that is one of your specialties."

"No problem, that's why we're here," Kate said. "I guess we should get to work now if we want to finish with the ivory before the end of the day."

6:30 p.m. Friday, January 25, 2013
Hyatt Regency Dar es Salaam - Kilimanjaro Hotel, Dar es Salaam, Tanzania

John and Kate spent the afternoon assisting the TAWA CSI team at the two Mikocheni houses, documenting the ivory pieces and other evidence found in the houses. To save time, the CSI team only numbered and photographed each ivory piece and then loaded them into a truck for transport to the TAWA headquarters. They would then weigh each piece and log it into the official evidence file. The ivory could then be put in storage to await the trials of the poaching syndicate criminals.

When John and Kate arrived back at the hotel at around six-thirty in the evening, they went to check on Denny and the dogs in Anna's room and found Anna and Denny playing cards and watching TV. They asked how things were going and Anna said, "Syd is doing better, although she's still limping a bit. We took them for a short walk and doggie bathroom break a couple of times to the park across the street along the waterfront, and she managed all right. She just ate her evening meal, so her appetite is fine. How did things go this afternoon at the Mikocheni houses?"

John and Kate went through the events of the afternoon and told them about the ledger books and shipping orders that were found in the houses. John said, "The total count at the two houses was 706 ivory tusks. Joseph Mitambo and his investigators will interrogate the three men arrested tomorrow morning at TAWA headquarters. He invited us to observe.

"On Monday, they plan to go to the port facility in Zanzibar and open the container recently shipped there from Dar es Salaam under the company name Brightline International. It is the front company the poaching syndicate is using for transporting the ivory out of Tanzania in shipping containers filled with products like dried fish and seashells. Joseph has also invited us to go to Zanzibar with him and his team. Since we have never been to Zanzibar,

Kate and I thought it would be an opportunity to help with the operation as well as see some of the island."

"That sounds great," Denny said. "We've been looking for an opportunity to go to Zanzibar, so it seems like we should take them up on their offer. I'm starving. Should we go downstairs for dinner and talk about it some more?"

After Denny left Anna's room to drop the dogs off in his room, Anna said to John and Kate, "Denny is doing better now, but he was pretty upset about what happened at the house. We should keep an eye on him for a few days to make sure he doesn't have problems again with his PTSD issues. He told me this morning that it was the first time he has had to kill anyone since he left the military, and it suddenly brought back a lot of his demons from those days."

John said, "Yes, he had a tough time the first couple of years he was with me following his military service. It took quite a while seeing the RCMP staff psychologists for him to come to grips with what he had to do as a sniper in the special forces. Killing people for a living for over ten years, even if they are enemy terrorists, can really mess with your head, even if you're as grounded as Denny. He once told me he stopped counting his kills after he reached one hundred. He found out the Taliban even had a bounty of ten thousand US dollars on him the last couple of years in Afghanistan. That's why he and Mike Giroux never talked to anyone about their missions at the bases in Afghanistan, and Denny was known as 'The Ghost.'"

"Yeah, I know, he told me some stories about his days as a sniper," said Anna. "But, being a tough guy, it's hard for him to open up about how that stuff affected him over the years."

"I don't blame him for being upset this morning," said John. "In fact, I think I might be more worried if he wasn't upset. None of us thought he would have to shoot those two men this morning, although Denny is always the first one in after the dogs, so I suppose it was bound to happen. Anyway, let's keep an eye on him and I'll ask him if he wants to talk about things when he seems ready."

9 a.m. Saturday, January 26, 2013
Tanzania Wildlife Authority Headquarters, Dar es Salaam, Tanzania

While Denny and Anna stayed at the hotel again with the dogs, John and Kate went to the TAWA headquarters the next morning to observe the interrogation, from an adjoining room, of the two Chinese men, Chen Xiao and Zhang Wei, and the Tanzanian, Stanley Muta. Joseph brought in a Chinese interpreter in case they claimed to not understand English, which he knew was not the case.

Chen Xiao still refused to answer questions unless he had a lawyer present, but Zhang Wei ended up being quite talkative after the prosecutor offered him a better deal than his colleague Chen Xiao, if he cooperated. He confirmed that the company called Brightline International operated from the two houses and that numerous shipments of ivory had occurred from the Port of Malindi in Zanzibar over the last few years.

He also said that a company called Zanzibar Seafood Products, based out of Stone Town, the oldest part of Zanzibar City, was the usual agent for the shipments. Zanzibar Seafood Products was a legitimate cover business that imported products like garlic and citric acid from China and exported seafood products from Tanzania. That was how they could hide the ivory trafficking activities and explain the delivery and shipping of cargo containers.

The employees of Zanzibar Seafood Products arranged for the exports from Zanzibar and facilitated the concealment of the ivory in shipping containers. Zhang Wei said he knew little about that end of the operation, other than two Chinese citizens who lived in Stone Town and another Tanzanian from Zanzibar operated Zanzibar Seafood Products. He said he had heard that one of the Chinese men was a former employee at the Chinese consulate in Zanzibar.

He also told them that two Tanzanians, Kelvin Kasembe and Moses Ladipo, were the main suppliers of the elephant tusks discovered at the Mikocheni houses. He said that Kelvin Kasembe lived in the Mbezi area of Dar es Salaam but was originally from southern Tanzania. He and Ladipo, who he thought still lived in one of villages on the outskirts of the Selous Reserve in southern Tanzania, were the main brokers for the syndicate, buying elephant tusks from the poachers in southern Tanzania and selling them to their Asian clients based in Dar es Salaam.

He said that he thought the two Tanzanians were connected to a man named Benjamin Malengo, also known as Shetani, but he had never met him or saw him at the houses.

11:30 a.m. Monday, January 28, 2013
Port of Malindi Container Depot, Zanzibar, Tanzania

Since Syd seemed to be feeling better after recovering over the weekend, they decided to all go to Zanzibar with Joseph Mitambo and his team of NTSCIU enforcement officers. Simon drove them the short distance to the dock area next to the ferry terminal, where they met Joseph at nine o'clock at the slip where the TAWA Defender B Class Response Boat was moored. The boat was used for maritime law enforcement in the harbor area and along the coast around Dar es Salaam.

There was room for up to ten people in the small cabin area of the thirty-foot-long boat. The boat was powered by two 225-horsepower outboard motors and could reach speeds of up to eighty-five kilometers per hour. There was a formidable-looking M60 machine gun mounted in the bow area.

Joseph had two of his senior investigators with him, plus the boat operator. The rest of his six-person team caught the seven o'clock vehicle ferry driving a twenty-six-foot truck and a Land Rover. The truck was required to transport the ivory they anticipated finding in the container back to Dar es Salaam.

After they were all onboard the boat, they left for the one- to one-and-a-half-hour trip to the Port of Malindi in Zanzibar, depending on how rough the ocean was. Luckily, it was a calm day on the ocean, and the swells were small. Anna was sometimes prone to seasickness but survived the crossing with no problems.

They had a beautiful view of the harbor area and the Dar es Salaam skyline as they left the port area, and then of the coastline as they proceeded out to the open ocean. Syd and Nelle always enjoyed riding in boats and seemed to be fascinated with the sights as the boat proceeded out of the harbor area.

Syd recovered quite quickly from her ordeal and was rapidly getting back to top form. Once on the open ocean, the humans went back into the small cabin area so they could get out of the cool wind as the boat picked up speed. Syd and Nelle enjoyed the wind though. It was the same as when they would stick their heads out of the car windows when riding with Denny or John.

Because the ocean was quite calm, they made good time and got to the Zanzibar Port in a little over an hour. As they approached the relatively small

Zanzibar Port of Malindi facility, compared to the much larger Port of Dar es Salaam, they noticed a large container ship docked at the main wharf. There were cranes loading containers onto the ship's deck from the adjacent container storage yard. The name on the ship's side said *Rota Finning*, which was also the name of the ship on the confiscated bill of lading at the Mikocheni house.

Joseph had called a senior Zanzibar Port Authority agent he trusted and told the port agents to locate the container from Zanzibar Seafood Products and ensure it didn't get loaded onto the ship. He got a search warrant for the business premises of Zanzibar Seafood Products in Stone Town and warrants for the arrest of any employees of the company. He also got a warrant for the arrest of the Zanzibar-based shipping agent, Makame Matembo.

The TAWA driver of the Defender B Class Response Boat motored around the *Rota Finning* container ship and to the far side of the port facility where there were docking facilities for smaller boats. The bay was filled with fishing dhows that serviced the nearby Malindi Fish Market. They found an open spot at the wharf reserved for government watercraft and secured the boat.

Joseph called the Zanzibar Port Authority agent, Noel Kinana, as they approached the port. He was waiting on the dock for them as they all got off the boat with a twelve-person port authority passenger van. Noel told them he had transferred the container to the quarantine impound enclosure and that the rest of the team of NTSCIU enforcement officers had already arrived from Dar es Salaam and were waiting for them.

They drove the short distance to the impound enclosure and were greeted by the other four NTSCIU officers who had taken the early morning vehicle ferry with the transport truck. They all walked up to the Zanzibar Seafood Products container and one officer started taking pictures of the container and the sealed locks on the rear doors. Another officer with bolt cutters cut the locks and opened the large doors of the container. The smell of dried fish was extremely strong when they opened the doors. The bill of lading said the container was filled with several types of dried fish and bags of seashells, which the Chinese used for making trinkets and jewelry.

The canvas bags of dried fish were loaded in the container's rear and the NTSCIU officers systematically removed them from the container and stacked them on the cement pad beside the container. A third of the way into the container, they started finding the canvas bags of ivory. As they continued removing the bags of dried fish and then the bags of seashells, they found bags of ivory mixed in with them.

It took about two hours for the NTSCIU officers to unload all the bags and separate them into stacks of dried fish, seashells, and ivory tusks. There were 102 bags of ivory with, on average, about ten pieces of ivory in each bag, for a rough total of approximately one thousand elephant tusks, representing about five hundred dead elephants — a truly sobering realization for all those gathered around the shipping container.

Their next emotion was anger! Joseph said emphatically, "Let's go round up the rest of these sons-of-bitches."

While his officers were unloading the container, Joseph had called the commanding officer of the nearby Malindi Police Station, a friend of his named John Sajilo. Lieutenant Sajilo had arrived at the port facility with three of his police constables a few minutes previously.

Joseph explained the situation to him and that he had a search warrant for the business premises of Zanzibar Seafood Products and warrants for the arrest of any employees on the premises of the company. He also had a warrant for the arrest of the Zanzibar-based shipping agent, Makame Matembo.

John and Kate went with Joseph and his officers and the Malindi Police Station officers to observe the arrests. Anna, Denny, and Simon skipped the arrests and opted to spend the time with Syd and Nelle on the waterfront just down from the ferry terminal at a beachside bar and cafe called Mercury's Bar. The bar was named after one of Zanzibar's most famous former residents, Freddy Mercury from the band Queen. John Sajilo recommended it, saying Mercury's Bar was a favorite after-hours spot of his officers.

Three Land Rovers, one filled with NTSCIU officers, including John and Kate, and the other two with Zanzibar City police officers, drove to the premises of Zanzibar Seafood Products, which was on Benjamin Mkapa Road in Stone Town, quite close to the port facilities. They did not expect any resistance; however, they were careful to cover all the exits anyway. They entered through the front door, weapons ready, and quickly went past the counter area displaying various seafood products to the rear office area. There, they found two Asian men and one Tanzanian man in three separate small offices.

Several officers went into each office at the same time and informed the three men they were under arrest for the illegal smuggling of elephant ivory. With no resistance, they put handcuffs on the three men and took them out to the waiting police cars.

There were three local workers, two men and one woman, in the front area behind the counter. They were also taken into custody but would likely be released after questioning. Unfortunately, they would now be without jobs since the Zanzibar Seafood Products business would cease to exist after the owners ended up in jail.

After the premises were secured, one police officer was assigned to remain onsite until Joseph could send a CSI team to go through everything in the offices. Their next stop was the office of Makame Matembo, the Zanzibar-based shipping agent. His office was on Funguni Road, a few blocks from the port facility.

They drove the short distance to the office and again entered in force and found Makame Matembo in one of the grimy offices of the small, three-room office building. A middle-aged woman, who said she was Mrs. Matembo, occupied one of the other offices. Both were handcuffed and informed they were under arrest for the illegal smuggling of elephant ivory. They were then placed in the back seats of two other waiting police cars for transport back to the Malindi Police Station.

As John and Kate entered the office building after the occupants were in custody, they saw several filing cabinets and stacks of papers on each of the desks in the offices. John said to Joseph, "It looks like your CSI people will have a good time here and at the Zanzibar Seafood Products premises going through all the files and shipping orders. Hopefully, it will lead you to the rest of the ivory trafficking syndicate at the ivory's destination points in Asia and China."

Smiling broadly, Joseph exclaimed, "This had been a phenomenal few days for me and my NTSCIU team. It's one of the first times we've been able to bring down an entire ivory trafficking syndicate. And we've been able to confiscate almost eighteen hundred elephant tusks before they got to their end market in Asia.

"I hope we find enough evidence here to arrest the people who were going to receive the ivory shipments in China. I know that is the main goal of

Project Wisdom and Operation Cobra, to dismantle the ivory trafficking syndicates at all levels, from the local poachers killing the elephants in the bush to the owners of the illegal carving factories in China."

After they finished securing the shipping agent's office, they went back to Mercury's Bar to meet up with Denny, Anna, Simon, and the dogs. Joseph sent his officers back to the container depot at the port to finish loading the bags of ivory onto the transport truck so they could take them back to the TAWA headquarters in Dar es Salaam.

Joseph said to John, "I think we all deserve a celebratory drink, so I'll join you for a beer and something to eat. I will stay here in Zanzibar City for a day or two to make sure everything is taken care of and to supervise the CSI team, who should be here tomorrow morning. You can return to Dar es Salaam on the boat this afternoon. Would you still be able to come into the office on Thursday for a couple of days to do a condensed version of your training workshop for my senior enforcement officers?"

"Yes, that should be fine," John replied. "We were planning on staying in Dar es Salaam for at least two weeks anyway before we have to be back in Nairobi."

The Mercury Bar and Restaurant was right on the waterfront so the 'people watching' was great, with lots of tourists and locals walking on the beach and dozens of fishing dhows and other boats anchored in the harbor area. The bar had lots of Freddie Mercury and Queen memorabilia on the walls. Mercury was born Farrokh Bulsara in 1946 in Stone Town to Parsi-Indian parents in what was then the British protectorate of Zanzibar. He attended English-style boarding schools in India from the age of eight and returned to Zanzibar after secondary school. In 1964, his family moved to Middlesex, England. Six years after leaving Zanzibar with his family at seventeen, he changed his name to Freddie Mercury when he helped form the band, Queen.

Syd and Nelle enjoyed their afternoon on the open-air patio at the bar. They went for several walks down the beach with Anna and Denny. There were lots of new and interesting smells, and they even got a few morsels of food from sympathetic patrons at adjoining tables on the patio.

After the team finished their beers and food and had discussed the events of the day, they headed back to the boat for the return trip to Dar es Salaam so they could get back before dark. The ocean was still calm, so they had another pleasant trip. Anna was happy about the calm ocean, especially since she had consumed a couple of beers and seafood wraps, and she and Denny split an appetizer platter with seafood and fruit skewers.

They all enjoyed the return trip to Dar es Salaam on the deck of the boat, breathing the early evening ocean air, and taking in the view of the Dar es Salaam coastline as they approached the port. As they were relaxing during the boat ride, they discussed what they would do for the next couple of days. They decided to go to the TAWA headquarters and help process and catalogue the almost eighteen hundred pieces of ivory confiscated over the past few days.

9 a.m. Thursday, January 31, 2013
TAWA Headquarters, Dar es Salaam, Tanzania

John, Kate, Anna, and Denny spent two days working with the NTSCIU team processing the ivory from the Mikocheni houses and from the shipping container in Zanzibar. The final count was 1,023 pieces of ivory in the shipping container, weighing approximately 2.9 tonnes, plus the 706 pieces from the two houses. It was a big job numbering, photographing, and weighing each individual piece of ivory; however, at the end of the two days, they had a complete inventory of the ivory. It would form the key evidence used by government prosecutors when the poaching syndicate criminals went to trial.

John and the team went back at the TAWA headquarters on Thursday to teach a shortened two-day version of their standard workshop for wildlife crime scene investigators and wildlife enforcement officers. When Joseph returned from Zanzibar, he told them what the CSI team had found in the offices of Zanzibar Seafood Products and the shipping agent, Makame Matembo.

Joseph explained, "We found various paperwork and records in the Zanzibar Seafood Products offices with the names of several companies in Hong Kong and the Chinese mainland. It looks like the owners of Zanzibar Seafood Products performed the function of arranging the export of the ivory from Zanzibar but were not the actual owners of the ivory. One name that appeared on several shipping orders and on some of the other paperwork was

Wang Fenglan, but we think this person is actually a well-known Chinese businesswoman named Wang Jin Li, and she is using the alias Wang Fenglan.

"Wang Jin Li is now in her mid-sixties and has lived in East Africa since the mid-1970s. From our intelligence work, we know she is often referred to as the 'Queen of Ivory.' We know she has connections to businesses in China; however, she also has lots of political connections in Tanzania and Kenya, and we are quite sure she has some politicians and key government bureaucrats on her payroll. We also suspect she has links to Benjamin Malengo, or Shetani, as he is more commonly known. As you know, he is one of the up-and-coming ringleaders of several poaching syndicates.

"Wang Jin Li seems to have disappeared from Tanzania in the past couple of years. We think she is now living in Uganda, at least temporarily. Wang Jin Li was originally from Beijing. She is thought to be quite wealthy and owns several properties here in Dar es Salaam. Back in the 1970s, because she learned to speak Swahili in China, she got a job in Tanzania as a translator for Tazara, the Chinese-owned company that helped build the new railway system.

"According to information we have collected, she has been involved in ivory trafficking since at least 2006, working with some of the most high-ranking poachers in East Africa. She is connected to various companies in Asia, all Chinese-owned, and circulates in the upper circles of Chinese citizens living and working in Tanzania. She has even been the vice president and secretary-general of the Tanzania China-Africa Business Council and we think she at least partially owns one of the biggest Chinese restaurants near the Dar es Salaam railway station.

"With the latest evidence from these two big takedowns, we are hopefully a little closer to nailing some of these top players in the ivory trafficking syndicates. We know that Wang Jin Li still owns a fancy house in one of the upscale neighborhoods north of the city center along the coast, so we have informants watching for when she comes back to Dar es Salaam to take care of her business interests."

John and the team decided to return to Nairobi on the weekend after they had completed the two-day workshop. They left Dar es Salaam early Saturday morning for the long nine-hour drive back to Moshi, where they stayed at the Parkview Inn again. On Sunday, they drove the remaining five hours to Nairobi and the Wildebeest Eco Camp, where they settled back into their cottages.

While driving from Dar es Salaam to Nairobi, they had lots of time to talk about the events of the previous couple of weeks and the raids at the Mikocheni house and the port in Zanzibar City. Syd recovered from her ordeal and seemed to be mostly back to her normal self. The real test would be the next time she and Nelle would be expected to take down the bad guys.

John, Kate, and Anna were also able to get Denny to talk about how he was feeling about killing the two poachers in the Mikocheni house. He was not the type of person to talk much about those types of things, but he had learned through many months of therapy with the RCMP psychologists after leaving the military that he couldn't keep things bottled up if he wanted to cope with the things he did as a special forces sniper. His PTSD was always lurking in his mind, but he learned about various coping mechanisms to combat the anxieties and feelings of guilt.

He and John had often talked about things over the years whenever Denny felt overwhelmed by the pressures of his job with the RCMP and their work with INTERPOL. After some earnest conversations while they were driving to Nairobi, and some friendly banter and kidding, Denny was getting back to his normal self. It helped him to know that they were all law enforcement officers with similar fears and anxieties, and that both John and Kate had, unfortunately, also killed people in the line of duty in the past and had their own demons to deal with.

CHAPTER 11

9 a.m. Monday, February 4, 2013
Kenya Wildlife Services Headquarters, Nairobi

John and the team arrived back in Nairobi on Sunday afternoon and settled back into their cottages at the Wildebeest Eco Camp. They had a nice dinner on the patio of the hotel restaurant then spent the evening relaxing and catching up on their emails from home. They were scheduled to spend the week in Nairobi helping the KWS forensic scientists and technicians set up their first in-house forensics lab.

With the addition of the modern technology, the KWS had the capability to independently analyze evidence gathered at wildlife crime scenes and do DNA analysis of seized wildlife and wildlife parts such as elephant ivory and rhino horns. To date, they had relied on the Kenyan National Police forensics lab and sometimes international forensics labs to do the testing and analysis, often creating lengthy delays in securing the evidence they needed to prosecute the wildlife criminals.

When he heard they were back, Joseph Mwangi came into their office to say hello and ask them how their trip to Tanzania had gone. John and Kate filled him in on the details of the operations in Dar es Salaam and Zanzibar. He was impressed with the success they had in helping to shut down a major ivory poaching syndicate. He said, "I've seen the reports of the takedowns through the Operation Cobra updates. It looks like the NTSCIU, with assistance from your team, has been able to dismantle one of the major ivory trafficking syndicates in Tanzania. I also read about what happened at the Mikocheni house. How is Syd doing?"

Denny answered, "She seems to be doing okay. I think she's still a little sore, but she should be good to go in a few more days."

"How about you, Denny, how are you doing?" Joseph Mwangi asked. "That must have been a pretty tense situation during the takedown."

"Yes, we never want to be in a situation where we have to use deadly force, but things just happen sometimes," Denny said. "Luckily, it all turned out and my team here helped me get through things. I guess I've dealt with a lot worse, so I'll get over what happened in Dar es Salaam as well. The two men I shot made their choices about what they were doing and suffered the consequences. It's a dangerous business, both on our side of the law and theirs."

Joseph then said, "I know you're here this week to help set up the new forensics lab, but I just wanted to let you know that we have a potential big takedown of our own planned for later in the week or on the weekend in Mombasa. We got a tip from one of our informants in Mombasa that a guy we've been after for the last couple of years, Fahad Mohamed Ali, has been spotted in Mombasa. We suspect he's probably organizing a major ivory shipment out of the Port of Mombasa. We have an undercover surveillance team watching for him, and we're hoping he'll lead us to the location of the syndicate's ivory storage facilities in Mombasa."

"Yes, we know about Fahad Mohamed Ali through INTERPOL alerts," John said. "He is supposed to be the ringleader of the biggest ivory trafficking syndicate operating in Kenya, Uganda, and Zambia, using the Port of Mombasa to export the ivory to Asia. I'm surprised he would show up in Mombasa himself, but it would be great if we could finally take him down. You can count us in if you need any help with the operation."

"All right, I'll keep you posted on how the surveillance is going," Joseph said. "We might have to move pretty quickly if we find out where the ivory is being stored and when and how it's scheduled to be moved to the port facilities."

After Joseph left the office, Kate asked Denny, "Do you think Syd would be ready for another takedown if they wanted to use the dogs for the operation?"

"Yes, I think so, but you never know for sure what will happen until you send them in. When the RCMP dog handlers were training them, they ran lots of simulations where they fired guns when they were in the middle of a training takedown to make sure the dogs maintained their focus. Syd and Nelle always passed, otherwise they wouldn't have made it through the program.

"They always take their cue from me, so if I'm there with them and give them the command to go, they are hardwired to obey me. I don't think they process impending danger the same way we do. Their breeding and training kicks in and they just go for it when they get the command. In many ways, they are the perfect law enforcement agents, not subject to the same rational thinking that we humans exhibit when faced with life-threatening situations."

John said, "Well, I guess we'll have to find out how they react at some point, so it might as well be sooner rather than later. We will just have to make sure we are more careful in the future about knowing who and what they are up against before we send them into a dangerous situation."

8 p.m. Friday, February 8, 2013
The Tamarind Village-Nyali Apartment Hotel, Mombasa, Kenya

John and the team spent the week at the KWS headquarters helping to set up and calibrate the new equipment for the forensics lab. Funding for the lab was provided through Operation Cobra and several wildlife conservation NGOs, as well as the US Fish and Wildlife Service and the Canadian Embassy in Kenya. Since John, Kate, and Anna were all senior forensic scientists who managed their own labs, they could provide valuable training for the KWS forensic biologists and technicians. Denny helped in the lab when he could but spent more time with Syd and Nelle taking them for long walks and making sure they would be ready the next time they might be needed.

As it turned out, it was to be during the upcoming weekend. The KWS surveillance team in Mombasa were watching Fahad Mohamed Ali at his hotel. They finally caught a break when they followed him and several of his associates to a small warehouse behind a tea wholesale and shipping office in the Chaani District of western Mombasa, a light industrial and business area north of the Port of Mombasa.

They watched the warehouse for a couple of days and saw a series of vans and SUVs coming to the warehouse and unloading bags of what they assumed was elephant ivory. They were consolidating the ivory at the warehouse to prepare for loading in a shipping container. The ivory would be concealed with the tea, which was packed in special multi-walled, paper bags then shrink-wrapped on pallets.

On Thursday afternoon, a truck with a shipping container on a flatbed trailer arrived at the warehouse. The surveillance officers called their boss, Joseph Mwangi, in Nairobi and told him it was time to come to Mombasa and take down Fahad Mohamed Ali and his ivory poaching gang.

After the call from his surveillance team on Thursday afternoon, Joseph told John and the team about what was going on. He told them he would be taking a team of enforcement officers to Mombasa on Friday afternoon. They planned to execute the raid of the warehouse on Saturday and arrest Fahad Mohamed Ali and any of his associates who were there. John, Kate, Anna, and Denny had already decided they would go to Mombasa and help with the takedown. The KWS intelligence officers from Nairobi would be joined by several KWS enforcement officers from the Mombasa office, as well as the tactical unit from the Mombasa Police Service.

John and the team left Nairobi at noon for the five-hour drive to Mombasa. They made reservations at the Tamarind Village Apartment Hotel. It was in the upscale Nyali District on the Tudor Creek waterfront, overlooking the Old Town of Mombasa. The hotel had fully serviced apartments with kitchen facilities, as well as a poolside restaurant.

The well-known Tamarind Dhow Restaurant was next door to the hotel, and they managed to get a reservation for dinner. Simon joined them at their table for five. The Dhow, now a floating five-star restaurant, sailed around the Tudor Creek Inlet. The patrons could enjoy a gourmet meal of seafood or steak while taking in the evening sights along the inlet waterfront.

While they were enjoying their meal, Simon said, "I like the way you guys roll. I've always wanted to have dinner at the Tamarind Dhow Restaurant, but I'm usually working when I come to Mombasa, and it's a little above my normal KWS meal allowance."

"Well, we don't usually eat at places like this either, being government employees ourselves," Kate said. "But we're on INTERPOL meal per diem allowances while on this field assignment, so we can splurge occasionally. Besides, it isn't every day we stay next door to one of the best restaurants in

Kenya. We might as well take advantage of the opportunity when we can. We still have to eat, right?"

Laughing, John said, "Can we put that on the INTERPOL expense report? The restaurant was recommended by a senior employee of the US Fish and Wildlife Service Office of Law Enforcement who said, 'Well, we had to eat someplace.'"

"Yes, I think my word should be sufficient," Kate responded, laughing. "After all, what are they going to do, ground us?"

"Well, that was one of the better meals I've had in a while," Denny said. "And sailing around Tudor Creek Inlet in Mombasa while eating a gourmet meal is not something you get to do very often, if ever."

While waiting for their dessert and tea to arrive, John decided to go over the plan for the following day.

"So, I guess we have to meet Joseph and his KWS officers at the Makupa Police Station tomorrow morning at nine," John said. "His surveillance team will watch the warehouse and let him know when Fahad Mohamed Ali arrives. How they organize the takedown will depend on how many of Fahad's people are at the warehouse. They don't know if they will have to use the dogs, but they want us there, just in case."

Denny said, "I think Syd is ready to go if we need her. She is moving well, and she didn't seem to have any issues when I ran them through some of their training routines."

"Well, it looks like we are back at the dock. We better go to our rooms and try to get some rest," Kate said. "Tomorrow will probably be a busy day."

9 a.m. Saturday, February 9, 2013
Makupa Police Station, Mombasa, Kenya

John and the team arrived at the Makupa Police Station at nine o'clock Saturday morning. The Police Station was only a ten-minute drive from the warehouse, which was just south of Airport Road on Port Reitz Road, in the light industrial and business Chaani District. Joseph was already there with his officers. The Mombasa Police Tactical Unit was on standby, waiting for the word to converge on the warehouse.

At nine thirty, they received a call from the surveillance team that Fahad Mohamed Ali had left the hotel with two of his men and were driving towards the warehouse in their SUV. At nine forty-five, they got another call that Fahad had arrived at the warehouse and was inside with his two men. Joseph sent an officer to the warehouse posing as a courier driver with a package to be delivered to the business. He hoped the undercover officer could get a look inside the warehouse and report how many other people were working there.

The officer relayed, to Joseph, his findings. "Sir, I counted six men altogether. One was driving a small forklift loading the pallets of tea into the container. At least two of the men had guns in shoulder holsters. Only one guy looked like he was a guard with an assault rifle slung over his shoulder."

Joseph called the whole team together into the meeting room of the police station, including the tactical unit team leader, so they could discuss how to organize the raid of the warehouse. The entire property was enclosed with an eight-foot-high chain-link fence with one main gate in the front. The loading bay was facing the front of the street beside the front office entrance door.

They decided to go into the warehouse yard in force and apprehend the men before they had the chance to mount any type of organized resistance. They prepared themselves for possible exchange of gunfire. However, the police and KWS officers had the definite advantage of surprise, superior manpower, and weapons. It was agreed the situation was too dangerous to use Syd and Nelle for the initial raid, but they would be on standby if any of the men in the warehouse tried to escape and make a run for it.

John and the team would not take part in the initial breaching of the warehouse but were all outfitted with their Kevlar vests, including Syd and Nelle. John, Kate, and Anna had their SIG Sauer P226 service pistols, and Denny also had one of the tactical unit's Colt C8SFW assault rifles.

The tactical unit van with six officers went through the front gate of the warehouse first, followed by two KWS Land Rovers with four officers in each vehicle. Simon drove their vehicle in last and proceeded to the back of the warehouse to watch for anyone trying to escape from the back. While they were driving around to the back, they heard shouting from the tactical unit officers inside and a couple of gunshots. Just as they rounded the corner of the warehouse, they saw two men come out of the back door of the warehouse, run to the back fence, and push through an opening and run down the alley.

Screeching to a halt, Simon assisted Denny and John as they prepared Syd and Nelle for pursuit. Denny pulled the section of fence back and gave the dogs the command "Capture." The dogs did not hesitate and took off after the two men, who were now about half a block away, running at full speed. The two dogs quickly closed the gap, but as he was running, one of the men turned and fired a shot at the dogs. The bullet missed the dogs, but unfortunately, grazed John's shoulder.

The dogs were unfazed and before the two men got another half block, the two dogs were on them, grabbing their lower legs and yanking them down to the ground. Denny and John were close behind the dogs and by the time they caught up, the two men were lying on their backs yelling for the dogs to let go of them. Nelle had clamped down on the forearm of the man with the gun, making him drop it on the ground.

Denny commanded the dogs to "Release" and he and John pointed their guns at them and shouted at them to get up. Denny reached down and retrieved the handgun from the ground and put it in his side pocket. Although John's shoulder was stinging and bleeding a little, they marched them back to the opening in the fence. While Denny covered the two men with his assault rifle, Kate and Anna put handcuffs on them.

After the two men were secured and on their knees on the ground, Kate finally noticed the tear on John's shirt sleeve and the patch of blood growing larger around the tear. Looking alarmed, she exclaimed, "Oh my God, John, did you get shot?"

"Yes, I guess the bullet must have grazed my shoulder when one of these guys took a shot at the dogs. It's nothing though, just a scratch."

"I'll be the judge of that. Let me have a look," Kate scoffed.

John rolled up his shirt sleeve so they could see the wound and Kate began wiping away the blood with gauze from the first aid kit Simon retrieved from the Land Rover. Luckily, the bullet just grazed his upper arm; however, there was a significant gash that would need a few stiches.

Kate said, "It looks like you'll live, but we'll need to take you to the ER to get some stitches. I'll put a bandage on it for now until we can get away from here and go to the hospital."

Looking at John and Denny, Anna said, "This is getting scary. First Syd gets shot and now John. Are we sure we want to be acting like SWAT officers all the time? I thought we were supposed to be scientists."

Smiling, John said, "What fun would that be, just being boring scientists? And besides, it's not like one of us gets shot during every takedown. We just hit a bad stretch on this trip."

In her sternest 'mother voice,' Kate said, "Well, I think we've reached our quota now for getting shot on this trip. No more heroics. We can let the police professionals do their jobs for the rest of the trip."

One of the tactical unit officers came out through the back door to see what was going on and told them they could bring the two men back into the warehouse where they had the other men in custody. They proceeded into the warehouse through the back door and saw five men in handcuffs on their knees on the warehouse floor, one of whom was Fahad Mohamed Ali.

They could see the shipping container was about one third full of bags of tea stacked on the pallets and then covered with shrink wrapping. Piled on the floor were dozens of canvas bags, hundreds of multi-layered large paper bags containing the processed tea leaves, and partially loaded pallets. One of the KWS officers opened a couple of the canvas bags and exposed several raw elephant tusks in each bag. It looked like the scheme was to put a couple of bags of elephant tusks in the middle of each pallet, stack the bags of tea around them, and then shrink wrap the whole pallet.

The tactical unit leader called the police station to send a prisoner transport van to the warehouse. After its arrival, the officers escorted the prisoners out to the van, securing each one inside. The tactical team then followed the transport vehicle to the police station.

As the KWS officers and John's team were standing around looking at the warehouse operation, Joseph said to Denny, "I heard your dogs chased down the two guys who escaped through the back door. I really appreciate your help with the raid."

He just then noticed the blood on John's shirt sleeve and the bandage on his arm and asked, "Are you okay, John? What happened to your arm?"

John said, "It's all right, one of the guys took a wild shot at the dogs in the back alley, and I was unlucky enough to get hit. It's just a scratch though, and we're going to the hospital to get it stitched up as soon as we're finished here."

"We're all happy to be here and be a part of this takedown," Denny said. "And it was good to get Syd and Nelle back on the job so they could put what happened in Dar es Salaam behind them. Syd seems fine, so I don't think we have to worry about her anymore. It looks like you have a major win here, stopping this shipment of ivory and finally catching Fahad Mohamed Ali and some of his senior gang members."

"Yes, we've been after Fahad for a couple of years now, so this is a momentous day for us," Joseph replied. "We knew he'd been operating primarily out of Mombasa for a while now, but he seldom came here in person, so we were lucky to get the tip that he was here this week. This looks like a long-term, well-organized operation, so hopefully we can figure out how the other parts of the ivory trafficking syndicate work now.

"I'll be getting my CSI team to come to the warehouse and hopefully we can find out the locations of the endpoints of the shipping containers, how that part of the trafficking syndicate works, and who the ultimate buyers of the ivory are. Through Operation Cobra and INTERPOL's Project Wisdom, we are now getting more cooperation from the law enforcement agencies in Asia. They can shut down that end of these international ivory trafficking operations.

"We'll also interrogate all the men we apprehended today, so hopefully we'll get some information about who is supplying the elephant ivory to the warehouse from areas in Kenya, and even from bordering countries like Uganda, the Democratic Republic of Congo, and Zambia. We also know there are shipping agents and customs officers working in Mombasa at the Kenya Port Authority who are helping guys like Fahad Mohamed Ali. They helped Fahad get clearances for the shipping containers so he could get them loaded onto the cargo ships.

"So, you better get John to the hospital now so they can get his arm fixed up. I think the closest hospital to here is Boma Hospital, which should be just a ten-minute drive north on Soweto Road."

They said their goodbyes to the KWS officers and Simon drove them to the Boma Hospital. The ER was not too busy, so John got in after a fifteen-minute wait. A young Kenyan ER doctor put six stitches in his arm. The doctor was quite interested to hear that John was from Canada, since she had done her residency in emergency medicine at the Victoria General Hospital in Halifax, Nova Scotia.

The group agreed to stay one more night in Mombasa at the Tamarind Village Apartment Hotel and return to Nairobi the next afternoon. On Sunday morning, they drove back to the warehouse to check on how things were going with processing the ivory and the collection of any other evidence the KWS officers found. Joseph was there and when he saw John and his team come into the warehouse, he said to them, "Good to see you again. How is your arm feeling today, John?"

"A nice young doctor stitched me up at the Boma Hospital. It's a little sore, but it should be fine in a few days. How are things going here?"

"Things are going well. We unpacked all the pallets that were already in the shipping container, and together with the other elephant tusks in the bags in the warehouse, we have counted 714 pieces. We have recorded and numbered each piece and will take them all back to Nairobi to weigh them on our scales and officially enter them into evidence against Fahad Mohamed Ali and his three accomplices, Abdul Kara, Ghalib Sadiq, and Pravez Noor Halim.

"We estimate the ivory will cumulatively weigh around twenty-one hundred kilograms. The other three men arrested are just local muscle types working as guards at the warehouse, so we will charge them with lesser offenses. Except for the one who shot at your dogs and hit you instead. We have also charged him with attempted murder, so he'll spend a little more time in jail than his two friends.

"The CSI guys are still going through the paperwork and files in the office area, but they've found some shipping orders and bills of lading for shipping container transactions from the past couple of years. Most of them have been signed by the same shipping agents and customs officers, so we'll pay these people a visit tomorrow when they are at work again.

"Most of the shipping containers seemed to be loaded on ships owned by one Chinese-owned shipping company, with stops either in Manila in the Philippines or Haiphong in Vietnam, and then Shuidong Port in the Maoming Region of Guangdong Province in China. We will contact the Chinese law enforcement agencies working with the Operation Cobra people to let them know what we've found so they can hopefully shut down that end of the ivory trafficking syndicate as well."

Kate asked, "Have you been able to find out anything about the identities of the local ringleaders who have been buying the elephant tusks from the poachers and bringing them here to the tea warehouse?"

Joseph replied, "Nothing much so far, but we still need to interrogate Fahad Mohamed Ali's three accomplices. They're in separate cells in the police lock-up. Maybe one is willing to sell out his brothers in crime for a special deal and fill us in on the details of the poaching operation. When we get that information, we can start rounding up the local poachers and middlemen."

"Well, congratulations, this is another big win for the good guys," John said. "We're going to head back to Nairobi now, so we'll see you there when you get back. We'll spend the rest of the week in Nairobi helping to get your KWS forensics lab up and running, and meeting with the people from the Lusaka Agreement Task Force about Operation Cobra.

"Anna, Denny, and the dogs will return to Canada next weekend, but Kate and I are off to Phuket in Thailand for a vacation. From there, we'll be attending the Conference of the Parties of CITES in Bangkok from March 3rd to the 14th."

Joseph said, "I've always wanted to go to one of the CITES conferences, but I'm not far enough up the KWS pecking order yet. I hear the next Conference of the Parties after Thailand is in Johannesburg in 2016, so maybe I can go to that one since it's close to home. I'll see you in a couple of days back in Nairobi."

CHAPTER 12

8 p.m. Sunday, February 10, 2013
Wildebeest Eco Camp, Nairobi, Kenya

John and the team drove back to Nairobi on Sunday afternoon and settled back into their cottages at the Wildebeest Eco Camp. They went for dinner on the open-air patio of the hotel restaurant and discussed the events of the last few days. While they were enjoying their second bottle of wine after dinner, Anna said, "So, John, how's your arm feeling?"

"It's a little sorer than yesterday, but I think that's normal. Kate changed the bandage before we came for dinner and it looks okay, no sign of infection or anything. It should be healed up by the time we leave for Thailand on the weekend."

"Wow, a week in Phuket not chasing after any bad guys," said Anna. "Are you sure you won't get bored just lying around on the beach and drinking fancy cocktails? I went to Bangkok and Phuket with a couple of my girlfriends from McGill University on spring break when I was in graduate studies. I recommend you try Sangsom, the local drink of choice in Phuket. It's a popular rum with a high alcohol content that's brewed locally from sugarcane and aged in oak barrels.

"I got really drunk one night on Sangsom and, although I couldn't remember doing it, I was told by my friends that I ended up dancing on a beachfront restaurant table with a fellow Canadian boy I had just met. We were apparently asked to leave the restaurant by the manager, not one of my finest moments."

Laughing, Denny said, "Wow, I would have definitely paid money to see that. Badass RCMP Corporal Anna Dupree getting drunk and dancing on a table and getting kicked out of a Thai restaurant. What happened to that wild and crazy gal?"

Anna said laughing, "I guess she grew up and got a job where getting drunk and dancing on tables is sort of frowned on. Not that I can't still have my wild and crazy moments. I just try to tone them down so I can still remember them the next morning."

Smiling, Kate said, "Well, I'm sure we all have those kinds of stories from our youth. Except John here, who says he's been a serious crime fighter since birth."

"Alright, I know you think of me as your mentor and a world-renowned crime fighter, but I do have some stories of my own from my youth that I prefer not to advertise," John said, smiling.

Denny interjected, "More than a few stories from some things I've heard from Michael Alden about your time together at the RCMP Training Academy in Regina. And then there was the time in Afghanistan when we needed to get driven back to the base by a couple of sympathetic MPs. And how about that time in Amsterdam in 2009 when we were on an overnight stopover on our way back to Edmonton from Nairobi. Not a pretty scene getting back to our hotel from that red-light district bar."

Laughing, John said, "Okay, okay, no one is interested in those stories. What's past is past. No need to dwell on any of our former indiscretions. We've all had those moments from our younger foolish days we are not too proud of."

"Well, it's refreshing to hear that the great Dr. John Benson does indeed have some human flaws," Kate said, smiling. "It's good having these talks among friends. Makes us all a little humbler knowing that others know some of our more embarrassing secrets."

"Well, look at the time," John said, trying to change the subject. "We better get back to our cottages and get some sleep. We're going to spend the next few days helping to get the new equipment operating at the KWS forensics lab. And then we have some meetings scheduled at the LATF office about Operation Cobra and the upcoming CITES Conference of the Parties in Bangkok."

9 p.m. Sunday, February 17, 2013
Outrigger Laguna Phuket Beach Resort, Phuket Island, Thailand

John and Kate had spent the previous week in Nairobi working at the new KWS forensics lab and going to several meetings with members of the LATF. Besides what John's team had been doing for the past few weeks in Dar es Salaam and Mombasa, there were several other aspects of Operation Cobra taking place in various other countries, both in Africa and Asia. They were to take part in a panel discussion about Operation Cobra at the CITES Standing Committee meeting on March 14th in Bangkok after the completion of the Conference of the Parties, so they wanted to make sure they were up to date on the progress of the overall operation.

Denny, Anna, and the dogs flew back to Edmonton on Friday morning on KLM Airlines with an overnight stopover in Amsterdam. John and Kate left Nairobi for Bangkok early Saturday morning on a Kenya Airways flight with a two-hour stopover in Dubai. After almost twelve hours of flying, they finally arrived and checked into the Modena by Fraser Bangkok Hotel for the night.

On Sunday, later in the morning, they took a one-and-half-hour flight on Thai Vietjet Airlines to Phuket Island. For once, they had booked a real vacation with a reservation for ten days at the five-star Outrigger Laguna Phuket Beach Resort. After a short taxi ride from the Phuket Airport, they checked in to their oceanfront one-bedroom suite.

Phuket is one of the southern provinces of Thailand. It consists of the island of Phuket, the country's largest island, and another thirty-two smaller islands off its coast. It's located off the west coast of Thailand in the Andaman Sea. The island is mostly mountainous, with a mountain range in the island's west running north to south. The population is about six hundred thousand, consisting of migrants, international ex-pats, Thais registered in other provinces, and locals.

Phuket is approximately 860 kilometers south of Bangkok and covers an area of 543 square kilometers. The island's length, from north to south, is forty-eight kilometers and its width is twenty-one kilometers. The most popular tourist areas in Phuket are the beach areas along the west coast, and most of Phuket's nightlife and shopping is in Patong, the capital city.

On December 26, 2004, Phuket and other nearby areas on Thailand's west coast were struck by a tsunami caused by an earthquake in the Indian Ocean. The waves destroyed several highly populated areas in the region, killing up to 5,300 people in Thailand and two hundred thousand more throughout the Asian region. About 250 people were killed in Phuket, including foreign tourists. Almost all the major beaches on the west coast of Phuket sustained major damage. Since the 1980s, they have developed the sandy beaches on the west coast of the island as major tourist destinations, with Patong, Karon, and Kata being the most popular. Following the 2004 tsunami, they restored all the damaged buildings and attractions; many new hotels, apartments, and houses were currently under construction.

The Outrigger Laguna Phuket Beach Resort was a five-star luxury resort on Bang Tao Beach on the west-central coast of Phuket Island. It was a sprawling, 220-room resort complex with both oceanfront and lagoon-front accommodations. John and Kate splurged and booked a ground-level, oceanfront, one-bedroom suite with a private patio area looking out onto the white sand beach and the incredibly blue ocean.

Although they had traveled and stayed together on many occasions over the previous three years since they had become a romantic couple, it was usually work related, and they hadn't had the chance to have an extended vacation together, completely away from work. John and Kate were workaholics, so taking vacations in exotic locations was not a priority for them. They intended to make the most of this vacation and try to just concentrate on being together and doing things just like ordinary people on holiday in one of the most beautiful places they had ever been to.

After they arrived from the airport and checked into their suite, they took a walk around the resort to check things out. The resort had three restaurants, several swimming pools with the requisite poolside bars and cafes, a large fitness center, and a spa featuring traditional Thai massages, reflexology treatments, and aromatherapy. As they walked by the spa area, Kate said, "I intend on spending quite a bit of time here at the spa. I've heard the Thai massages are phenomenal."

John said, "Yes, I agree, why don't we make it a daily activity? My body doesn't seem to recover as quickly as it used to, and I could use some pampering after the last few weeks, to say nothing of getting shot."

"Your arm looks like it's healing well since you got the stitches out in Nairobi," said Kate. "I've never been on a vacation to such a beautiful place, and I'm so happy we finally got the chance to come together. Let's not talk about work and just enjoy our time here as much as possible."

"Okay, it's a deal, no shop talk, just rest and relaxation and seeing the sights of Phuket."

Over the next ten days, they spent lots of time just relaxing on their private patio, taking long walks on the beach, eating at the resort restaurants, going for drinks at the poolside bars, and having almost daily half-hour Thai massages at the spa. They went on several excursions around the island including a visit to the Phuket Elephant Sanctuary, the Khao Phra Thaeo Wildlife Conservation Development and Extension Center, which conserved several wild animals that would otherwise have gone extinct in Phuket, and the Phuket Aquarium at the Phuket Marine Biological Center. They took two evening trips south to the town of Patong and strolled down Bangla Road, which had the biggest collection of nightclubs, bars, shows, and general nighttime fun in Phuket.

They went on a day trip by ferry to Phi Island, which was one of the more popular smaller islands located about forty kilometers east of Phuket Island in the Andaman Sea. Most of the island was a national park and had an abundance of coral reefs and marine life; limestone mountains with cliffs and caves; and long, white, sandy beaches.

Phi Island was eight kilometers long and three and a half kilometers wide and, since the re-building of Ko Phi Phi after the 2004 tsunami, had paved paths and narrow roads covering many areas of the main tourist spots; however, all the roads were for pedestrian use only with push carts used to transport goods and tourist luggage. The only permitted motor vehicles were for emergency services. Kate and John spent the day leisurely hiking around the island and having an extended lunch and drinks on the patio of a beach-side café.

On their last evening on Phuket Island, they had a romantic dinner with two bottles of wine delivered to their patio overlooking the ocean. After they finished their dessert and had opened the second bottle of wine, Kate said lovingly, "This has been one of the nicest vacations I've ever had. I can't remember the last time I've spent ten days not thinking about work. And I think we've gotten to know each other on a whole new level, just as best friends and romantic partners, without the backdrop of an impending mission."

Smiling, John replied, "Yes, for me too. I didn't realize how much I needed a break from our crazy busy lives. And spending the last ten days with you here, with no work distractions, has been the best time I've had in a long time. We should make a point of having these longer breaks together at least once a year, even though we usually end up traveling together for work more often. Life is too short to only spend it working at jobs like ours."

After a momentary pause, John continued, "Lately, I have been thinking about how random life is. A couple of weeks ago, I was shot, and if the bullet would have been a few inches over, it could have killed me. During a very random event that I had no way of foreseeing. I guess what I'm saying is that, especially in our line of work, we can't take anything for granted. We must take more time to enjoy our lives and our families and each other."

Smiling, Kate said, "Well, it looks like we both did some serious thinking these past couple of weeks. Why don't we take the rest of the bottle of wine inside and make use of that nice king-sized bed for one last night before we have to go back to the real world."

7 p.m. Wednesday, February 27, 2013
Modena by Fraser Bangkok Hotel, Bangkok, Thailand

John and Kate caught their flight from Phuket back to the Suvarnabhumi Airport in Bangkok late Wednesday morning. It was a shocking adjustment to go from the relaxed Phuket Island lifestyle to the frenzied traffic and pedestrian congestion in Bangkok. On the taxi ride from the airport, they were amazed by the sheer numbers of other taxis, tuk tuks, motorcycles, bicycles, buses, and cars driving on the roads.

They finally got to their hotel in the late afternoon, the Modena by Fraser Bangkok, a very modern four-star hotel within walking distance to the Queen Sirikit National Convention Center (QSNCC), the site of the CITES Conference of the Parties. After unpacking, getting settled in their studio executive suite, and relaxing for a while, they ordered dinner from room service, staying in for the evening with a bottle of wine, catching up on emails, and watching world news — something they hadn't done for a couple of weeks.

John called his daughters to let them know that he and Kate had finished their vacation in Phuket and were now in Bangkok. He still hadn't told them about getting shot, or about Syd getting shot. He didn't want them to worry about him while he was away. He'd tell them when he returned home. He knew they would be angry at him for not telling them sooner, but he realized they worried a lot about him and his crazy globe-trotting job. It was better they knew as little as possible about his assignments. Kate also called her daughter Dianna in Portland. She also refrained from sharing details about the events in Dar es Salaam and Mombasa.

John also called Anna to see how things were going in Edmonton, to let her know how their vacation had gone, and to tell her they were now in Bangkok. Anna told him how jealous she was of him and Kate since the temperature in Edmonton was minus fifteen and it had been snowing for the last two days.

Laughing, John told her he was sorry for her pain, but even though it was plus twenty-eight in Bangkok, the humidity was extremely high, so it was quite uncomfortable without the air conditioning. It didn't seem to impress Anna, who told him she hoped there was a big snowstorm in Edmonton when he got home so he didn't completely miss the joys of the Edmonton winter.

This was the first time either of them had been to Bangkok for an extended period, and they were going to spend the next few days at the International Law Enforcement Academy of Bangkok (ILEA) before the start of the CITES conference on March 3rd. The ILEA, which operated as a joint effort between the Royal Thai government and the government of the United States, was established in 1998 to strengthen the regional cooperation network through the provision of state-of-the-art law enforcement training to the fifteen participating Asian countries.

To date, over twenty-two thousand law enforcement personnel from participating countries had taken part in the training programs, which also included training to combat international wildlife trafficking. Because they were 'back on the clock' and official members of their respective country's delegations, the bill for their stay in Bangkok was being picked up by a combination of their government employers and INTERPOL's Wildlife Crime Unit.

John and Kate were scheduled to participate in Operation Cobra update meetings over the next few days as representatives of Environment Canada, the US Fish and Wildlife Service, and INTERPOL's Wildlife Crime Group. They had prepared briefing reports about their recent participation in the takedowns of the ivory trafficking syndicates in Dar es Salaam, Zanzibar, and Mombasa. Although not their original goal, they were now known as two of the big players in the world of on-the-ground international wildlife crime law enforcement.

7 p.m. Thursday, March 14, 2013
Modena by Fraser Bangkok Hotel, Bangkok, Thailand

John and Kate had spent the previous two weeks attending meetings and workshops, listening to many speeches and presentations, some interesting but many boring and often delivered in halting English or by an interpreter through earpieces. However, they also renewed friendships and met many new people from all over the world involved in wildlife conservation and wildlife crime law enforcement.

The 16th Meeting of the Conference of the Parties of CITES was attended by delegates from over 180 countries, plus invited guests from many of the major international environmental conservation NGOs. These were the organizations, foundations, and trusts that funded a lot of the on-the-ground wildlife conservation efforts around the world, and they had a significant amount of lobbying power with countries involved in CITES.

The conference was held at the QSNCC, the largest convention center and exhibition hall in Bangkok. The main meeting place for the conference was the Plenary Hall, a theater style hall, which could accommodate up to six thousand people. The center was named after Queen Sirikit in honor of her sixtieth birthday.

There were committee meetings going on simultaneously with the main conference proceedings, where voting took place on resolutions and decisions to be adopted by the Conference of the Parties. In many ways, it was like the international wildlife conservation version of the United Nations.

Organizations such as INTERPOL's Environmental Security Unit were well represented at the conference since they were often involved in enforcing wildlife trafficking laws in countries around the world.

When not attending conference events and meetings, John and Kate tried to see some sights in Bangkok, which is the capital and most populous city in Thailand, with a population of over eight million. Over fourteen million people live within the surrounding Bangkok Metropolitan Region. Bangkok is in the Chao Phraya River delta in Thailand's central plain. The river meanders through the city in a southerly direction, emptying into the Gulf of Thailand.

The city is flat and low-lying, with an average elevation of one and a half meters above sea level. Most of the area was originally swampland, which was gradually drained and irrigated for agriculture by the construction of canals which took place from the sixteenth to nineteenth centuries. The course of the river as it flows through Bangkok had been modified by the construction of canals, which are now used to transport goods and people.

Bangkok is also one of the world's top tourist destinations. John and Kate went on several excursions in a tuk-tuk, the auto rickshaw that seemed to be one of the most common forms of urban transport in Bangkok. Drivers also used their tuk-tuks to transport all manner of goods around the city. There were several urban parks near their hotel, Benjakitti State Park and Lumphini Park, which they visited to get some fresh air and find some respite from the crowds of people at the conference.

Although they weren't much for shopping, Bangkok is a paradise for shopping enthusiasts. If you don't want to pay higher prices for original designer brand names, you can always find someone selling high-quality knockoffs of everything imaginable, from Rolex watches, to handbags, and all kinds of clothing.

One afternoon during their first week in the city, they took a taxi to the famous Pratunam Market, which is one of Bangkok's major markets and Thailand's largest clothing market. It was extremely chaotic and hot, with hundreds of kiosks, so they didn't stay long. They managed to buy some gifts for family members back home, like silk scarves, T-shirts, and shorts for John's grandkids, and knock-off, expensive-looking handbags for their daughters.

Kate splurged and bought a couple of leather handbags, several silk scarves, and a new dress for herself for the upcoming gala banquet at the end of the conference. On the previous Sunday morning, they went to the Chatuchak Weekend Market, a sprawling market in the Chatuchak District of Bangkok only open on Saturdays and Sundays. John bought a new watch for himself and one for Denny and a couple of bottles of Sangsom rum. He also purchased several intricately carved wooden animals — an Asian elephant, a Sumatran rhinoceros, and a Sunda pangolin — for Anna to add to her collection of wood carvings from Africa.

Pangolins are among the most heavily poached and exploited protected animals. Like other pangolin species, the Sunda pangolin, native to Thailand and other countries in Southeast Asia, is hunted for its skin, scales, and meat, and used in clothing manufacturing and in traditional medicine. Scales are made into rings as charms against rheumatic fever, and Indigenous people eat the meat.

Despite having protected status almost everywhere in its range, illegal international trade, largely driven by Chinese buyers, has led to rapidly decreasing pangolin populations. The Sunda pangolin is currently listed as being critically endangered and Pangolins were a major topic of discussion at the CITES conference.

Although John and Kate were not big fans of nightclubs, Bangkok was famous for its nightlife scene and there were hundreds of nightclubs, rooftop bars, and cocktail bars in Bangkok, and particularly in places like Khao San Road. On a couple of evenings, some of their colleagues from the conference persuaded them to go to fancy restaurants with adjoining nightclubs on Khao San Road.

The area was internationally known as the center for dancing and late-night partying in Bangkok. There were also shops that sold handicrafts, paintings, clothes, local fruits, unlicensed CDs, DVDs, and a wide range of fake IDs. After dark, the bars opened, the music started, and food hawkers sold barbecued insects and other exotic snacks for the tourists. There were also hawkers selling evenings with Bangkok's famous 'party girls' for those interested in that type of entertainment. Despite their misgivings about the scene, John and Kate had a fun time and experienced the chaotic nightlife in the heart of Bangkok's party district.

On Friday, March 15th, they caught their Air Canada flight back to Canada. Kate went to Edmonton with John, stayed a couple of days, then flew to Portland to visit her daughter before driving back home to Ashland, Oregon. Their first leg of the flight was a little over six hours to Tokyo, with a twelve-hour layover, which they spent part of on a bus tour of Tokyo since they had nothing better to do while they waited for their next flight, and they had never been to Tokyo before.

The next leg was an eight-and-a-half-hour flight to Vancouver, with a shorter two-and-a-half-hour layover, before their last leg to Edmonton. They both laughed when they touched down in Edmonton at three thirty in the afternoon and saw the snow coming down and the wind blowing. Anna must have ordered the snowstorm out of spite for having had to come home early before winter was over.

Anna was waiting for them in the terminal once they'd gone through customs and retrieved their luggage. Following the welcome home greetings and hugs, John said, "Well, it looks like you got your revenge, the weather is crappy, and winter is still here in Edmonton."

Laughing, she said, "Okay, I must admit that I'm a little happy the weather is horrible for when you got back. But tomorrow, I'll be ready for spring to start."

Anna brought Syd and Nelle with her to the airport because they had been staying with her since she and Denny got back from Kenya. They were extremely excited to see John and Kate, with lots of squirming, tail wagging, and whining. After some pats and greetings from John and Kate, they eventually settled down. Now that John was back, the dogs would move back home with him. On the drive into the city, John and Kate told Anna about their vacation in Phuket and the CITES conference in Bangkok.

When they got to John's house, he gave Anna the wooden carvings he bought for her. She was overjoyed and marveled at the craftmanship of the Thai wood carvers. Once Anna left, John and Kate ordered pizza from John's favorite pizza place, Dallas Pizza, and settled into an evening of TV watching. John phoned his daughters to let them know he was home, and Kate did the same with her daughter in Portland.

While they were eating their pizza on the couch, with Syd and Nelle on the floor looking intently at them, hoping for a few morsels of pizza crust,

Kate said, "I really like your house, and the view of the river valley is great, even though it's winter."

John said, "I've been here since 2004, after my divorce. It's a great neighborhood and good for the dogs with all the walking trails in the river valley. You'll have to come into the office with me tomorrow morning and meet all the staff. Anna is always telling the other people in the office about how great you are, so they're all eager to meet the famous Dr. Kate Beckett, one of the senior forensic scientists at the United States National Fish and Wildlife Forensics Lab."

Smiling, Kate said, "Well, now I'm worried they'll be disappointed when they find out that I am just a mere mortal. Do you have a cape or something I could wear?"

"I'm sure I could find something around here we could make into a cape. Don't worry though, they're great people and are just excited to meet one of their own who has done so well."

"Alright, it'll be great to see where you work and to meet your staff. Then I need to get home. I think my flight to Portland leaves at four tomorrow. I guess it will be a while before we see each other again. Our next trip to Africa is in October to do the training workshops in Zambia, Tanzania, and Kenya again. Maybe we can take a vacation together later this summer. I know some beautiful places along the coast if you wanted to come down for a week or two."

"That sounds great," said John. As they snuggled lovingly on the couch, they both wondered how long they could continue with their unconventional relationship. The times they spent apart were becoming increasingly difficult. Yet, bringing their lives together on a permanent basis seemed impossible without one of them giving up their current career path. In the meantime, they would continue to make the best of their situation and find ways to be with each other whenever they could.

CHAPTER 13

8 p.m. Sunday, October 20, 2013
Wildebeest Eco Camp, Nairobi, Kenya

John and the team finally arrived back at the Wildebeest Eco Camp after their two-day trip from Edmonton. As usual, they flew with KLM Airlines and stopped overnight in Amsterdam to break up the flights and give Syd and Nelle a chance to get out of their travel kennels.

Kate flew to Edmonton on Thursday, October 10th to spend a Canadian Thanksgiving weekend with John and his family, then stayed with John until they left for Africa later in the week. They arrived in Nairobi at five o'clock in the afternoon and were picked up at the airport by Simon. They settled into their usual cottages and went for dinner on the outdoor patio of the hotel restaurant.

It had been seven months since their last venture to Africa together, and they were looking forward to the next couple of months. After getting back home in March, they had settled back into their regular jobs: Kate in Ashland, Oregon, and John, Anna, and Denny in Edmonton. Despite their concern for what was going on in East Africa, there was also plenty of wildlife-related criminal activity happening on their home turf in Canada and the US.

Illegal hunting and poaching of trophy big game animals was an ongoing problem, especially in the National Parks. Illegal importation of live exotic animals, reptiles, and birds and smuggling of animal parts or products made from restricted or endangered species at the airports or through courier companies or the postal service was also a constant occurrence. There was never a shortage of work for the understaffed law enforcement and border service agencies trying to keep up with the many ways the smugglers and criminals devised to traffic their illegal wildlife products.

John and Kate had talked to each other as often as possible on the phone over the previous six months, and John even drove down to Oregon in July for two weeks. Kate lived in a nice bungalow in Ashland backing onto Bear Creek, about a five-minute drive from her office in the National Fish and Wildlife Forensics Laboratory on the campus of Southern Oregon University.

They rented a twenty-eight-foot travel trailer from one of Kate's coworkers and went to the Mystic Forest RV Park on the coast of northern California for a week. It is a beautiful area in Redwood National Park, just north of the town of Klamath, California. The area is famous for preserving the few remaining gigantic redwood trees that were once plentiful in that part of the state. There are also long sandy beaches to walk on. They spent their evenings talking and sitting in front of the campfire in their camping spot — quite different from their last vacation in Phuket, Thailand, but very enjoyable, nonetheless.

While they were finishing their second bottle of wine on the patio of the Wildebeest restaurant and discussing their last few months of cases back home with Kate, Anna said, "It seems like a long time since we were last here, it's good to be back in Nairobi. So, do we have our schedule completed for the next few weeks?"

John answered, "Yes, I think things are finally sorted out. We already knew that after this week here helping at the KWS's new forensics lab, we were going to do training workshops for the KWS again, and that we were supposed to go down to Dar es Salaam again to do workshops for TAWA. Just before we left, I got a request from Roberta Mulenga, the head of intelligence for the ZAWA, to come to Lusaka to assist with a training workshop for a new initiative they are implementing.

"ZAWA has recruited eighty-four Honorary Wildlife Police Officers (HWPOs), who will assist ZAWA in areas of conservation, law enforcement, and anti-poaching activities. Out of the eighty-four officers, fifty-five are renewals, while the rest are new appointees who are required to complete an orientation exercise to make sure they conduct their activities safely and professionally.

"The recruitment period is three years, after which an evaluation exercise will be conducted to allow the renewal of the appointment for those who want to continue and have a good record of performance, and the release from service for the rest of them. The HWPOs are volunteers recruited from the public and include lawyers, doctors, scientists, and other professionals who have offered their expertise, time, and resources to the conservation of Zambia's wildlife resources."

Kate continued, "As we know, the Zambia Wildlife Authority is an autonomous agency of the Zambian government established to manage and conserve Zambia's wildlife resources and protected areas, consisting of twenty National Parks, thirty-six Game Management Areas and one bird sanctuary, which together cover thirty-one percent of the country's land mass.

"The reorganizing of the National Parks and Wildlife Services Department into ZAWA reoriented the new wildlife authority towards a direction that revamped the country's wildlife management sector. Although not as well-known as some of the Kenyan and Tanzanian parks, the Zambian National Parks, such as South Luangwa, Kafue, and Lower Zambezi are among the finest game parks in the world. Kafue National Park is Zambia's largest National Park and the second largest in the world."

"So how are they going to run the training program?" Denny asked.

John answered, "I don't know all the details yet, but Roberta told me they are going to have a classroom session for three days at the Twangale Park Hotel and Conference Center. I guess it's one of Lusaka's premier hotels and event venues and is on seven acres of manicured grounds. It even has one of Lusaka's best art galleries, with an extensive collection of Zambian art."

Looking excited, Anna said, "That's great. I can't wait to check it out. Maybe I can add to my collection of African art and carvings."

Kate added, "Me too. I still have a spot on one wall in my office for a nice African painting, depending on the prices at the gallery, of course."

John continued, "Roberta said they are also trying to organize a few days of field training at Kafue National Park, which they hope we can attend, as well. They want to show the new HWPOs what goes on at the park and how the park rangers do their jobs. There will be some firearms training, which they hope Denny might assist them with. And they are interested in getting some demonstrations of how we work with Syd and Nelle in the field."

"Well, that sounds like fun," Denny said. "And I'm sure Syd and Nelle wouldn't mind showing off a little." At the mention of their names, the two dogs both looked up at their humans from napping beside the table. Things had been quiet for the dogs back in Canada for the past few months, so they were looking forward to some bad guy takedowns now that they were back in Africa. Syd's last brush with death in Dar es Salaam was a distant memory. It didn't seem to have affected her willingness to rush headlong into dangerous situations, a testament to her breeding, training, and absolute loyalty to her human team.

8 p.m. Saturday, October 26, 2013
Twangale Park Hotel and Conference Center, Lusaka, Zambia

John and the team flew from Nairobi to Lusaka's Kenneth Kaunda International Airport on the KWS Cessna 425 Corsair plane they usually used when they were in Kenya on official business. The INTERPOL Wildlife Crime Unit reimbursed the KWS airwing for the use of the plane, and it was much more cost effective and expedient than trying to take commercial flights. The flight was three hours long and they landed in Lusaka at four in the afternoon. A ZAWA park ranger who worked with Roberta Mulenga picked them up at the airport in a twelve-passenger shuttle bus and drove them to the hotel. Lusaka is the capital and largest city of Zambia, with an urban population of about two and a half million.

They had spent the previous week in Nairobi working out of their usual temporary office at the KWS headquarters and staying at the Wildebeest Eco Camp. The biologists and technicians at the new KWS forensics lab were pleased to have them back so they could check that all the equipment was operating properly. It also gave them an opportunity to review some of the more difficult cases with John and the team and get their advice on how best to handle them.

The team also attended a two-day training workshop for wildlife law enforcement officials from twenty-one countries on October 24th and 25th at the Laico Regency Hotel in Nairobi to prepare for the initiation of Operation Cobra II, the next phase of Operation Cobra. The training workshop was organized by the ICCWC in collaboration with the LATF.

It was designed to strengthen the skills of law enforcement officers from across Africa and Asia to combat transnational organized wildlife crime more effectively using a broad range of innovative and specialized investigation techniques. It also exposed the officers to firsthand training on the use of tools and services available to them through ICCWC partner agencies and highlighted the importance of increased international collaboration.

The training was followed by a pre-operational planning meeting organized by LATF and supported by ICCWC. The planning meeting discussed and formulated strategies for executing operation Cobra II, as well as the secure communication system to be used during the operation. Coordinators were going to rely on CENcomm, the World Customs Organization's secure and encrypted communication tool, to exchange actionable intelligence and to coordinate their operational activities.

Operation Cobra II was to be coordinated from two ICTs based in Nairobi and Bangkok. As representatives from both Canada and the US, as well as INTERPOL's Wildlife Crime Unit, John's team were recognized as key players in the execution of Operation Cobra II. Their upcoming training workshops in Zambia, Kenya, and Tanzania would be instrumental in bringing the operational, on-the-ground African wildlife law enforcement agencies up to speed on what was happening with the operation.

After arriving from the airport, John and the team checked in to their rooms at the Twangale Park Hotel and Conference Center. They assigned John and Kate a one-bedroom suite that came with a kitchenette and lounge area opening to a spacious private balcony overlooking the lush garden areas of the hotel grounds. Denny (with Syd and Nelle) and Anna had executive rooms, which also had kitchenettes, mini-bars, and private balconies. Roberta Mulenga's wildlife crime intelligence unit was based out of the ZAWA headquarters in Lusaka. She met them for dinner at the hotel restaurant to discuss the upcoming week's activities.

They started dinner at seven o'clock and had a pleasant discussion about the accomplishments of Operation Cobra over the last year and the new initiatives planned with Operation Cobra II. They also told her about the dismantling of the ivory trafficking syndicates in Dar es Salaam, Zanzibar, and Mombasa earlier in the year. Roberta updated them about the aftermath following the raid on the ivory storage warehouse in Livingstone on April 10th, 2012.

She explained, "We contacted Dr. Saul Waters from the University of Washington in Seattle and he agreed to come to Lusaka and take samples of the tusks for DNA testing so we could try to figure out where the 108 individual elephant tusks we confiscated at the warehouse had come from. It took a few months, but when we got the results of the DNA analysis, they showed the tusks had come mostly from the Chobe National Park region in Botswana and from Kafue and Lower Zambezi National Parks in Zambia. There were also a few from Hwange National Park in Zimbabwe and Etosha National Park in Namibia. It's really amazing how accurate the DNA analysis is at locating the geographic origins of the tusks."

Kate said, "Yes, it's amazing and has really helped anti-poaching agencies like yours in narrowing down the problem areas where the poachers are operating out of. I collaborated with Dr. Waters when I was doing my post-doctoral research at the University of Cambridge in England from 1992 to 1994.

"I was working with a research team who were also developing similar genetic bioassay techniques for tracing confiscated African elephant ivory to the elephant's geographic origin. When I returned to the US in 1994, I was offered a job at the United States Fish and Wildlife Service Office of Law Enforcement. Since then, I have worked with Dr. Waters quite a few times over the years. By the way, did you ever track down that manager of the ivory storage warehouse in Livingstone, Moses Aladele?"

"Yes, we issued a country-wide warrant for his arrest, and finally in October last year, we got a tip that he was back in Livingstone, and we were able to arrest him. He switched his base of operations for buying poached elephant tusks to Francistown in Botswana but made the mistake of showing up in Livingstone to see some of his family. His trial was just last month in Lusaka, and he got sentenced to ten years in jail. He never told us exactly who he was working for, but we suspect the main trafficking ringleader is Benjamin Malengo, or 'Shetani, which is the name most people know him by. I believe you are familiar with Mr. Malengo's work?"

John answered, "Yes, unfortunately, we are quite familiar with his work. The Tanzanian Wildlife Authority know he was the guy calling the shots for the ivory trafficking operations we helped take down in Dar es Salaam and Zanzibar in February. He's now the top priority for Joseph Mitambo and TAWA. So far, they haven't been able to catch him, but it's only a matter of time before he makes a mistake, or somebody sells him out and tips off the police or TAWA."

"So, what is the itinerary for the training workshop over the next week?" Kate asked.

Roberta answered, "All the HWPOs not living in the Lusaka area should arrive over the weekend and then we'll start the three-day classroom portion of the orientation workshop on Monday morning with all eighty-four of the HWPOs. We will then take the thirty new recruits to Ngoma in Kafue National Park, where the Southern Park headquarters is located. It's a short way south of the town of Itezhi-Tezhi and the Itezhi-Tezhi Dam. The Ngoma headquarters is the home of the head warden for the south half of the park, and for around two hundred game wardens and their families employed by ZAWA.

"The head warden, Martin Afumba, has three days of exercises planned to give the new recruits a taste of what the game wardens need to know to do their jobs. We hoped you might come as well and take part in the field exercises, especially instructing them on wildlife crime scene evidence gathering and anti-poaching methods. We were also hoping that you could do some demonstrations on how you work with Syd and Nelle capturing poachers. If you haven't been to Kafue National Park before, it would also give you a chance to check it out. We can arrange for a game drive and a sightseeing tour for you after the training workshop is over."

"That sounds great to me," said Denny. "None of us have been on any safari tours of national parks in Zambia, so it would be interesting to see some of Kafue National Park. And Syd and Nelle would be happy to show off a little for the new recruits. Maybe we can get a few of them to volunteer to pose as poachers and the dogs can demonstrate their poacher-capturing skills."

"All right, that's great. We'll be driving to Kafue on Thursday. It takes about five hours to get there from Lusaka. The instructors and your team will drive ZAWA vehicles, and we have rented a bus for the recruits. They will be roughing it and staying in field tents in the park headquarters grounds, but we have booked rooms for you and the senior ZAWA instructors at the

Musungwa Safari Lodge, just a few kilometers north of Ngoma on the shore of Lake Itezhi-Tezhi. The lodge is a few kilometer from Musa Gate, which is the main entrance to the southern sector of Kafue National Park."

Continuing, Roberta said, "I have stayed at the lodge several times and it's very nice. Musungwa's central complex consists of three large, thatched rondavels comprising the reception area, bar, and restaurant. The food in the restaurant is usually exceptionally good and has fruits and vegetables from their own garden and fresh fish from the lake. It's also well known for traditional open-air barbecues. They even have a bar and lounge. There are eleven twin chalets and twelve four-bedded chalets which are simple but nicely furnished and have individual shower and toilet facilities. Each chalet also has a private verandah overlooking Lake Itezhi-Tezhi."

"That sounds wonderful," said Anna. How big is Lake Itezhi-Tezhi?"

"Lake Itezhi-Tezhi is actually a reservoir about 1.8 kilometers long and covers an area of around 390 square kilometers, which has flooded a section of Kafue National Park," said Roberta. "The Itezhi-Tezhi Dam is on the Kafue River and was built between 1974 and 1977 at the Itezhi-Tezhi Gap in a range of hills where the river eroded a narrow valley, leading to the broad expanse of the wetlands known as the Kafue Flats.

"The purpose of the dam is to store water for the Kafue Gorge Upper Power Station over 260 kilometers downstream. The town of Itezhi-Tezhi came into existence when the dam was constructed and has a population of around four thousand, mostly employees of the electricity company ZESCO."

After they finished dinner, Roberta left to go to her home in Lusaka, and they retired to their rooms in the hotel for the night. When John and Kate were settled on the couch in their room and had turned on the TV to watch the BBC world news channel, Kate said, "It sounds like we'll be having an interesting week here. I'm really looking forward to staying at the Musungwa Safari Lodge and going on a game drive in the park."

"Yes, it sounds like the Safari Lodge should be a great place to stay, and I've read there are a few wildlife species in the park we probably haven't seen before, plus all the standard ones," John said. "We should probably spend some time tomorrow with Denny and Anna going over our presentations for the classroom part of the workshop. We'll have to adjust some of our standard talks for the HWPO recruits, since they won't be doing the standard park ranger or wildlife enforcement officer jobs."

"Yes, that's a good idea," said Kate. "It's a good thing we came a day early, so we have some time before the workshop starts. This is a nice suite. Maybe we should climb into bed and watch TV."

Smiling, John said, "All right, but I hope watching TV is not all you have in mind."

CHAPTER 14

8 p.m. Thursday, October 24, 2013
Musungwa Safari Lodge, Kafue National Park, Zambia

John and the team had spent the previous three days listening to Roberta Mulenga and the other ZAWA training officers give talks on various subjects. They had also delivered their own presentations on the role of forensic wildlife biology in wildlife crime enforcement, wildlife crime scene evidence gathering and documentation, issuing and using search warrants, and an overview of the current global efforts to combat wildlife crime through initiatives like Project Wisdom, Operation Worthy, and Operation Cobra.

Many of the HWPO recruits were particularly interested in the last topic. There were a lot of questions about how these operations worked and who was involved. To illustrate his point, John told them about their recent involvement in dismantling the elephant ivory trafficking syndicates in Dar es Salaam and Mombasa, and the follow-up actions by law enforcement agencies in various Asian countries, including China.

Although John, Kate, Anna, and Denny didn't think of their lives as being special, the HWPO recruits, plus the ZAWA training officers, listened to John in fascination as he described what he and his team did for a living. Most of them had not been outside of Zambia and could not imagine traveling the world like John's team did and mingling with the top policy makers and bureaucrats from agencies like INTERPOL, CITES, and the LATF, as well as executives from the world's most prominent wildlife conservation NGO's, foundations, and trusts.

On Thursday morning, they made the five-hour drive from Lusaka to the Musungwa Safari Lodge in Kafue National Park. They traveled in a ZAWA extended Land Rover with a driver. Roberta and three other ZAWA training officers drove in another Land Rover. The thirty new HWPO recruits crammed into a charter bus. When they got to the Southern Park headquarters at Ngoma, the recruits set up a tented field camp, like what they would do if they were temporarily stationed at a park ranger outpost in one of the National Parks or Game Management Areas.

The Musungwa Safari Lodge was a significant upgrade from the tented camp the new HWPO recruits were staying at — the privilege of being visiting foreign trainers and ZAWA senior training officers. They each got one of the twin chalets, with John and Kate sharing and Syd and Nelle bunking in with Denny. The restaurant lived up to the glowing review by Roberta Mulenga, and dinner consisted of fresh vegetables from the lodge garden, fresh fish from the lake, and sirloin steak grilled on the large barbeque on the open-air patio overlooking Lake Itezhi-Tezhi. Since it was a slow time of the year for tourists, there were only a few other guests at the lodge.

After dinner, they all went for coffee and drinks to the lodge's bar and lounge in the large rondavel, the local name for the traditional circular African dwelling with a conical thatched roof. They had a lively discussion with the ZAWA training officers about the state of Africa's wildlife populations, African politics, and what Zambia and some of the other neighboring African countries were doing (or not doing) to quell the problems of poaching and wildlife trafficking.

After they went back to their chalet, John and Kate sat in the deck chairs on their private verandah for a while, finishing their glasses of wine and looking at the moonlight glistening on the waters of Lake Itezhi-Tezhi. John looked over at Kate sitting next to him and, smiling, said, "We are incredibly lucky to do what we do, and also get paid for it."

Kate, leaning over and putting her hand on his arm, said, "You got that right, and doing it together makes it that much better."

9 a.m. Friday, October 25, 2013
Ngoma Southern Park Headquarters, Kafue National Park, Zambia

In the morning, after breakfast at the lodge restaurant, they drove the short distance south to the Ngoma Southern Park headquarters and had a short meeting with the head warden, Martin Afumba, to discuss the plans for the next three days. He had put together an ambitious schedule for the HWPO recruits that only partly involved John and his team.

Each day before breakfast, the recruits would go on a ten-kilometer hike on trails in the park. They were then split into smaller groups to participate in concurring instructional exercises such as hand-to-hand combat, map reading and orienteering, and marksmanship on the shooting range.

The head warden asked Denny if he could put together a demonstration with Syd and Nelle to show some of their training and how they captured fleeing poachers. After lunch, for a break during the heat of mid-day, he asked John, Kate, and Anna if they could show some of the field crime scene evidence gathering procedures to the recruits in the mess tent. They were more than happy to oblige.

Denny put together a few demonstration scenarios for Syd and Nelle to show the recruits what types of things they were trained to do. One involved chasing down two fleeing recruits posing as poachers. He brought along some protective arm padding from the ZAWA canine training unit in Lusaka and convinced a couple of recruits to volunteer to be the fleeing bad guys. With all the HWPO recruits and ZAWA training officers watching, he sent the two recruits off running with a seventy-five-meter head start then gave the dogs the "Capture" command.

As expected, the dogs took off at full speed and closed the gap quickly. Each dog grabbed a man on their padded arm protector and dragged him down onto the ground. Denny was close behind them and after the two men were down, looking very alarmed with their arms firmly in the grasp of the two dogs, he gave the "Release" command. The dogs backed away and sat down beside the men while they waited for Denny to put handcuffs on them. All those watching gave the dogs a short round of applause.

Another exercise involved tracking down two recruits posing as bad guys. After giving Denny their jackets, they were told to go off somewhere in the park headquarters complex and hide. Once out of sight, Denny took their jackets and let Syd and Nelle smell them and then gave them the command "Track."

The dogs both started sniffing the ground and once they picked up the scent of the two men, started following it. After about fifteen minutes, they located both men hiding in one of the storage sheds on the far side of the compound. Denny followed the dogs with the rest of the group close behind. When they got to the shed, the dogs both sat down and looked at Denny with the implied message, "They are in the shed, what now?"

Bringing the exercise to closure, Denny told the men to come out of the shed with their hands on their head. When they sheepishly obeyed, Denny put them in handcuffs. The group gave the dogs a short round of applause again and then returned to their other training exercises.

During dinner that evening at the lodge restaurant, there was a lot of discussion about how the day's training exercises had gone and about the exploits of Syd and Nelle during the last couple of years since joining John's team. The second day of training exercises was to be much the same, except Denny would be putting on a demonstration with the dogs taking down two armed bad guys in a house-breaching scenario.

On the morning of the third day, when they got to the park headquarters, they were told by Martin Afumba that he had received a disturbing report from one of the ranger stations in the southwest part of the park. Looking very upset, he said, "Three elephants were found dead by rangers out on a regular patrol. Based on the condition of the elephant's remains, they were killed by poachers who used chain saws to remove their tusks.

"The site where the elephants were killed is about fifty-five kilometers from here along the D769 road going south through the park. I will be heading there tomorrow morning after the HWPO training is over, but I was wondering if you could go there with a few of my park rangers and Roberta this morning to check out the scene to see if we can get an idea of who the poachers are and where they might have gone with the elephant tusks?"

"Yes, of course we can do that," answered John. "We'll just go back to the lodge and get our gear and then drive there and do what we can to figure things out."

The ZAWA driver drove John, Kate, Anna, Denny, and the dogs back to the Musungwa Safari Lodge to collect their crime scene forensic gear, plus some extra clothing, food, and water. They met up with Roberta and three senior park rangers at the park headquarters then drove south on the D769 public road running through the park from the north and eventually intersecting with the M10 Highway about one hundred kilometers west of Livingstone.

The road was bumpy and full of potholes, so it took them over an hour to drive the fifty-five kilometers. One of the park rangers who found the dead elephants met them on the road and they followed his vehicle cross-country for about a kilometer into the bush where the butchered elephants lay.

When they got to the site, another park vehicle was there with two rangers standing guard over the dead elephants. After introductions, they walked over to where the elephants were lying dead, all within fifty meters of each other. Looking like she was going to be sick, Kate said, "Oh my God, this is horrible."

They walked up to the dead elephants and could see there was one large bull and two smaller cow elephants. Their heads had been brutally mangled with a chain saw to get to the base of the tusks so the poachers could cut off the maximum length of each of the six tusks. The elephants had been dead for less than forty-eight hours so had not decomposed too much yet, but there were lots of flies buzzing around and some birds had already started pecking at their eyes. Without the presence of the park rangers, more scavengers would have taken advantage of the fresh meat.

It was a truly grim scene, one which they had all seen before; however, the team were usually involved in the aftermath of the killing — the storage and trafficking of the elephant ivory. This was the reality of what happened in the bush. They all walked around the three magnificent animals with tears in their eyes, now dead for the few dollars the poachers would get for their tusks.

One of the park rangers said he knew the bull elephant very well. He was one of the larger and older bulls in this part of Kafue National Park and had one of the largest set of tusks of any elephant in the area, making him a prime target for the poachers.

The park rangers showed them where the elephants had been shot: several times each in the heads and on their sides. The poachers, who had probably been scouting their movements, were waiting in the adjacent shallow creek bed as they passed by the area. They were ambushed. There were probably at least three poachers, each picking an elephant to shoot. The doomed elephants had no chance to escape once the gunfire started.

After surveying the general scene for about thirty minutes, and trying to keep their anger in check, they all went into forensic crime scene scientist mode and started documenting and recording the evidence. John volunteered to do the unpleasant task of retrieving the bullets from the elephant's bodies. Anna started taking pictures of the scene, and Kate and Denny began scouring the area for any pieces of evidence the poachers might have inadvertently left behind.

Since the poachers didn't expect professional CSIs would scour the site, they weren't particularly careful about what they left behind. There were several cigarette butts on the ground close to each elephant and an empty pack of matches with the name of a business on the cover: "Dynest Club - Sichili, Zambia."

One of the park rangers said that the Dynest Club was a popular bar in the small town of Sichili, which was one of several towns just west of the park. They also found eight bullet casings in the creek bed, which were the common caliber of bullets used in AK-47 rifles, one of the common guns used by poachers. It was common knowledge that poachers bought the guns cheaply from illegal arms dealers who came into Zambia from neighboring Angola or the Democratic Republic of the Congo.

They also found a crumpled-up receipt, mostly hidden in the sand in the creek bottom, from a gas station in Sichili, dated from two days earlier. It was processed with the old-style credit card swipe machine, so it had the imprint of the name of the credit card owner still on it, Chanda Kombe.

When Kate showed the receipt to Roberta, she smiled and said, "Well, isn't that handy that Mr. Kombe left his name for us at the crime scene. These local poachers are not criminal masterminds, and unfortunately consider elephant ivory poaching as easy money. Way more lucrative than working at a menial job that pays them a few dollars a day."

After several hours searching the site, taking pictures, and collecting any evidence they could find, they returned to the Ngoma Park headquarters and told Martin Afumba what they had discovered, including the book of matches and gas receipt from Mr. Chanda Kombe. Roberta said she would contact the local police station in the Sichili area and see what she could find out about Chanda Kombe. Since it was getting late, they all drove back to the lodge to clean up before dinner.

At dinner, they discussed the disturbing events of the day. Roberta said, "Before dinner, I called the police chief at the local police station who services the communities west of Kafue Park and asked him about Chanda Kombe. He said he knew who Kombe was and that he lived in Sichili and was frequently involved in petty crime in the area. The police chief said he had arrested Kombe himself three times.

"When I told him we suspected Kombe might be involved in killing elephants in Kafue Park, he said it didn't surprise him. He told me about a couple of the men Chanda Kombe usually associates with in his criminal activities, who also live in the Sichili area. The police chief also gave me the most current address that he had for Kombe."

Over dinner, they discussed a plan to pay Mr. Chanda Kombe a visit in Sichili in the next couple of days.

7 a.m. Tuesday, October 29, 2013
Sichili, Zambia

The plan came together quickly. Roberta spoke again with Charles Kapawa, the Sichili area police chief, who confirmed Chanda Kombe still lived at the same address with his girlfriend, and likely one or two of his criminal friends. She told him about their plan and confirmed that he and a couple of his police officers would be available to help with the takedown.

On Monday afternoon, John, Kate, Anna, Denny, and the dogs, as well as Roberta and three of the senior ZAWA trainers, drove for three hours to Mulobezi, a small town about thirty-five kilometers east of Sichili. They booked three rooms at the Woodland Guest House so they could get a few hours of sleep before driving the rest of the way to Sichili early on Tuesday morning.

They met the police chief, Charles Kapawa, and three of his police officers on a side street on the outskirts of Sichili at six thirty the next morning to go over the takedown plan.

Just before seven, they converged on the shabby-looking residence of Chanda Kombe, with the four ZAWA officers, John, and Denny in full tactical gear, brandishing assault rifles. Syd and Nelle were outfitted as well. As usual, half the breaching force went to the front door and the other half went around to the back of the house.

The front door was quite flimsy and took only a light tap with the battering ram to fly open. Denny gave the "Capture" command to the dogs, and they rushed into the small house looking for the occupants. They were still in bed sleeping. A man and a woman were in the bedroom, and a single man was sleeping on the couch in the living room.

Syd took the man on the couch, and Nelle went for the man just coming out of the bedroom. They had them both down on the floor in seconds, then Denny, John, and the ZAWA officers came into the house right behind them. Denny gave the dogs the "Release" command, which they did immediately. The ZAWA officers put the two groggy and bewildered men and the woman in handcuffs and marched them out to the waiting police vehicles.

Kate and Anna then came into the house and, together with John and Roberta, started looking around the messy house. One of the ZAWA officers who had gone around the back came into the house and said there was a small shed in the back with a lock on the door. They all went into the backyard area and one of the ZAWA officers cut the lock off the door with a set of bolt cutters. Inside, laying on the dirt floor, wrapped in a blood-splattered tarp, were the six elephant tusks. Two of the tusks were quite large, between five and six feet long. Wrapped in another tarp and sitting beside a blood-smeared chainsaw were three AK-47 rifles.

Roberta looked at John and Kate and said, "Well, that puts a stop to this little criminal enterprise. What a shame those three beautiful elephants had to lose their lives to finally bring these three low-life poachers down."

Looking sadly at the six bloody tusks lying on the floor of the grimy shed, Kate said, "Yes, it's a shame, but unfortunately, this is still happening daily in countries all over southern Africa. Although it's very satisfying to take down these poachers, we need to catch the guys buying the elephant tusks from the poachers, and those responsible for consolidating all the pieces of ivory and shipping them to the buyers in Asia."

CHAPTER 15

8 p.m. Friday, November 1, 2013
Wildebeest Eco Camp, Nairobi, Kenya

John and the team flew back to Nairobi from Lusaka on Friday on the KWS plane. However, since the unexpected takedown of Chanda Kombe and his poacher friends had interfered with their planned game drive in Kafue National Park, they did an impromptu game drive on their way back to the park headquarters after the events in Sichili on Tuesday morning.

The ZAWA driver knew the area very well, so he took them on a tour of the southern part of Kafue Park. They saw many of the common wildlife and bird species in the park, such as breeding herds of elephants, several prides of lion, as well as cheetahs and leopards. They also encountered a few packs of the endangered Cape wild dog, which was quite rare, plus Cape buffalo, zebra, blue wildebeest, and various antelope species like impala, puku, sable, hartebeest, bushbuck, roan, red lechwe, grysboks, and defassa waterbucks. Along the Kafue River, they came across several pods of hippos and a few of what the ZAWA driver said were the largest crocodiles in southern Africa.

Because of the diversity of habitats in Kafue National Park, it was also one of the best locations in Africa for birding. The Kafue River, wetlands, savannah, and woodlands provided habitats for about 478 of Zambia's 733 recorded bird species. On their tour, they saw African wattled and crowned cranes, fish eagles, woolly necked storks, saddle-billed storks, Goliath herons, ground hornbills, African finfoots, Pel's owls, purple-crested louries, Chaplin's barbets, and numerous other smaller, less impressive species.

They stayed one more night at the Musungwa Safari Lodge and then drove back to Lusaka on Wednesday and stayed overnight at the Twangale Park Hotel and Conference Center. On Thursday, they spent the morning at the ZAWA headquarters in Lusaka meeting with Roberta Mulenga and some of the senior ZAWA managers reviewing the training workshop and the takedown of the poachers in Sichili.

Chanda Kombe and his two poacher friends, Francis Mambwe and Halima Sakala, were transferred to the jail in Livingstone to await their trials. It turned out that Chanda Kombe's girlfriend, Halima Sakala, was actually the third shooter in the poaching operation, so at least the poaching business provided local employment for women as well as men.

During his interrogation in Livingstone, Francis Mambwe was persuaded to divulge the name of the usual buyer of the elephant tusks from the local poachers in the region east of Kafue Park. His name was Daniel Chiyaba. Kombe also said he had heard that Daniel Chiyaba worked for a guy they called "Shetani," although he didn't think that was his real name.

They spent some time on Thursday afternoon just relaxing at the hotel and getting ready for their return trip to Nairobi. Kate and Anna went back to the art gallery at the hotel and finally decided which paintings they'd buy for themselves. The art gallery was one of the best in Lusaka and featured artwork by many local Zambian artists. Anna picked a watercolor painting of the African savannah with a herd of elephants and several giraffe eating leaves from an acacia tree. Kate picked a more abstract acrylic painting of two southern white rhinos standing next to a waterhole. Both were excellent choices.

They were scheduled to participate in another three-day training workshop for the newest graduating class of KWS wildlife enforcement officers at the KWS Training Institute at Naivasha on Monday through Wednesday of the upcoming week. Then, they were scheduled to go back to Dar es Salaam in Tanzania for a couple of weeks to work with Joseph Mitambo at the NTSCIU.

They planned to relax on Saturday at the Wildebeest and then drive to the KWS Training Institute at Naivasha on Sunday to be ready for the Monday morning workshop. Denny was scheduled to spend time again during the three days with the KWS canine training unit at Naivasha.

8 p.m. Sunday, November 10, 2013
Hyatt Regency Kilimanjaro Hotel, Dar es Salaam, Tanzania

After the three-day training workshop at the KWS Training Institute at Naivasha, the team returned to Nairobi on Thursday and spent Friday morning at the forensics lab at the KWS headquarters complex. On Friday afternoon, they drove from Nairobi to Moshi so they could spend Saturday at the CAWM, located about fourteen kilometers north of Moshi. When they had visited the CAWM earlier in the year on their last trip to Tanzania, they promised the dean of the college they would do a half-day lecture and workshop for the senior Wildlife Management and Conservation students.

The two hundred students in the lecture theatre were fascinated with the lecture topic but were particularly interested in John and Kate's description of the world of international wildlife crime law enforcement. Being college students with an interest in wildlife management and conservation, they were still quite innocent and uninformed about the harsh realities of international wildlife crime and the agencies in the trenches of the war against the poachers and traffickers.

They told the students about agencies such as INTERPOL's Wildlife Crime Group, the Lusaka Agreement Task Force, and CITES, including government agencies like TAWA's National and Transnational Serious Crimes Investigation Unit, and the numerous wildlife conservation NGOs.

John also briefly told the students about INTERPOL's Project Wisdom and their current activities with Operation Cobra, the International Consortium on Combating Wildlife Crime, and the operation of the two International Coordination Teams running Operation Cobra based in Nairobi and Bangkok.

Finally, they had to put an end to the many questions from the students since they had exceeded their scheduled time by at least an hour. However, the students would talk for days about the team of INTERPOL wildlife crime fighters from Canada and the United States who told them about the fascinating world of international wildlife crime.

The dean invited them for dinner at the college's faculty club with several of the instructors, where they continued their discussion about the fate of Africa's wildlife populations. On Sunday, the team drove the rest of the way to Dar es Salaam. The weather was cloudy and overcast while they were in Moshi, so unfortunately, the top half of Mount Kilimanjaro was not visible, as it was on their previous drive earlier in the year.

Based on what had happened the last time they were in Dar es Salaam in January, they decided to bring their full arsenal of firearms with them, which included their RCMP issued SIG Sauer P226 sidearms, and John and Denny's Colt C8SFW (special forces weapon) assault rifles. Simon always traveled in the Land Rover with his own KWS-issued SIG Sauer sidearm and a Remington 870 Police Magnum fourteen-inch barrel, twelve-gauge shotgun tucked between the two front seats. Then there were Syd and Nelle, also dangerous criminal deterrents. Potential carjackers and criminals would be wise not to mess with the occupants of their particular Land Rover.

They were all tired from the nine-hour drive from Moshi when they finally arrived at the hotel in Dar es Salaam. They all just checked in and ordered dinner from room service, John and Kate in their suite, and Denny, Anna, Simon, and the dogs in Denny's suite.

9 a.m. Monday, November 11, 2013
Tabata House, NYSCIU Operations Center, Dar es Salaam, Tanzania

After breakfast at the hotel coffee shop, Simon drove them to Tabata House, the operations center for the NTSCIU, to meet with Joseph Mitambo. After exchanging some pleasantries about what John's team had been doing since they were last in Dar es Salaam and how their drive from Nairobi had gone, they got down to business.

The NTSCIU had been busy since John and the team had last been in Tanzania in early February. Joseph Mitambo told them that two Tanzanians, Kelvin Kasembe and Moses Ladipo, who were the main suppliers of the elephant tusks discovered at the Mikocheni houses, were now in custody. Kelvin Kasembe was arrested at his house in the Mbezi District of Dar es Salaam. Moses Ladipo, who lived in one of villages on the outskirts of the Selous Reserve in southern Tanzania, was also arrested together with half a dozen other local poachers and a few local game wardens and police officers who were collaborating with the poachers.

They were the main brokers for the now defunct ivory trafficking syndicate, buying elephant tusks from the poachers in southern Tanzania and selling them to their clients based in Dar es Salaam and Zanzibar. Joseph Mitambo said, "Under interrogation, Kelvin Kasembe confirmed they were associates of Benjamin Malengo, or 'Shetani,' but seldom saw him at the ivory storage houses or in the Selous Reserve area. Kasembe said that Shetani is always on the move and doesn't stay in one place for more than a few days. However, he thinks Shetani has a secret house on the outskirts of Dar es Salaam where he stays when he comes to take care of business in the area."

Joseph continued, "Through some informants we have working at the Port of Dar es Salaam, and the Tanzania-China Africa Business Council, we are keeping track of the activities of the Chinese businesswoman, Wang Jin Li, affectionately known as the 'Queen of Ivory.' She has been living in Kampala, Uganda, for the last couple of years, keeping her head down. But we suspect she is still calling the shots between upper-level guys like Benjamin Malengo and her associates in China, who operate the illegal ivory carving factories and finance the ivory shipping operations between Africa and China. We think she sneaks back into Dar es Salaam quite often, using small aircraft that land on private airstrips in the region, to check on her business interests here, but we haven't been able to catch her yet."

"What about Shetani? Do you have any leads on where this secret house of his is in Dar es Salaam?" John asked.

"Yes, we know it's in the Mikongeni District west of Julius Nyerere International Airport in western Dar es Salaam, and we even have it narrowed down to about a six-block area based on the information we've gotten from a few of his people we've arrested so far," responded Joseph. "We have a couple of undercover agents stationed in the area at the local shopping mall who are watching for him and the men who travel with him."

At the request of the NTSCIU, John and the team scheduled another three-day training workshop at the TAWA headquarters for thirty of the new TAWA wildlife enforcement officers who had been promoted from their regular service as conservation officers in various Tanzanian National Parks. The officers had recently completed additional para-military and anti-poaching training from the Tanzania People's Defense Forces and had acquired enhanced skills and techniques to manage armed adversaries in the field.

Before being re-assigned to the parks and wildlife reserves with the most serious poaching problems, the TAWA also wanted them to receive additional training in wildlife crime scene investigative techniques and evidence documentation. This new generation of young wildlife enforcement officers were mostly graduates of the College of African Wildlife Management in Moshi and were critical in the future management of Tanzania's wildlife resources. With this higher level of training for the front-line wildlife enforcement officers, TAWA hoped to increase their success in not only catching the poachers and criminals, but in successfully prosecuting them as well.

John and the team had delivered various versions of the workshop on many occasions over the past few years. They were each responsible for specific parts of the workshop, depending on their particular skills and areas of expertise. John concentrated more on the legal issues related to the issuance and serving of search warrants and chain of custody issues. Denny instructed the participants on various tactical maneuvers for apprehending the poachers or suspects of various criminal activities. Kate and Anna focused more on the Crime Scene Investigation (CSI) aspects and the collection and documentation of evidence.

Syd and Nelle were mostly there for moral support and as a welcome distraction for the trainees during coffee and lunch breaks. The fact they could be extremely focused and dangerous law enforcement officers in their own right, but also mingle with the trainees like ordinary house pets, was a testament to their training and temperaments.

In the field, the wildlife enforcement officers rarely had the luxury of relying on a CSI team coming in to do the work as would normally happen in a big-city police service. They usually had to do their own CSI work. That also meant they were responsible for the veracity of the evidence that government prosecutors would rely on to get convictions of the bad guys.

9 a.m. Friday, November 15, 2013
Tabata House, NTSCIU Operations Center, Dar es Salaam, Tanzania

When John and the team arrived at Joseph Mitambo's office at Tabata House on Friday morning, he was quite excited about news he'd received the previous evening from an informant who was working at the office of the

China-Africa Business Council of Tanzania. The informant overheard two of his coworkers talking about the Chinese businesswoman Wang Jin Li, known in TAWA circles as the "Queen of Ivory." She was back in Dar es Salaam for the weekend to check on her two core business interests — the Shanghai Restaurant and the Shanghai-Tanzania Investment Company, located above the restaurant in the same building.

Joseph was hoping she would eventually make the mistake of coming to Dar es Salaam from Kampala, Uganda, and that one of his informants would find out about the visit. The sixty-six-year-old Wang was born in Shanghai, China, in the late 1940s. She graduated from the Shanghai People's University in Foreign Studies, where she majored in Swahili.

In 1975, they assigned her to Tanzania, where she worked as a translator in the construction of the TAZARA Railway, linking Zambia's landlocked copper belt with Tanzania's coast. After the project, she returned to China, and then in 1998, she came back to Tanzania and set up her two businesses in Dar es Salaam. She also served as vice-chairwoman and secretary-general of the China-Africa Business Council of Tanzania for several years until she had to move to Kampala in early 2011 to avoid arrest and prosecution.

The NTSCIU knew Wang was one of the kingpins behind the illicit trade of elephant ivory worth millions of dollars, using her ties to the Chinese and Tanzanian business communities to move ivory from Africa to Asia. It was reported she even supplied the poachers with guns and ammunition through her network of poaching go-betweens. She was the connection between the upper-level African ivory brokers like Shetani and the international ivory market.

The NTSCIU had suspected Wang for several years and steadily uncovered her role in the trafficking network. They also suspected she was using her restaurant in downtown Dar es Salaam as a cover, sneaking ivory from outside of the city into food shipments that went to the restaurant. She would then transfer the ivory to upscale houses in Dar es Salaam, like the ones they raided back in February in the Mikocheni District, When enough ivory was collected, it was consolidated and transferred in bulk to shipping containers for delivery to various Asian countries, and eventually to China. It was thought she was ultimately responsible for the killing of thousands of elephants in Tanzania and other neighboring countries.

She still owned a large estate house in the upscale Masaki District of Dar es Salaam, about four kilometers north of the Embassy of the People's Republic of China along Toure Drive, the ocean-side street in the Oyster Bay and Masaki neighborhoods. When Joseph got the tip from his informant the previous evening saying she was back in the city, he'd sent two teams of undercover officers to watch her house. At eleven o'clock on Thursday evening, they reported that a Mercedes Benz sedan with what appeared to be three people inside arrived at the house and drove into the gated compound.

As of nine o'clock the following morning, the Mercedes had not left the estate, so they assumed she was still there. Joseph said to John and the team, "We are planning to raid her house this morning and arrest her and anyone else who may be at the house with her. I assume you would be interested in being involved in the takedown?"

"Yes, you bet. We would be extremely interested in helping any way we can," John said enthusiastically, while looking around at the rest of the team, who were all nodding in agreement. "So, do you have a plan put together?"

"Yes, but we're still working out the details," Joseph said. "I've contacted the Dar es Salaam Police Service Tactical Unit and told them to meet us a few blocks from the house in the Masaki District. I will take two teams of NTSCIU enforcement officers, and your team can also come in your own vehicle. I don't think we can use your dogs when we breach the house because we don't know how many men may be there. We will just have to breach the estate in force and hope there isn't too much resistance."

After a little more discussion, they all went to their vehicles, put on their gear, and got their firearms ready. Simon followed the two TAWA Land Rovers north to the Masaki District. As they were approaching Mahando Street where the house was located, they got a call on the radio from the undercover officers watching the house that the Mercedes Benz sedan had just left the estate and was heading east on Mwaya Street to the T-intersection with Toure Drive.

The teams immediately changed tactics and headed to Toure Drive hoping to intercept the Mercedes. After a few blocks driving south on Toure Drive they spotted the Mercedes stopped at a red light. There were several cars between the lead TAWA Land Rover and the Mercedes, with Simon next in line. When the light turned green, all three Land Rovers turned on their flashing lights and sirens and pulled out into the opposite lane to try to get behind the Mercedes.

The three occupants of the Mercedes, seeing and hearing the Land Rovers behind them, immediately sped up, trying to get away. The Chinese Embassy was only about three kilometers further south on Toure Drive, so it was obvious that it was probably the destination of the Mercedes' occupants. They were hoping to reach the Embassy before the TAWA Land Rovers could stop them.

Suddenly, the Mercedes stopped on the north end of Coco Beach, and two men got out and started running towards a small marina about four blocks away on the waterfront. The Mercedes, with the tires screeching, took off again south on Toure Drive.

John radioed the other officers, "Our team will take down the two men, you catch up with the Mercedes before it reaches the Chinese Embassy."

Simon pulled over to the side of the road and Denny, John, Syd, and Nelle all jumped out. Simon, Kate, and Anna continued after the Mercedes as soon as the doors closed.

The two men were running fast and were about halfway to the marina. Denny gave the dogs the "Capture" command, and they took off running flat out after the two men. Within seconds, they caught up to them. They each picked one man and grabbed a leg before they reached the entrance to the marina. Both men hit the ground hard, gripped firmly by powerful canine jaws.

Denny and John caught up to them and, with their assault rifles aimed at the two men, Denny gave the dogs the "Release" command. The dogs both released their hold and John shouted at the men to lie on their stomachs and put their hands behind their backs. As John kept his assault rifle aimed at them, Denny put handcuffs on both men.

Meanwhile, with the Mercedes speeding south on Toure Drive, Simon demonstrated his KWS driving skills and maneuvered his vehicle immediately behind the Mercedes. Then, at the first opportunity, he quickly sped around it and forced it to stop at the side of the road. Kate, Anna, and Simon, with their handguns drawn, jumped out of the Land Rover and surrounded the Mercedes. Kate tapped on the driver's window and yelled at the middle-aged

Asian woman driving the car, "Get out of the car with your hands on top of your head."

By this time, the two TAWA vehicles had arrived on the scene. Joseph and the other NTSCIU officers got out of the vehicles. Realizing there was no escape, Wang Jin Li opened her car door and slowly got out of the car with her hands on top of her head.

Joseph walked up to her, nodded, smiled at Kate, and took out his handcuffs. Turning Wang Jin Li around and pressing her against the side of the Mercedes, he put her arms behind her back and secured the handcuffs on her wrists. As he was doing this, he said, "Wang Jin Li, you are under arrest for the smuggling of elephant ivory and any other charges we can come up with." He then recited the standard Miranda rights.

Once his prisoner was secured, he instructed the driver of one of the TAWA Land Rovers to go back to the Coco Beach marina with another officer and pick up the two men John and Denny had captured. Wang Jin Li's two poaching lieutenants had obviously not counted on the NTSCIU officers having the help of two very well trained and fast Canadian German shepherd police dogs when they had made a run for it.

Simon said to Kate and Anna, "I'll go back and pick up Denny and John and the dogs."

Simon followed the TAWA Land Rover back to the Coco Beach marina, where John, Denny, and the two dogs were standing guard over the two men still laying on the ground with their arms handcuffed behind their backs. Upon arrival, the TAWA officers put the two men in their Land Rover, and John, Denny, Syd, and Nelle got in the vehicle with Simon.

As soon as he saw Simon, John asked, "So, what happened with the Mercedes chase?"

Simon described how he ran the Mercedes off the road and the ultimate takedown of Wang Jin Li. Smiling and patting Simon on the back, Denny said, "So, how does it feel to be part of the team that took down the infamous Ivory Queen?"

With a big grin, Simon replied, "Damn, it feels good. You guys always seem to be in the thick of the action. My life is always more exciting when you're here in Africa." Laughing, he continued, "My family back in Nairobi is always eager for me to get back home so I can tell them about the latest crazy things you've gotten me involved in."

Smiling, John said, "Well, today is another win for the good guys and, as usual, you are an important part of our team. We are fortunate to have you working with us."

Looking pleased with the compliment, Simon said, "Thanks, John. Why don't we get back to Kate and Anna now? They're probably anxious to see that you're all right."

When they got back to the scene of the Wang Jin Li takedown, things were wrapping up. Kate and Anna gave each of them a big hug, thankful that everyone was safe. Syd and Nelle were wagging their tails enthusiastically, rushing from person to person, happy their humans were all safe and excited about what had just happened with the bad guys.

The dogs enjoyed the outdoor rundowns and capture of the bad guys the best. They were always excited when they were part of a successful operation, mostly because they could sense their humans were pleased with them, which was their biggest reward for what they were trained to do.

It was still early in the day, so they stopped for lunch on the patio of a Coco Beach beachside restaurant before heading back to Tabata House. Joseph joined them while his NTSCIU officers took Wang Jin Li and her two poaching lieutenants, Jackson Mtutara and Eric Nsemo, to the Dar es Salaam Police Service headquarters lock-up facilities.

They finished their lunch on the outdoor restaurant patio overlooking the beach but were still recapping the events of the morning and what it would mean to the ivory trafficking industry. Just as they were about to leave, Joseph's cell phone rang.

Seeing who the call was from, Joseph held up his hand and said to the rest of them at the table, "It's from one of my undercover officers." As Joseph listened intently to what his officer told him, John and the team watched him, anxious to hear what was being said.

After the call ended, Joseph looked up at them smiling and said, "My officer just told me they spotted Malengo with two of his men in a coffee shop at the Pugu Mnadani Shopping Mall, close to where we think his secret house is located. I told them to be careful not to get spotted by Malengo or his men, and to call in a second surveillance team so they could follow Malengo when he left the coffee shop, hopefully back to his house."

After a short pause, Joseph said excitedly, "Well, it looks like the day's adventures might not be over."

"That's great news, Joseph," exclaimed John. "So, what do you want to do?"

After thinking for a few seconds, Joseph said, "Maybe Shetani is in Dar es Salaam to meet with Wang Jin Li. We should probably keep her arrest quiet until we deal with Malengo. Let's go back to Tabata House so we can figure out how to proceed."

Exited with anticipation, they left the restaurant and went back to Tabata House to wait for an update from the surveillance teams. Was the possibility of capturing the two most sought-after ivory traffickers in Tanzania on the same day, or couple of days, be too much good luck to hope for?

2:30 p.m. Friday, November 15, 2013
Tabata House, NTSCIU Operations Center, Dar es Salaam, Tanzania.

Around two-thirty, they received a call from one of the officers who had followed Malengo's Nissan Pathfinder SUV after he and his men left the coffee shop. Over the speakerphone device in the boardroom, the officer explained, "Malengo drove to a house with a small warehouse in the back of a fenced and gated lot in the Mikongeni District on the western outskirts of Dar es Salaam, just as we suspected. There were two men with Malengo, and they drove into the warehouse through an overhead door. They then closed the overhead door so we couldn't see what was going on inside. Our two surveillance teams are parked at opposite ends of the street right now. We both have good views of the entrance into the compound in case Malengo leaves the house again."

After the call, they discussed several options about how they could do the raid and subsequent takedown. Joseph spoke with the team leader of the Dar es Salaam Police Service Tactical Unit, who had helped them earlier in the day, but was told the tactical unit would be busy on another operation. They decided they couldn't wait for the tactical unit and would have to proceed with just the NTSCIU enforcement officers and John's team with Syd and

Nelle. They didn't want to risk losing the opportunity to capture Shetani when they had the chance.

Joseph assembled all eight of the available NTSCIU enforcement officers at Tabata House, plus John's team, and organized an impromptu tactical meeting in the basement training and meeting room. He went over the layout of the lot where the residence and warehouse were located, and together, they came up with a plan.

At five o'clock, two TAWA Land Rovers and the KWS Land Rover driven by Simon left Tabata House for the forty-minute drive to the house in the Mikongeni District. They agreed one of the TAWA Land Rovers would go to the rear of the lot down the rutted and cluttered back alley. The other TAWA Land Rover and John's team would break through the front gate of the fenced compound and, as quickly as possible, breach the front door of the house and take down the occupants.

The other team would do the same with the small warehouse in the rear of the lot behind the house. Because they didn't know exactly how many people were in either the house or the warehouse, John's team, with Syd and Nelle, were going to drive around to the back of the house and provide backup for the two NTSCIU teams in case any of the poachers inside came out and tried to make a run for it. The two NTSCIU undercover surveillance teams were also still at the site, so were available to provide backup for the assault teams.

As they approached the lot, one NTSCIU team broke off and went down the back alley as planned. The other two Land Rovers sped down the street, and when they got to the lot, the TAWA Land Rover with the reinforced front bumper crashed through the chain-link gate and stopped a few feet from the front door of the house. Simon drove the KWS Land Rover around the side of the house and stopped between the back of the house and the warehouse's front entrance.

Simultaneously, the action began. The NTSCIU team at the front of the house used their battering ram to break open the front door. The four officers, plus Joseph Mitambo, rushed into the house with their assault rifles ready and found Benjamin Malengo and a woman sitting in the living room watching television. The tactical unit leader immediately shouted at them both to get down on their knees and put their hands on top of their heads, which they did with no resistance. Joseph and one other officer put their arms behind their backs and locked handcuffs on their wrists.

Meanwhile, at the warehouse, because the entrance door of the warehouse was made of heavy steel, explosives were needed to breach. An NTSCIU officer attached three small explosive devises to the door, one each close to the two hinges, and one next to the deadbolt. Ordering everyone to take cover, he detonated the explosive devices. The door blew off its hinges and fell into the warehouse.

The four officers rushed into the warehouse with their assault rifles ready to fire at anyone in the warehouse who offered any resistance. There were three men in the warehouse and two of them immediately put up their arms when they saw the four officers come in after the door came crashing down.

The third man ran to the back of the warehouse and picked up a chair, pulled back the metal screen on the window, and broke the glass in the small window facing into the back alley. Before any of the NTSCIU officers could get to him, the man launched himself through the window and landed hard on the ground. With a rolling motion, he got up and took off down the alley. One of the officers came back out the front doorway and yelled at Denny, "One of the men escaped into the back alley. Can you send the dogs after him?"

John and Denny immediately ran to the back alley with Syd and Nelle where they could see the man running about fifty yards ahead. Denny gave the dogs the "Capture" command and they took off at a dead run after the escaping poacher. Since they were extremely fast runners, it took them only seconds to catch up to him. Syd grabbed one leg and he went tumbling head over heels. With both dogs hovering over him and growling, the man curled up in a fetal position with his hands over the back of his head and started yelling, "Get them off me, I give up."

When John and Denny arrived, Denny gave the dogs the "Release" command, and the dogs backed away and sat down about three feet from the cowering poacher, ready to spring into action if he tried to get away again. While John pointed his assault rifle at the poacher, Denny told him to get up. He slowly got back on his feet, looking warily at the two dogs who were staring intently at him, with low growls coming from their throats.

Denny put the poacher's arms behind his back and handcuffs on his wrists. They then marched him back down the alley to the front of the warehouse where the other two poachers were on their knees on the ground in handcuffs. Denny told the third poacher to join them on the ground, which he did.

Just then, Joseph exited the back door of the house. With a big smile on his face, he said cheerfully, "We got him, we got Shetani!" He then walked up to the group of people standing around the three poachers and began shaking each of their hands. When he got to John Benson, he gave him a quick hug, shook his hand, and said, "Thank you, my friend, for your help today."

Approaching Denny, he also shook his hand, gave him a hug, and said, "Thank you, as well, my friend. You and your two dogs have helped make this one of the best days since we formed the NTSCIU." To complete his heartfelt expression of gratitude, he gave Kate and Anna brief hugs, shook their hands, and told them how thankful he was for their help.

After he shook each of his NTSCIU officer's hands, he turned to John and the team and said, "Let's see what's in this warehouse."

They entered the warehouse through the opening where the door used to be and began looking around. Parked to one side was the Nissan Pathfinder SUV, and on the other side was an older-looking Land Rover hooked up to a trailer with four dirt bikes secured with straps to the side railings. On the opposite wall were shelves loaded with dozens of elephant tusks of varied sizes. On another set of shelves were an assortment of rifles, including AK-47s, and boxes of ammunition for the rifles. Also on the shelves were chain saws, machetes, and axes.

Kate said sarcastically to the others, "Looks like your standard elephant poacher's supply warehouse."

Joseph, with his hands on his hips and shaking his head in disbelief, said, "This is unbelievable. Shetani was running his poaching operation like a business empire. Who knows how many warehouses he has like this in different countries where his people are operating?"

"Well, we have him now, so he won't be killing any more elephants," John said. "We just have to make sure that some other up-and-coming poaching ringleader doesn't step in to fill the void."

"Yes, our work isn't done, but we certainly have had a momentous day," said Joseph. "I would never have dreamed we would capture both the Ivory Queen and Shetani on the same day. Let's get things finished here and transport our prisoners to the Dar es Salaam Police Service lock-up facilities. Then it will be time for a celebration!"

9 a.m. Monday, November 18, 2013
Tabata House, NTSCIU Operations Center, Dar es Salaam, Tanzania

The team was back in Joseph's office at the Tabata House on Monday morning following a weekend of celebration and relaxation. They were there to say goodbye before returning to Moshi on Tuesday and then on to Nairobi the following day. They would be flying back to Canada and the US via Amsterdam on Friday morning.

Joseph joined them at their hotel on Friday evening for dinner and toasted to their good fortune in finally capturing the two most wanted elephant ivory poachers and traffickers in Tanzania.

Joseph told John and the team that he and the senior managers at the Tanzania Wildlife Authority were going to make a major press announcement about the takedowns on Saturday morning. He invited John and his team to join them; however, they declined, saying they were grateful for the invitation, but the accolades from the world press should be for the NTSCIU and TAWA, not for them.

9 p.m. Thursday, November 21, 2013
Wildebeest Eco Camp, Nairobi, Kenya

The return drive to Nairobi, with an overnight stay in Moshi, was without incident. John and the team arrived back at the Wildebeest late Wednesday afternoon and spent Thursday morning at the KWS headquarters saying their goodbyes and the afternoon packing and getting ready for their flight home.

They had just finished dinner on the patio of the Wildebeest restaurant and were enjoying their second bottle of wine when a large birthday cake arrived at their table with fifty-six candles. As the server set the cake on the table, several other servers and kitchen staff gathered around the table and sang “Happy Birthday” to John Benson.

John looked at Kate with an expression of accusation on his face, and Kate threw up her arms and said, “Don’t blame me, it must be from Charles Jelani and the staff at the KWS Wildlife Protection Department. He insisted they send a cake here when he found out it was your birthday today.”

“And how did he find that out, I wonder,” John said, smiling at Kate.

Smiling back at John, Kate said, “I have no idea. Maybe it was in one of today’s INTERPOL alerts.”

THE END

EPILOGUE

In October 2014, INTERPOL announced the creation of a dedicated team to tackle environmental crimes at its newly formed Regional Bureau for East Africa in Nairobi, Kenya. As part of the Regional Bureau, the team would collaborate with national law enforcement agencies and INTERPOL National Central Bureaus in the region to increase information exchange, support intelligence analysis, and assist national and regional investigations, focusing particularly on wildlife crime.

During 2013 and 2014, Operation Cobra II, coordinated by two International Coordination Teams based in Nairobi, Kenya, and Bangkok, Thailand, resulted in the seizure of unprecedented amounts of wildlife parts and products, including thirty-six rhino horns, over three metric tonnes of elephant ivory, over ten thousand turtles, over one thousand skins of endangered species, over ten thousand European eels and more than two hundred metric tonnes of rosewood logs. The operation also resulted in the arrest of over four hundred criminals in Asia and Africa. Several of those arrested were trafficking kingpins.

In June 2014, Feisal Mohamed Ali, along with four suspected accomplices, were found in Mombasa, Kenya, with 228 elephant tusks and 486 other pieces of ivory stashed at a warehouse. The ivory cumulatively weighed 2,152 kilograms. The Kenyan national was charged with crimes in Kenya, and two suspects were arrested during the ivory seizure, but Ali quickly skipped bail and fled to neighboring Tanzania. In December 2014, Ali was arrested in Dar es Salaam, Tanzania, and two days later was extradited to Kenya on charges of dealing in wildlife trophies and suspicion of being involved in an international wildlife trafficking ring. In July 2016, a Kenyan magistrate sentenced Ali to twenty years in prison.

Tanzania's most notorious poacher, Boniface Mariango, nicknamed "Shetani" or "The Devil," was sentenced to twelve years in prison for running an ivory trafficking network across five African countries. The PAMS Foundation, which helped finance the Tanzanian government's fight against poaching, said he was one of Tanzania's most notorious ivory traffickers. He was believed to be responsible for killing thousands of elephants as the head of fifteen poaching syndicates operating throughout Tanzania, Burundi, Zambia, Mozambique, and southern Kenya. He was also accused of leading a poaching network supplying a sixty-six-year-old Chinese citizen and Tanzanian businesswoman known as "The Ivory Queen."

A Chinese businesswoman, Yang Fenglan, labelled "The Ivory Queen," was sentenced to fifteen years in prison by a Tanzanian judge for smuggling the tusks of hundreds of elephants. They had charged her, along with two Tanzanian men, with smuggling ivory to Asia worth over six million US dollars over several years. She was a key link between poachers in East Africa and buyers in China for more than a decade. The court in Dar es Salaam also ordered that all her Tanzanian property be repossessed. Under tight security, she was escorted to the Ukonga prison in Dar es Salaam where she is to serve her jail time.

In December 2015, INTERPOL announced that Operation Worthy II, supported by its Project Wisdom, resulted in 376 arrests, the seizure of four and a half tonnes of elephant ivory and rhinoceros horn, and the investigation of twenty-five criminal groups involved in the illicit wildlife trade in Africa. The operation, which took place across eleven African countries, also resulted in the seizure of 2,029 pangolin scales; 173 live tortoises; warthog teeth; big cat, pangolin, and python skins; and impala carcasses.

On April 30, 2016, the government of Kenya set ablaze the world's largest stockpile of elephant and rhino horn ever burned. It took Kenya's Wildlife Service ten days to build the outdoor crematorium that contained the 105 tonnes of elephant ivory, 1.35 tonnes of rhino horn, exotic animal skins, and other products such as sandalwood and medicinal bark. The event brought together heads of state from several African nations and hundreds of onlookers to watch Kenyan President Uhuru Kenyatta set fire to over $172 million dollars' worth of illicit wildlife goods. This was the most significant demonstration against poaching in the region and the largest burn of illegal wildlife products in history.

In September 2016, US President Barack Obama and China's President Xi Jinping made a joint commitment to impose near-total elephant ivory bans in their countries. The US finalized new regulations in June that would help shut down commercial elephant ivory trade within its borders and stop wildlife crime overseas. In December 2016, China made the game-changing decision to end the domestic ivory trade by 2017. The new regulations came as part of their government's efforts to reduce demand for elephant ivory and help end the global elephant poaching crisis.

In August 2017, Wayne Lotter, fifty-one, was shot in the Masaki district of the city of Dar es Salaam. The wildlife conservationist was being driven from the airport to his hotel when his taxi was stopped by another vehicle. Two men, one armed with a gun, opened his car door and shot him.

Wayne Lotter was a director and co-founder of the PAMS Foundation, an NGO that provided conservation and anti-poaching support to communities and governments in Africa. The PAMS Foundation funded and supported Tanzania's elite anti-poaching National and Transnational Serious Crimes Investigation Unit, which was responsible for the arrests of major ivory traffickers, including the "Ivory Queen" and "Shetani" and several other notorious elephant poachers. Since 2012, the unit has arrested over two thousand poachers and ivory traffickers.

The global battle against the illegal poaching and trafficking of wildlife continues.

ABBREVIATIONS

ATV	All-Terrain Vehicle
AWF	African Wildlife Federation
BC	British Columbia
BDF	Botswana Defense Force
CAWM	College of African Wildlife Management
CITES	Convention on International Trade in Endangered Species
CSI	Crime Scene Investigation
CSIS	Canadian Security Intelligence Service
DNA	Deoxyribonucleic Acid
DWNP	Department of Wildlife and National Parks (Botswana)
ER	Emergency Room
FBI	Federal Bureau of Investigation
F&W	Fish and Wildlife
HWPO	Honorary Wildlife Police Officers
ICCWC	International Consortium on Combating Wildlife Crime
ICT	International Coordination Team
IFAW	International Fund for Animal Welfare
ILEA	International Law Enforcement Academy
INL	International Law Enforcement Affairs
INTERPOL	The International Criminal Police Organization

IOB	International Operations Branch (RCMP)
KWS	Kenya Wildlife Service
KWSTI	Kenya Wildlife Service Training Institute
LATF	Lusaka Agreement Task Force
NATO	North Atlantic Treaty Organization
NGO	Non-Governmental Organization
NTSCIU	National and Transnational Serious Crimes Investigation Unit
PTSD	Post Traumatic Stress Disorder
QSNCC	Queen Sirikit National Convention Center
RCMP	Royal Canadian Mounted Police
RV	Recreational Vehicle
SIG	Special Investigation Group
SUV	Sport Utility Vehicle
TAWA	Tanzania Wildlife Authority
TISS	Tanzania Intelligence and Security Service
U of A	University of Alberta (Edmonton)
USC	University of Southern California
WCO	World Customs Organization
WCS	Wildlife Conservation Society
WED	Wildlife Enforcement Directorate (Environment Canada)
WWF	World Wildlife Fund
ZAWA	Zambian Wildlife Authority

AUTHOR'S NOTE

I would like to point out to readers that although I have been a professional biologist and environmental consultant for the last thirty-plus years with a B.Sc. in Wildlife Biology and an M.Sc. in Forest Science, I am not a wildlife forensic biologist and have never worked in law enforcement. However, I did a fair amount of research to educate myself about the fascinating world of international wildlife crime law enforcement.

I have tried to capture the spirit of the real events that occurred during the 2012 to 2016 period when the world came together to stem the tide of rampant elephant ivory and rhino horn poaching in Africa, threatening the survival of both animals in the wild.

I have borrowed from some of my background in the development of the John Benson fictional character. I am a professional biologist and live in Edmonton, Alberta, Canada, and have three married daughters and seven grandchildren. I had an Australian shepherd/blue heeler cross dog named Sydney (Syd) for seventeen years, and a border collie cross dog named Nelle for fifteen years. They both unfortunately died of the afflictions of old age within about three weeks of each other in early 2018.

I would like to thank my three daughters, Sarah, Andrea, and Lisa, and my two sisters, Jane and Nancy, for their encouragement and support during the writing of this fiction novel.

I also thank the staff at Friesen Press in Victoria, British Columbia, for their assistance, and in particular the editors and publication specialists for their help in getting the book ready for publication. I would also like to thank Emily Poppel for her editorial services.